Children of AMBITION

J. J. McAvoy

Copyright

This is a work of fiction. Names, characters, places, and incidents are either products of the writer's imagination or are used fictitiously and are not to be construed as real. Any resemblance to actual events, locales, organizations, or persons, living or dead, is entirely coincidental.

Children of Ambition

Book ISBN-13: 978-1981520411
ISBN-10: 1981520414

NYLA Publishing
121 W. 27th Suite 1201 New York, NY.10001
http://www.nyliterary.com

VICE

noun **\'vīs**

a: *moral depravity or corruption:* WICKEDNESS

b: *a physical imperfection, deformity, or taint*

c: *an abnormal behavior pattern in a domestic animal detrimental to its health or usefulness*

AMBITION

noun **\ am'biSH(ə)n/**

a: *an ardent desire for rank, fame, or power*

b: *a desire to achieve a particular end*

c: *a strong desire to do or to achieve something, typically requiring determination and hard work.*

PROLOGUE

"She slept with wolves without fear,
for the wolves knew a lion was among them."
~R.M. Drake

DONATELLA

One day the wolf will dwell with the lamb, and the leopard will lie down with the young goat, and the calf and the young lion and the fatted steer together; a child would lead them all... That is what the church told me. But that time never came and so, when I grew older, my mother taught me to slaughter the wolves, skin the lambs, shoot the leopards and behead the goats. Have the calf for my feast and the lion as my goal. None needed to be together. The child would grow and rule over them all.

All of nature, not just human nature, abided by one law... Rule or be ruled. Which meant to solidify one's position of dominance was inherent in all things, whether man or beast, because man was a beast.

People were not people.

People were animals.

Beasts on two feet.

Fearsome creatures...and yet so many lived in a perpetual state of fear of themselves and other people. Why? ...Rule or be ruled... Many people like to believe they are the master of their own fates, that nothing controls them. But in reality, fear and the need to survive ruled over everything in their lives. Why did people get married? Because they sought to survive loneliness. Why work in jobs they hate? They fear poverty. People even offer a fraction of their freedom to governance, in order to be protected from those who'd tried to rule over them.

Everything in the end came down to surviving. Ironically, at the end of that long or short life, the grim reaper punishes everyone's efforts with death.

So, there are two truths.

A person will do anything to survive, but will never survive because death will come. When I realized this, when I realized that death was the ultimate ruler, I decided since I cannot be death I would become the bringer of death until death came for me.

My mother used to say *everyone is ruthless, they just don't know it.* I say, it doesn't matter if they know or not, so long as I'm the most ruthless of them all. As long as I am not ruled.

"We'll be there in four minutes," Toby said, releasing the secret hatch for the backseat of the Range Rover beside me where a small black box waited for me. It looked like a lunch box…because it was a lunch box, the red metal Mulan box I used as child and spray painted black when I was teenager.

"We don't have to do this," Toby added, his brown eyes meeting mine in the rear-view mirror; he was mistaking my hesitation for doubt.

So, I ignored him and took the square box out of its hole, flipping open the tabs and lifting the lid, staring down at the used, scratched, hand-me-down Glock that sat at the bottom, the few old, round-headed bullets with it, and the letter I'd written in anger and had wanted to read aloud during my graduation speech.

"It belonged to your mother, didn't it?"

"Toby," I said softly, placing the box on my lap, lifting the gun and ejecting the magazine, "I understand you are trying to make conversation, but I have nothing to say today."

He nodded like he understood me. I doubted he did, though. Sitting up straighter, I turned to look out the window. Toby Valentino, my elder brother's childhood friend and my longtime lover. He was stern, emotionless, cold, desperate but had pledged his loyalty to me alone.

He's not going to be able to help himself. I thought as I loaded the gun. With each bullet I put in place, I couldn't help but see my brother's face in my mind.

"We didn't account for Wyatt coming back so soon," Toby spoke up just as I thought.

"You and I know both Wyatt won't do anything to me." Grinning, I handed him the gun. "You on the other hand...I make no promises."

He glanced down under his arm, confused as to why I was giving it to him.

"This outfit's tight." I shrugged, leaning back in to my seat and tossing the lunchbox into the hole it came from.

"Is white really the best choice?"

"It's called symbolism," I said.

Turning from him, I stared at the landing strip, the place my brother—my brothers—would both be momentarily. I wished I felt my heart pounding or my pulse racing, instead I felt still, cold...partially dead inside. My own reflection often gave me a chill. It reminded me of my mother's... Maybe that's why they, the Italians who had felt excluded by our family, came to me. They saw my mother's ruthlessness in me.

A ruthlessness she never even spared me from.

DONATELLA- 12 YEARS OLD

"It hurts." She wasn't asking a question. My mom rarely asked questions. She just told us reality…I hated her for it.

Breathing in through my nose, I knelt down beside him.

"Did you let me have Doval just so I'd have to kill him?" I asked, petting the gray-haired hound lying in the green grass in front of me, his chest rising and falling with each pained breath he took, his pink tongue hanging outside of his mouth. Each time I petted him, he let out a soft whine like it hurt him, but each time I stopped he whimpered and looked up at me like he was upset I had stopped.

"A sick dog appeared on our lawn, you fed it, you kept it warm, you demanded we save it. You knew he was sick, you named him anyway. You knew nothing could be done, yet you cared for him anyway. I'm sure he loves you too, that's why he wants to die with you petting him even though it hurts. You traded your smile for the love of a dying dog, Donatella; was it worth it?"

I bit my bottom lip, trying to stop the tears in my eyes from falling, but it hurt. It hurt so much that the tears were like fire ants in my eyes. I had to let them fall, but I didn't want to cry so I screamed at her. "YES! Doval made me smile and I'm happy I kept him! Just because he was sick doesn't mean I should have let him die!"

"Then don't blame me for what you have to do next Donatella; you chose what you wanted, now you have to deal with whatever the consequences are."

"I'm not shooting him!" I wasn't going to kill him.

She knelt beside me and I lifted my chin so I could look at her. It was so hot outside but not a strand of her black hair was out of place. It was long and thick and curly, like mine, but she didn't seem hot at all. I had to pull mine into a bun to keep from roasting. It was like the sun didn't touch her, she didn't even tan as much as I did when we went outside…How? Because she was her, just different.

"You're beautiful, you know that?" She said to me… Even though that was what I was thinking of her. *I wouldn't tell her that.* "Your eyes, your face, every part of you is beautiful, especially this part."

She tapped my chest, right over my heart. The corner of her lips turned up as she brushed the strands of my hair out of my face, the sun behind her made it look like a halo was behind her head.

"Your heart is beautiful Dona, which is why I need you to own it...Everyone loves beautiful things. Everyone wants to *have* beautiful things. Why do you think roses come with thorns? Because even flowers know that just because they are beautiful doesn't give you the right to touch them." She kissed both my cheeks before saying, *"Donatella, lo sai no moderazione, è fame di tutto, sei come il caos in una bottiglia, il tuo amore è come un vello d'oro, e la tua rabbia vaso di Pandora. Tu sei, come me. Non voglio che tu cambi quel. Voglio che chiudi gli occhi, prendi un respiro profondo e pensi innanzitutto. Avere grandi aspettative, non dubitare di te e non compromettere. Essere più intelligenti e avere più pazienza di tutti gli altri. Vedi la grande immagine e prosperi."*

"You're going too fast! I don't understand, Mommy." I frowned, looking up at her.

"I know." She smiled, really smiled, as she spoke to me. "Just remember that until you do understand. Remember that when you are faced with much harder choices than killing a dying dog, Dona."

When she got up, she didn't look back at me. She climbed the stairs on the slope of the green hills. There, at the very top of the hill, was my dad, who nodded to one of the guards before he came out of side of the manor. This side was covered in dark red vines and was where we could go to play. Every time I looked at it, the house appeared as though one side had been eaten alive by the vines and the other was fighting it off. Mommy hated them, she said it made the house look hideous. But Daddy wouldn't let her get rid of them, he said *'the Irish aren't supposed to look pretty,'*

"What?" he asked Mom, fixing the watch on his wrist and looking at her the same way he always did when he wanted to know what was going on. I didn't know what face Mom made back, but it didn't answer his question, so he glanced down towards at me, his eyes narrowed on something. I wasn't sure why until I looked where he did.

Doval!

He was barely moving, his eyes closing, all because of the needle in his side, right next to were my mom had been kneeling.

"Doval?" I shook him gently and he didn't whimper or whine. He was gone. *I didn't even get to*... Pulling out the needle, I threw it as far as I could, into the field of grass while hugging Doval. I got up angrily; marching, then running to the stone steps to get to her, but before I could, Daddy grabbed me.

"Let GO!" I tried yanking my arm away, but he wouldn't let go. I screamed to the house instead, knowing she'd hear me, "I hate you! I HATE YOU! YOU MURDERER!"

"Dona! Dona! DONATELLA!" Daddy shook me. Kneeling before me, he pulled my arms in front of me and held them there. "Don't ever say you hate your mother in front of me. Do you understand?"

I couldn't stop the tears from pooling in my eyes as I glared at him. I glared directly into his green eyes, "Why are you always on her side?! No matter what, you always pick her side over mine!"

"Donatella—"

"No!" I yanked myself out of his arms. "I'm not going

to let you talk me down! She's a monster! I hate her and I hate you! I hate everyone! One day you're all going to be sorry! One day you're going to wish you were on my side!"

I thought he was going to holler at me again, but he just stood up, stuck his hands in his pocket, and smirked. Staring down at me before shaking his head, he didn't say a word. Like he didn't see or hear me.

"You'll see." I whispered softly to myself, balling my fists as he walked away. *They'd all see one day.*

DONATELLA - NOW

"Donatella," Toby called out to me. The door was open, the cool Chicago morning air drifting into the car. I stepped out of the car one black heel at a time. I stopped, and Toby moved to close the door behind me, allowing me to see old man Moretti... As in Savino Moretti, the man who had a much more sinister reason for wanting my brother dead. His graying brown hair was combed back in waves and as he came to stand beside me, I saw he was so short that I could have rested my elbow on his head. He grinned at me before lighting the cigar he'd taken from his jacket and inhaling the scent deeply.

"Beautiful day, isn't it?" he asked, placing the cigar between his chapped lips. His mustache looked like it was trying to cover them up, but barely reached the top lip.

"Depends on who you are," I replied, taking my sunglasses off my head, my dark hair falling slowly over my shoulder as I perched them on my nose.

"True," Savino muttered, glancing up as the jet began its decent.

Out of the corner of my eye, I saw his knuckles flex.

Well, he's anxious. Then again, why wouldn't he be? Ethan had killed his daughter, and now he would never see Ethan alive again.

"Just distract yourself." Toby whispered into my ear. "Everything you are, everything you've gone through, has been for this moment."

In the mafia, there is an unspoken rule; you don't kill family... Unless you have to kill family. Why? Well because family wasn't just people, it was the name. The name Callahan was both a shield and a weapon. Sometimes in order to protect the name, you had to kill a person.

"I'll do what I must do," I whispered to myself as

the jet pulled in across from us. Just like I'd planned, Ethan was the first one out. He raised his brow in question as he glanced down at us...only us; none of his men present as they should have been.

"Welcome back, big brother," I replied sweetly.

"This doesn't feel like a welcome, little sister." He replied emotionlessly, walking further down the stairs towards me.

I grinned. Of course, he'd sense it. "You're right, big brother." His green eyes, the same green eyes as mine, glared at me, trying to read what exactly I was thinking. And what I thought was...*I will never be able to wash my hands of this.* But what I said was, "I believe the correct word for it would be a coup d'état."

"The correct word for it would be betrayal." He frowned, shaking his head as if I were a little kid, as if he didn't really believe I was capable.

Well, wasn't he stupid?

Toby handed me the gun. Before Ethan could get another word in, I pointed the gun and said,"Let's call it betrayal then."

I fired.

His wide eyes were the last thing I focused on before twisting my wrist to the left. I fired once into Savino's skull and then once over my right shoulder, not looking at Toby as I fired directly into his chest.

"Dona..." He gasped behind me, before stumbling back against the Range Rover. I didn't stop firing, feeling the heat of the gun burn in to my shoulder, until there were no bullets left. When I finally glanced back up, the man I'd shot first - the pilot - lay dead at the entrance of the jet, his rifle slipping from his hands on to the step below him. His blood splattered the inside wall of the jet.

Wyatt and Ivy stepped forward to the entrance of the jet. Wyatt's wide brown eyes stared down at the pilot at his feet and then glanced over at me. Ethan, who'd dropped down in order to dodge the bullet he thought was meant for him still hadn't gotten up. He remained on one knee, his green eyes fixed on me...along with the gun in he'd pulled out. Even now, he still didn't drop it, his finger on the trigger.

Staring back at him, I lifted my hands but didn't drop my gun either.

"You would have lost," I told him. If I'd wanted to,

there was no way I could have missed him when he was so close. It would have been a perfect shot between the eyes, he'd never have had a chance to point his gun at me. *I could have done it. It would have been so easy.*

"Maybe." He couldn't even admit it as he winced, rising from the ground and standing like a pillar in front of me. Walking over to me, he just glared before putting his gun to my cheek. I allowed him to turn my head to the side so he could inspect my eardrums.

"You're bleeding. Are you alright?" he asked softly, finally taking his gun off my face and tucking it behind his back.

"Is she alright? Ask me if I'm al-fucking-right!" Wyatt yelled, stepping over the pilot and getting a good footing before reaching back to help Ivy, who he'd been holding back, over the body as well. "I've been in this city for less than a bloody minute - *one minute!* - and I've had a shotgun in my face, and blood on my shoes. Why can't we ever have a normal welcome home? You know, balloons! Maybe a banner or some shit like that?"

Closing my eyes quickly, I inhaled deeply and counted to ten mentally, before opening my eyes again and tilting my head to the side, looking around Ethan's body to see Wyatt. "Got it. Next time balloons. So… You're done with Boston now?"

"Donatella," Ethan interrupted.

Ignoring him, I focused on Wyatt. "You're wearing a dress shirt…and a tie. *Gasp*, you must really be home. I should have gotten a '*he's a man now*' balloon."

"We can get Wyatt his balloons later; right now, I'm much more curious about the blood at our feet," Ethan interrupted, and I looked down at Savino's blood, which crawled over the gravel to where our feet were directly opposite one another.

"Does it look like I give two shits about your curiosity?" I asked him when I lifted my head to look at him directly.

Ethan's eyebrow rose as he spoke, "Keep your shit; tell me what happened."

"So, am I supposed to take sides here or just watch you two glare at each other all day?" Wyatt asked, standing off to the side.

"Wyatt, hold this." I tossed my gun to him and, not a second later, pulled my fist back before bringing right across Ethan's jaw.

"I guess I'm watching then," Wyatt muttered, stepping back from the both of us.

Ethan reached up, touching his cut lip while flexing jaw. His eyes focused back on me. He didn't get a chance to speak, and I didn't get a chance to get another hit in because before either of us had time, *she* got in between us.

"Hit him again and you'll regret it." Ivy—messy haired, raccoon-eyed, pale-faced Ivy—had the nerve say to my face as if I wouldn't beat her down where she stood.

"*Belladonna*, believe me when I tell you this..." I stepped closer to her, "Even if both my brothers were married to you and every last Irishman knelt at your feet, you still wouldn't have the power to make me regret a *goddamn* thing. You have your lane, and it's not in front of me. So move, or I will move you!"

Before I could step any closer to her, Wyatt grabbed my arm, squeezing tightly as he muttered; "*Sister dearest*, whatever this is...breathe."

"Wyatt, take Ivy to the car. Now," Ethan said seriously as more than three other Ranges pulled on to the air strip.

Wyatt, to my surprise, didn't even argue; he let go of me and placed his hand on Ivy's shoulders. She still had the audacity to glare at me with those icy blue eyes of hers as he forced her away. She was lucky… If she was anyone else I'd make her eyes my earrings.

"Don't get her involved." Ethan's stern voice reached my ears.

I laughed bitterly, looking to him; "Why? What are you going to do, oh wise and great one? Lecture me to death? Threaten me? Kick me out of the family?"

He inhaled slowly through his nose, placing his hand on stomach. "I can see you are upset, Donatella—"

"If you can see then you'd already know that while you and your wife were playing house, terrorizing Boston, and almost dying…*nice one*," I smiled brightly, lifting my hands and stretching my arms, "I saved your damn city…you're bloody welcome."

"I wouldn't have left you in charge if I didn't believe—"

"Keep talking to me like I'm a fucking idiot and I really am going to fucking kill you Ethan." He said nothing. Of course, he said nothing. So, I continued. "You didn't believe in me at all. You wanted me to get rid of Toby…and test my loyalties…you set us both up!"

"If Tobias fell into a trap it's his own bloody fault for not watching WHERE THE FUCK HE WAS GOING!" He roared into my face.

"AND ME!" I screamed back. "You set a trap for me! Your sister! If I fell chasing the fake carrot you put in my face is it my fault too?!"

"Good thing you didn't fall little sister so we don't have to answer questions like that," he replied, walking around me toward the cars.

Balling my fist, I turned back to him as I said, "Wyatt and I may be twins, but we do not react the same way to manipulation. I will not come crawling to you. I AM NOT YOUR PUPPET, ETHAN! There are no strings on my back! Next, you'll want to test your—"

"Your lover; your problem, Donatella! I gave you time and space to deal with him before I had to do it myself…because you are my fucking sister, *so you are* bloody welcome," he snapped back at me before I heard the door slam behind him and the wheels of his car pull away.

"Keep pushing me Ethan," I murmured, still trembling with rage. Closing my eyes and relaxing my shoulders, I tried to calm down.

"Is it safe to approach?" Wyatt asked, coming to stand in front me.

"No."

"Oh well, then," he said grinning as he hugged me tightly. I didn't hug him back but I didn't move away either.

"I'm fine," I muttered.

"I'm not. Remember, I had gun in my face…it was *scary*." He spoke in a child-like voice, and I just rolled my eyes, pushing him away and standing up straight again.

"Give me my gun." I reached out for it.

"Sorry." He shrugged his shoulders. "I left it in Ethan's car."

"Wyatt."

"Let's use words."

"I am using words! Would you like me to use my fists?"

He sighed, reaching inside behind his waist and giving me the Glock, but not before asking, "What happened, Dona?"

"What do you think happened, Wyatt?" I replied, taking my gun from him. "*Il maestro di burattino mi ha fatto sentire che le sue stringhe mi tirano attorno al mio collo!*" (The puppet master wanted me to feel his strings pull around my neck!)

"And whatever the master wants, he gets," Wyatt stated. For the first time since he'd gotten off the jet, his face was completely expressionless and all the humor in his voice evaporated.

"I have no master, Wyatt."

Turning around, I looked to Toby's lifeless body slumped over the hood of my white Ranger...his blood splattered over the windshield...over me...staining my suit. No matter how badly you scrubbed or washed, blood never came out of white. I'd known him since I was child, he'd been in my bed, in me, and now the only permanent thing between was a ruined suit, because he, like Ethan, thought he could control me. Unfortunately for him, he wasn't my brother...so I couldn't forgive him.

"No one controls me...but me." Because I was Donatella Aviela Callahan, only daughter of Liam Alec Callahan, head of Irish mob, and Melody Nicci Giovanni

Callahan, head of the Italian mafia... I was a Callahan...and a Callahan was a bringer of death.

ONE

"She wears strength and darkness equally well, the girl
has always been half goddess, half hell."

~ Nikita Gill

DONATELLA – 30 DAYS AGO

"Has it been like this since Sunday?"

"Yes, ma'am," Toby replied, stepping up behind me, blocking the sun with his body and casting a shadow over me. "The explosion came from the right side of the church; I don't know if we should be thankful or not."

"Not," I replied angrily, stepping forward into the OS center, the facility my parents had built right in the heart of the city to honor their fathers, Orlando *"Iron Hands"* Giovanni and Sedric *"The Butcher"* Callahan. Two great men I'd never met, but grew up constantly reminded of. My mother rarely spoke of her father, but when I shipped off to boarding school in Italy, I'd heard stories of him. Those who did remember him spoke of him like he was the boogeyman. Some believed he wasn't dead. That he was out there enjoying the mass fortune he'd "earned."

My father on the other hand, couldn't shut up about his father. Apparently, dear old grandfather hated his nickname so much, he forbade them to bring it up… I had no idea why, though, and it didn't matter now. What did matter was their legacy. The edifice my parents had built in their honor was supposed to show how far our families had come. It wasn't just a soup-kitchen or recreation center. It was reminder of their greatness, only the best of the best of the best went to it. First-class facilities, groceries, and even help with job search. Once a week, every week, we fed anyone who came through the door. The other six days it was open to the public to not only find work and train for better jobs, but for necessities like showers and haircuts. Even people who weren't Irish or Italian came here... And now... Now it looked like a World War II Triage Center, all because of the Finnegan Brothers and their grunts had placed a bomb in our family church.

"Now I know why Ethan left for Boston so quickly, Tobias," I said, walking down the corridor and looking at the sleeping mats that were all laid out. It's easy to get revenge; the aftermath was the messy part.

"Why, *ma'am*?" He stood directly behind me, closer than I preferred in public.

I glanced over my shoulder at him, "Haven't you realized my brother has only two facial expressions; Fear Me and Get the Fuck Out My Way, You Bore Me."

He tried not to smirk, but I saw the corner of his lip

turn up. And I couldn't help but think that he was cute. His long, shoulder length dark-brown hair was pulled back into bun, his light brown eyes staring down at my lips.

"How many children?" I asked suddenly, turning from him and walking on.

"Twenty-nine," he replied, following.

"And adults?"

"Fifteen."

"Fuckin' hell," I muttered to myself. The bombs went off on the right side of the church, the side where most of the parents sat in order to be able to see their kids in the children's choir.

"Before, Ethan had the center open to any children whose guardians couldn't be reached—"

"How nice," I replied sarcastically, "but this center isn't an orphanage. Are social services here?"

"Yes, however..."

"I hate dramatic pauses, Tobias," I said as we walked towards the silver double doors to the main cafeteria.

"Ethan spoke to the major... This is a *family* matter."

"Ethan." I gritted my teeth.

"He simply wants to prove to the people that he will—"

"You don't need to explain my brother's reasoning. I know what he wants. I just don't agree. Since I'm here and Ethan is not, we're doing this my way and they're going to have to go."

"Dona, they're children—"

"It's not up for debate. And even if it was, it wouldn't be a debate with you. The door." I waited, allowing him to go in front me. He pushed the door open and the moment I stepped through, I wanted turn around and walk back right out.

Clenching my teeth, I wave my hand out to the chaos in front us. "You said twenty-nine children and fifteen adults… Does this look like forty-four people?"

His eyebrows furrowed together as he stared at the herd of people now in the cafeteria…the watering hole of grown-ass men and women, whom I'm sure weren't in the church at all, stuffing their faces with our food.

"People are selfish by nature; they came because they heard the Callahan name and thought, 'So what if I wasn't affected directly, they can afford to give up a few extra plates, drinks, blankets...or straws." I said the last one looking directly at the freckle-faced woman stuffing straws, into her daughter's pockets. *Of all things...straws?*

"Ma'am." I turned my head to the side as Greyson appeared beside me. His orange hair and thick beard didn't make him stand out as much normal in this crowd...it was his large build that did that. "The kitchen said they've run out of breakfast and will need time to bring out more."

"More food isn't necessary," I said, watching the line grow at the counter. "Less people are."

"What do you need me to do?" Greyson asked, standing up straighter.

I glanced to Toby, waiting for him to stand up straighter as well. He forced a smile before doing the same.

"We can start asking people to leave," he said.

"I'm not asking; get me a microphone," I said, walking them to the front of the room when all of a sudden, a young voice yelled out.

"FIGHT!"

And like the craven people they were, everyone turned to watch yet no one attempted to stop it, not even my brother's men.

Father, give me strength, I thought as moved toward the "fight", Toby immediately pushing against the rising crowd.

"Take it back!"

"You take it back, you stupid—"

"GET OFF HIM!" a blonde-haired woman in her late forties screamed, pushing one of the boys away and hugging her son or grandson to herself. "How dare you?"

"He started it!" the other boy yelled, wiping his nose on his arm, ready to charge again. And if it wasn't for his friends holding him back, he would have.

"Marco, stop!" One of them yelled as they tried to hold on to his arm.

"Say it again," the boy—Marco, apparently—sneered at the other one. "Say it again! Call me *Guido* again!"

The moment the word came out of his mouth, more than few of the men who hadn't been paying attention turned to look at the coward with blond hair.

"I don't know what you are talking about!" he lied.

"How dare you make up such a lie!" she yelled back.

"I'm not lying—"

"You are, too!"

"And why don't we just stop there," I said politely, a fake smile on my face as I walked into the makeshift circle. Everyone's eyes turned to me. "It's been a stressful time for all of us—"

"I want an apology!" Marco yelled, yanking his arm away from his friends to stand on his own. He wasn't look at me. I wasn't sure if he could see anything other than the target of his rage. So, I stepped in front of him and snapped my fingers.

"Hi," I smiled again. *I just know I'm going to have massage my cheeks tonight.* "Do you know who I am?"

He frowned, looking at me for long time, until one of his friends whispered more than a little loudly, "It's Ethan Callahan's sister."

You little shit.

"Orlah." A few others whispered.

"Ethan Callahan's sister has a name and it's Donatella." I tried to speak with as little venom as possible. "And I said this fight is over. So, it's over. Am I clear?"

His hands balled into fists, he breathed through his nose, but didn't say anything.

"Thank you, Donatella, kids like him have no training or respect," the woman said from behind me.

I turned slowly to face her. She put her hand on her son's head, petting him as if he were a prized dog. "I'm sorry, I don't know what you mean? Kids like him?"

She tensed but didn't back down, "I just mean kids who are spoiled. The ones always trying to blame other people for their problems."

She's joking. She had to be.

"He's my problem!" Marco yelled at her.

"Marco, didn't I say this fight was over?" He muttered something under his breath and turned to walk away. "Don't walk away from me when I'm talking to you!"

If it wasn't for the older, white haired, half-drunk man who put his hands-on Marco's shoulders, he would have ignored me and kept walking.

"So, rude." I shook my head and turned back to the woman "What is your name?"

"Claire Eilis, my husband works for your brother," she said with a smug grin on her face; almost identical to the brat next to her lifting his chin as he glared at Marco.

"Really? Thank you for all your hard work. I haven't

met your husband personally, but I'm sure he's a good man. Is this your son?" *Keep smiling, Donatella. Just keep smiling*.

"My nephew, Declan."

"What a coincidence! I have an uncle named Declan too; do you know what the name means?"

The boy stepped forward, shaking his head and pretending to be innocent, "No, I don't ma'am."

"It means full of goodness," I said, putting my hand on his head and petting him just like his aunt had done for a second before grabbing a fistful of his hair and pulling his head back. "So why are you such a little shit?!"

"AH!" he reached up to grab my wrist. "Aunty!"

"Yes, Aunty Claire, please explain to me why your nephew is spitting out slurs in my center?" I asked, tilting my head to look at her clearly.

"He didn't do that—"

"So, Marco here just decided that out of all the kids here, he was going to frame your nephew and disrespect me using a term not commonly used in Chicago, in order to...? I'm sorry, but you're going to have to fill in the blanks for me, Aunty Claire. It must be the *Guidette* blood in me that makes it difficult to comprehend."

"I... He—"

"In fact, the more I think about it," I spoke, yanking more of the boy's hair, "the less this whole situation makes sense. Who gave you the right to call me Donatella? Why is your nephew a little gobshite? If your husband works for my brother, I'm sure you don't need to be here—?"

"We came to volunteer!"

"Tobias!" I called out, knowing he'd be somewhere close.

"Yes ma'am?"

"Is there a Claire Eilis on the volunteer's list?"

He checked his phone and before saying; "No, ma'am."

I gasped, still not letting go her nephew's hair; "See, now I have more questions, but I don't know if I can trust you, Aunty Claire. You seem like you've been lying to me. Are you lying to me, *Aunty Claire*?"

Her pink lips parted but she said nothing; she looked like a goldfish, her mouth opening and closing, her eyes wide and dead. So, I looked down to the boy in my grip trying his best not to cry. Toby came over to me, standing at my shoulder to whisper. "The kids are recording you."

Ignoring him, I spoke to the boy again, "Do you know why no one is coming to help you?"

His bottom lip quivered.

"I asked you a question, Declan."

"N...no."

"It's partially because you are a spoiled little gobshite; do you know what a gobshite is?"

"No."

I sighed; "You should ask your uncle when you see him next..."

"What's the other part Ms. Callahan?" I looked over at Marco, who spoke as he stood surrounded by friends all grinning at Declan. "You said no one is stopping him partially because he's...because he's a...goa...gobshite?"

"Gobshite! You have to say it with feeling Marco, come on, try again, all of you,"

Excited they said it loudly, proudly, and yes, with feeling and they weren't the only ones. A few others joined in... I noticed many of them...most them were Italian. The Irish looked uncomfortable and, as if to play on their pride, Declan started to cry.

"He's just a kid—" his aunt said.

"He's what? Ten?" I asked her.

"Twelve." Someone coughed but there were so many people around, I couldn't tell who it was.

"TWELVE? Now I'm upset." I pulled Declan over to Marco and stood them facing each other, "If you're old enough to know how to use slurs, you're old enough to repent for them. So repeat after me and then you're free to go."

"Okay."

"I, Declan the gobshite,"

He didn't say it.

"Declan..."

"I, Declan the gobshite," he repeated making Marco and his friends break out in laughter.

"Am very sorry for insulting not just you, Marco,"

"Am...very...sorry for insulting...not just you, Marco," he hiccupped.

"But every Italian person in the world."

"...I didn't..."

"Declan, my hand is getting tired; I can ask one of my *friends* to told your head if you'd like."

"But every Italian person in the world," he said quickly.

"I swear—"

"I swear—"

"To be less of a gobshite,"

He took a deep breath; "To…be…less of a gobshite."

"And never use that word or any other word like it again in my life."

Once he was done repeating my words, I flung him over to his aunty but not before letting her have it, "I'll get answers to my questions, Aunty Claire. And when I do, I'll personally visit you and your husband to tell you what I know. In the meantime, why don't you spend less time worrying about other people's children and fix the one rioting next to you because I swear on my mother's grave, if he ever insults my blood again…he'll see his. GET OUT!"

She left like fire was under her feet. As she was leaving, Marco and his friends began to cheer and make faces.

"Do I need to make show out of you all, too?" I asked and they immediately shut their mouths, looking down. It was silent, so I took the opportunity to address them all.

"Most of you do not know me personally. Consider yourselves blessed. Because if I have to get involved personally, I will not only embarrass you and your whole family, I'll make you wish you lived in a hole so deep you'd never see the sun, let alone my face. So take note, these are the things I get personally involved with: one, people abusing my family's generosity; two, people disrespecting my family or my heritage; and three, people causing trouble for my family. I'm sure you all can see the running theme here. If not, please let me know?" I asked politely again, looking around.

"Brilliant," I said, flipping the mental switch in my mind to kind and gentle as I spoke now. "I'm glad so many of you were able to enjoy today's breakfast. Please let anyone and everyone you know who plan on coming tomorrow that unfortunately my family and I will only be serving those affected by this horrendous terrorist attack. Of course, those of you who are suffering financially, our city's poor and needy, will always be welcome. It truly means so much to me. As you know my grandmother was one of the victims of this horrendous act and I want to make sure no-one is overlooked. The Mayor has also said he'll be allocating funds to help with any children who have been displaced either by the loss of guardian - and my heart goes out to those - as well as those of you whose parents are being treated at the hospital. I wish you could stay here, but we've been told by emergency services that this building isn't suitable for temporary housing. My cousin Nari will give you more information tomorrow. Thank you so much for your support and understanding."

I nodded to all of them before walking forward towards the double doors, my cobra-skin Gucci heels clicking on the floor as I tried to exit. I'd just made it into the hall when I heard the doors open again behind me as someone called out.

"Ms. Callahan!"

Pausing, I took a deep breath before turning back to Marco, he glanced up at me and blanched before looking back down. Toby's eyebrow raised and he glanced over at me, that small grin on his face again.

"Are you going to thank me or are you going to keep admiring the tiling?" I asked Marco.

"Uh...thanks. I mean thank you! Uhh..." he said this while looking directly at me and then rubbed the back of his head, trying to think of what else to say. I just nodded and was about to walk away when he said, "I wanna work for you!"

I paused, observing how grown up he was trying to make himself seem. Standing up taller, he stuck out his chest as if he were enlisting in the army…*he kinda is.*

"What is it you think I do, Marco?"

He blinked like I'd just slapped him, and then tried to think.

"You've got no idea," I answered for him.

He frowned, regaining his grown-up stance, "No, I got no idea. My pa says you guys run a lot of businesses and are really important people, so you've got guards because people always hurt you. I can fight! You saw. I could protect—"

I cut him off, "I protect myself, Macro. And besides, I'm *just* Ethan Callahan's little sister; you should speak to him—"

"No." Under his breath he muttered, "I don't want to work for the Irish."

I stared at him for a long time before moving over to Tobias. I flip open his jacket, reaching into the inside pocket and pulling out the pen. Hearing me walk over to him, Marco swallowed and took half a step back.

"Give me your arm."

"Why?" he eyed me carefully, putting his arm behind his back.

Rolling my eyes, I held onto his chin while he bunched up his face, closing his eyes like he was getting ready for a punch he couldn't avoid…or praying. Clicking the pen, I brushed his hair out of the way before writing directly on his forehead.

"Only the best work for me. So, if you want to join me, you're going to need more than your fists, you're going to need this." I used the pen to tap the top of his head before clicking it again. "And I'm going to need certification that you've used it. So that's after high school and college. Once you do all of that, call this number."

"High school and college?" he stared me like I was insane. "That's forever!"

"That's ten years; good luck." I gave him the pen before moving to leave.

"What happens if this number isn't working!" he yelled after me.

"It will work," I hollered back at him, stepping out into the wind as it blew in between the buildings. Toby opened the door to my car as it pulled up to the front of the building.

"Poor kid," Toby sighed, shaking his head, "He'll never find a girl that will live up to his first crush."

"Are you speaking from experience?" I questioned.

"Are you thinking you're my first crush?"

"I don't care either way," I told him honestly as I sat inside. "She wouldn't be able to live up to me even still."

"Would it kill you to be jealous once in a while?" He muttered something in Italian to himself, closing the door before I could reply.

I would have told him I heard him but in that moment, hearing someone else speaking Italian, something clicked at the back of my mind. I turned back to look at the glass, pyramid-shaped building.

"Marco, what is his last name?" I asked when Toby took his seat behind the wheel.

He grabbed his phone, scrolling, "Marco Forte. His mother died when he was young and his father, Joe, was injured during the bombing. But he's going to be alright, the kid's probably—"

"What does his father do? Does he work for us?"

He sighed, twisting his jaw to the side, "No. He's just a plumber."

"Find out how life has been going for Joe just-a-plumber."

"Alright, what am I looking for?"

"I don't know," I whispered mostly to myself, not able to get this nagging feeling out of my head. "Drive."

"Where to *Ms. Callahan*?" Toby questioned. When I didn't reply, he called again, "Dona—"

"Anywhere. I need to think."

Something felt off here, but I wasn't sure what.

TWO

"The sun watches what I do

but the moon knows all my secrets."

~J.M. Wonderland

DONATELLA - 24 DAYS AGO

The handcrafted yew-wood table was centered between the double doors where I stood with the large bay windows at the back. The chandelier, forged from iron and glass, was long, stretching almost the length of the table, but due to all the natural sunlight coming through the large bay windows, wasn't switched on. The chairs were like elegant wooden thrones and the china set in front them changed depending on the seasons. It was always, without exception, set for fifteen. With no else here but me, the dining room looked like it belonged on the cover of a luxury home and style magazine.

Everyone had their respective seats. Even myself…always on the left, one seat down from the head of the family, once my father, but now my brother, Ethan. Directly across from me sat my twin brother, Wyatt.

Order.

We all had our place and unless some died, there wasn't any reason to deviate from it. I walked directly to Ethan's seat.

"Good morning, Miss," O'Phelan, who had been the

head butler of our little Chicago castle for the last seventeen years, greeted me as he came from the side door to fill my glass of water. "I wasn't aware you wished to eat in the dining room today. I had your breakfast sent to your room."

"I'm eating here today," I said, running my hands over the groves of the first chair, walking around it once before taking a seat comfortably on it.

"Would you like the same breakfast I sent up—"

"No. Fresh fruit, vanilla yogurt, a croissant, and a deviled egg with a glass of grape juice," I told him, rolling my neck. He nodded, walking away for a minute only to return with a few documents, a tablet, and pen for me.

"Your publicist left a message saying they've pushed back the release of your next novel until Christmas."

Before I could reply, the doors at the other end of the room open and in walked Toby, dressed head-to-toe in black and wearing an expression befitting of Severus Snape.

"Good morning..."

"What's the matter today?" I asked, reaching for my

water.

"Marco Forte..."

"How many times has he called that number already?" I couldn't help but chuckle, shaking my head at thought of the little punk.

"He's dead," Toby replied.

I stared at him, though I wasn't looking *at* him or anything else for that matter. It was only when O'Phelan rolled out my food on the trolley and began to set my plate that I snapped out of it, plucking the grapes from the vine and tossing them into my mouth as I leaned back.

"From the look on your face. I'm guessing he didn't die of natural causes?" I finally replied.

"The police are saying he accidentally fell down the fire escape."

"Thank you." I nodded to O'Phelan when he moved to leave before I looked back to Toby. "I know what the police are saying...what are people saying?"

"Declan Eilis...or at least someone in the Eilis family."

"Of course," I rolled my eyes, lifting my spoon and yogurt.

Toby frowned, confused, "You don't believe it's him?"

I swallowed the spoonful in my mouth before replying "It's a little stupid, don't you think? I make the Eilis boy apologize to the Forte boy, and when I turn around the Eilis boy pushes the Forte boy down a fire-escape, killing him? Why? It's too obvious and too soon. He knows I'd find out and he wouldn't try it."

"Dona, he's a kid, not a trained assassin. I doubt in the moment he was thinking about the optics or with any rationality at all. Worse, if Marco might have taunted him…he could have snapped."

"Or…someone is testing me." Who, though? The Irish? The Italian? Ethan? "Someone wants to know what happens when I get involved."

"Dona, I really think you're overthinking this. Who would do that?"

"I don't care what you think!" I snapped at him. "I'm not sure why you keep asking me questions that you should already have answers to. Isn't this your job?"

He inhaled deeply through his nose, then exhaled. I kept eating my yogurt. Finally, he replied, "My job is to help you look at the optics... Irish kid kills an Italian kid—"

"Allegedly," I cut in, licking my spoon.

"You know as well as I do that a rumor is as good as a signed confession for many of these people, Dona. Some people are going to be looking to your family...no, to you... to handle it the way such matters have always been handled."

I dug into the bottom of the cup for the last bit of yogurt as I spoke, "So since you are also supposed to look at the optics, explain to me how would it look to have two dead kids?"

"One dead kid and a dead murderer."

"A kid who murders is still a kid," I said reaching for the eggs before looking up at him. "And if he's gone, especially so soon, the blame will fall on me. People will say 'oh, this is her fault, she made a big deal out of such a small issue, which should have been left to the boys to resolve. Now look what happened'...bad optics...for me."

He didn't reply, instead he moved closer and closer...until he was too close. He reached inside his jacket pocket, pulling out an origami dandelion. Holding it up between us, he twirled it in his fingers as he spoke, "I remember when you used to take your time picking dandelions one by one and everyone thought you were crazy, but I realized you did that to see which dandelions were the strongest. Which ones wouldn't blow away because of the wind as you walked. You were testing each flower and when you collected the perfect ones you'd use them to make a crown, place it on your head, and with this enormous hallelujah grin on your face, you'd get up and run and spin and jump as hard as you could, until every last petal came off the stems and it was floating all around you. You'd close your eyes and make wish…and each time you did…I did too."

"You wished to have me," I stated, reaching to take the paper flower from his hand, but he moved it. His fingers barely touched my ear as he brushed my hair behind it and placed the paper flower there, too.

"No, Dona," he said softly, "I wished that whatever you were wishing for would come true. Because in my mind, any wish from someone as sweet, kind, and innocent as you deserved to come true."

I wasn't sure what to say, so I stood up and he leaned back, allowing me to move around the chair.

However, I didn't leave. Instead, I kissed him, and like all our kisses it started off gently, tenderly. His hand fell to my waist, pulling me to him, both of our bodies pressed against each other...his hand sliding down to grab my ass when I stopped him, and pulled away.

"The cameras," I whispered to him, wiping the corner of my lip. "Later."

He just nodded and let me go. Walking around him, I headed back out the door. And just as I was about to make my escape he spoke.

"It is bad optics...for you, I know. However, it's worse optics for you to look weak. The public only remembers you as that sweet, kind, innocent little girl who cried her heart out the day her mother died... They need to see and know that you are no different than Ethan," he said. I turned around to tell him not to lecture me, however he spoke again before I could. "My job is also to tell you things you don't want to hear. Yes, I know, annoying. Ethan hates it, too."

The shit-faced grin on his lips as he ate my leftover strawberries killed the whole mood he had worked so hard to set with the damn dandelion.

"And you know what I said about later... I need to cancel." His mouth dropped open. I smiled. "You should have stopped while you were ahead, Tobias. Ethan can simply hate you... I can blue ball you."

I left and I didn't look back, allowing the doors to close him in as I walked towards the large grand staircase, to the elevator which lead to our private rooms, taking the paper flower from behind my ear.

*Someone as sweet, kind, and innocent as you...*he had said. I couldn't help but chuckle a little to myself as I twisted the paper flower between my fingers. Closing my eyes and blowing on it, even though I knew it wouldn't fly away, and made my childhood wishes all over again.

"Dandelion. Dandelion. As you float up beautifully dying. Grant these wishes from my throat. Give me the King's coat. Give me the Queen's Ring. Chop the Princelings to their knees. Send a swarm of killer bees to those who try to hurt me. And oh yes! Let it always be spring."

I couldn't help but grin, looking up from the paper flower at the distorted mirror of the elevator doors opened on my floor. I stepped out, wondering what Tobias, or any of them would do, if they knew my wishes back then were only sweet to me and neither kind nor innocent to others.

Pushing the handle down and entering my room, I moved towards my soft pink and cream-colored circular bed, dropping the paper flower on top of it and picking up the remote control. After entering my passcode, my bed spun around to face wooden wall that split open from the middle, revealing my brother's former master bedroom...now my closet.

Inside, I paused at the first mirror, fixing the strap of my silk emerald jumpsuit before moving to the second one near my bags, pressing my whole palm to the glass.

"Access granted," it said before the glass slid down, inside each of my guns and knives were displayed like fine china. I lifted the gold-engraved pistol, pressing the wood panel underneath it, taking out the old flip-phone, dialing quickly before lifting it to my ear. It rang once before she answered. She didn't speak, but I knew she was there.

"A boy named Marco Forte was killed today. Find out by who and why, Jackal, and find out fast. I need to know how deep this goes and how many people need to die."

Her reply was to hang up immediately, and I knew

that meant I'd have an answer within forty-eight hours.

Flipping the phone closed, I put it back in its place, the wood panel clicking closed. The glass of the mirror slid back up, showing my own reflection, my green eyes staring right back at me.

"All warfare is based on deception. Hence, when we are able to attack, we must seem unable; when using our forces, we must appear inactive; when we are near, we must make the enemy believe we are far away; when far away, we must make him believe we are near. But remember... To win one hundred victories in one hundred battles is not the acme of skill. To subdue the enemy without fighting is the acme of skill...this is The Art of War," I said to my own reflection, a small smirk appearing on my lips. I hadn't put the gun away.

Walking from the mirror, I wondered if I should feel insulted or grateful that my enemy, whoever it was, thought I was so stupid...

What was the fastest way to take power from my family?

It wasn't money... Anyone with half a brain knew my family had more than enough hidden all over the world to get by for generations, if not longer. My father had taught us all The Callahan Family Rules, and the moment I'd heard Marco say he wanted to work with me, I knew that he saw Ethan as Irish. I knew something wasn't right in that, which is why I remembered Rule 28: *"Remember that it is the clan that gives us our power."*

The fastest way to take power from my family...was to destroy the clan.

In the *Art of War*, the greatest test of skill was to subdue the enemy without fighting... What better way to do that than to pit the Irish and the Italians against each other... To restart the blood feuds between them.

"It's exactly what I would do..." I whispered to myself as I took a seat in my leopard-print chair, placing my gun on the side table, before reaching for the bottle of Pink Moscato at the bottom it. I filled a glass and turned the television screen to the cameras Ethan had secretly placed in the home of the man he hated so much, he had fucked his daughter just to spite him.

"I'm sure you remember the old blood feuds, Savino Moretti," I said, bringing the glass to my lips as I watched as Moretti screw yet another woman that was far too young for him in his office... Ethan and Ivy had killed his daughter, Klarrisa Moretti, only days ago and this was apparently how he mourned.

"To each their own," I whispered, drinking. Wine made everything, even this gag-worthy performance, bearable.

Soon—the moment I knew for sure it was him—I'd leave holes in him for the worms to fuck.

DONATELLA - 23 DAYS AGO

"Your screams are for the many and mine for the one. So, I am alien to you and you are alien to me." I typed on my laptop from inside the gazebo overlooking the koi pond at the edge of our private property.

"Your tea, ma'am." One of the maids filled my glass for me. However, I didn't look up. My fingers were trying to keep up with the words racing through my mind, when all of sudden a tablet was thrust in my face. I stared at the machine for a moment before looking up at the hand holding it there; when I finally got to his face, he was smiling down at me.

"I was waiting for you to get to a break but knowing you, that could be hours," Toby said.

"This about Marco?" I asked, lifting my hands from the keys, and taking the tablet from him.

"It is and I'm not sure if it's a good thing or a bad thing that it's not what you thought." He sighed, reaching over to press play. "There wasn't a camera in the alley but there was one across the street."

I watched as the blond-haired Declan, running as

quickly as possible out of the alley across the street, tried to wipe the blood on his hands onto his jacket, checking behind and in front of him, panicked.

"He later ditched his clothes," Toby explained, showing me the next video, which was a little grainier, but I could still see him as he threw his jacket into a dumpster behind a restaurant.

"No one else has these videos?" I asked him.

He nodded. "I bought it off the owners. What they'll say to others, though, is beyond me."

"Nothing should be beyond you," I corrected, handing him back the tablet. "Where is he now?"

"His mother's house. Hiding under the bed, I'm sure, which gives us time to enjoy our anniversary before paying him a visit." He grinned, grabbing my arm and lifting me off my seat.

"Anniversary? We do not have—"

Placing a finger on my lips, he smiled then looked me dead in the eye as he said; "For tonight, forget you're a Callahan and all the baggage that comes with that and simply have fun with me."

He looked like a puppy…that was the excuse I gave

myself as I followed him out of the gazebo and on to path towards the house, just as Greyson walked towards us. I tried to pull my hand away, but Toby held on tighter.

"Greyson, whatever it is, it can wait—"

"No, it can't. Don't speak for me!" I yanked harder, ripping my hand from his and turning to face Greyson, who looked between us both for a moment, glaring at Toby before looking to me.

"The new shipment has come in. However, they're short."

I froze, my whole-body stiffened. "How short?"

"Short enough that there needs to a very good excuse—"

"No excuses," I cut him off, stepping closer I asked him again. "Does Ethan often give anyone a chance to give him an excuse?"

"No, ma'am." He stood straighter.

"So, why should I?" I tilted my head to the side. He didn't answer. "Do the major cities have enough?"

"The Golden Three paid for more this time but they haven't gotten it," he replied.

"Since Boston is on hold for now, have them send

their shipment to the new Golden Three; Charlotte, Charleston, Jackson. Then, if anyone has anything they aren't moving, have it sent to Miami and Savannah."

"We have reverses—"

"No. That reeks of desperation. Do I look desperate to you?" I asked him.

"No, ma'am," Greyson said, with a slight laugh in his voice, and I turned to Toby.

"You come with me!" I snapped, already heading off the path into the woods. I walked for at least five minutes before turning to him and bringing my hand across his face as hard as I could. "WHAT THE HELL IS WRONG WITH YOU?"

His head was still turned to the side as if he couldn't believe I'd hit him.

"Do you feel good about that?" he asked, his eyes shining with rage, his fist clenched at his side. I wanted to smack him a second time. "Slapping me when you know I can't slap you back? And believe me, if you were anyone else, I'd do it."

"THAT IS THE PROBLEM!" I yelled. "I am not anyone else. I cannot forget I am a Callahan! Do not act upset. Do not pretend to be my victim; you are victim of yourself! You wanted to be with me and I made it clear that if we were, I was not going to treat you any different to anyone else and yet you keep insisting that I do! You keep forcing my hand. Who are you to decide whether or not I hear news about my family's business! News YOU should be giving me! Instead, you are making me look weak!"

"YOU CAN'T BE EVERYTHING YOU WANT TO BE!" he roared back at me. "For now, you are the head of this family, but what happens when Ethan returns? You're just going to sit in the corner with your blood boiling because he's taken over again! What are you going to do? Never marry anyone? You said you wanted to be loved! THAT IS WHAT I AM TRYING TO DO! You don't seem to get that you're going to have to give up on something, Dona, because you can't be Callahan and stand above everyone while still trying to find your equal! NOT UNLESS you plan on screwing your own—"

This time, I punched him dead on the nose, his whole head going back and for the first time, he hit me back. Something erupted between us. His fist slammed into my side.

"UGH!" I screamed, bouncing back into the ring, hopping in place, keeping my body moving and fighting the pain. He grinned, flicking the tip of his nose with his finger as he glared at me. When he came forward again, I ducked down and he shifted his punch, coming towards my face, replaying the punch he'd give my side. With an elbow right into his balls, I sent him curling forward before I grabbed his fingers and bent them back, twisting his whole arm while rising up and bringing him to his knees.

When Toby reached up, grabbed my blouse, and flipped me over him and onto my back, I couldn't think; the pain shooting up my body like lightening in a tree.

I rolled away from him on the ground of the woods; dirt, dry leaves all in my clothes, before he could grab ahold of me. I got to my feet and charged the small distance between us, head-butting him right in the nose and mouth. I felt his teeth hit my skull, but I didn't stop. When his head was thrown back, I punched him as quick and as many times as possible. He dropped his arm down, and I took the opportunity to hit him, but his arms wrapped around me like a snake, giving him enough time to lock his arms, pick me up off my feet, and run my back right into one of the trees. I lifted my arms to block him, but he grabbed them, holding them over my head and kissing me; his tongue in my mouth, his body pressed hard against me, and I couldn't help it, going from pain to that…felt…

"OH…" I moaned into his mouth, grabbing on to his shirt when he let my hands go, only to hike my skirt up to my waist.

"Fuck, you're beautiful," he gasped when our lips broke away for only a second. But I didn't want to talk, I wanted to fuck, so I reached down and undid his pants, grabbing his cock.

"Tell me something I don't know," I whispered back, before kissing him again.

THREE

"My mother always told me,
no monsters lived beneath my bed,
but she had failed to warn me,
it laid on top of it instead.
~ Poet E.h

DONATELLA - 22 DAYS AGO

I was sore.

And I wasn't sure if it was from the sex or the fight before the sex... I had a feeling it was a bit both, but mostly the fight.

I wanted to spend the day soaking in the bath to stop the bruises from getting bad. However, at five in the morning, I found myself in the Contemporary Art section of The Art Institute of Chicago, staring at a massive abstract painting of a woman sinking underwater, her skin cracking; above her was an eagle with a crushed butterfly in its claws and below her, in the water, was the tail-end of a shark disappearing behind the rocks.

"You're late," I said, hearing the footsteps behind me. I didn't bother turning around. She walked up beside me, standing at exactly my height, looking up at the painting as well. Turning to her, as she turned to me, and had anyone else had seen her, they would have flinched; her face was covered in deep, jagged-edged scars. They cut across the nose, cheek, and mouth...but none of them were as bad as the one she hid under her scarf, the one that ran right over her vocal cords. "You're never late, Jackal, what happened?"

She didn't answer. Not because she wouldn't, but because she couldn't. Not vocally, at least.

Reaching into her large tote bag, she handed me a thick yellow file.

Turning away from her completely, I walked to the bench within the exhibit and sat down.

"This is a lot of information on one kid."

When I looked back at her, she simply shook her head.

Furrowing my eyebrows together, I tried to read her expression, but she was keeping it blank on purpose.

"I'll just read then," I replied, opening the page. The very first thing I saw was an imagine of Toby and Savino from last Christmas. "What is this?" I asked, knowing she couldn't speak...but I'm sure she knew I was asking myself, not her.

The photo looked innocent enough, like Savino had accidentally bumped into him. In the back of my mind, I remembered that party. Savino had gotten drunk and started singing to the embarrassment of his daughter...something that was typical of him...and yet, in the image I could clearly see him slipping something into Toby's hand. Turning the page, I saw another photo, this time of the same alley Toby had shown me, where he'd said Declan had killed Marco...however...he shouldn't have been there, in that alley. Nor should he have been chasing down Declan.

Hearing her footsteps, I looked up at Jackal as she pointed to the photo of Toby.

"He killed Marco." I wasn't asking. I just knew. It was the only thing that made sense, and yet, seeing her nod made me inhale sharply. Swallowing the pool of saliva in my mouth, I looked down at my papers and photos again. On them, several of our suppliers...all of them from different regions of Mexico, Colombia, and Venezuela...all of whom had come short for this shipment. I remembered an old conversation Ethan had had with one of our uncles about a power struggle after the death of one of our point men.

"Toby is working with Savino," I whispered, nodding to myself, all the pieces coming together perfectly in my mind. "The drug lords and cartels in South have been changing. The new bloods, the second generation, has no respect for us... Savino wants control of the Italians...what better way to do that than restarting the blood feuds with the Irish, over the death of a proud Italian boy. Thus, cutting off the power of the Callahan's, especially now that Ethan's trying to reign in Boston."

Jackal snapped her fingers in front of my face, and when I looked back at her she held up a photo of Toby, confusion clearly on her face.

"Why would he betray us for Savino?" I asked her question and she nodded, putting the photo back down in my lap. I wish I didn't know that answer...but I did. "Me. He did it for me."

The fucking idiot.

"He'll kill Savino the moment he can. Then he'll be the Don of the Italian mafia. He'll go to my brothers and try to broker a truce...if I marry him. The Callahan's still have an in with the Italians; he's my equal and Ethan's equal. He gets everything he wants. He loves me, but he hates being under me. He hates being under my family. He's not working for Savino, he's working for himself. For his own ambitions."

It was brilliant; he was close enough that we trusted him and he was already respected by association from everyone we knew. On top of that, he knew how to run the business. If it failed... He could pin it all on Savino and wait to strike again.

Jackal crouched down to her knees in front of me and she lifted up the photo of Savino and Toby again. Pointing from Savino to Toby then to me.

"Take their plan?" I asked and she nodded again.

Let Toby kill Savino, then kill Toby. I'd have control over the Italians and Ethan would have the Irish...he'd already married Irish and, in doing so, caused a rift between himself and the Italian side of the family.

Do it, a voice in my mind whispered, rising from the deepest part of me. *This is it. This how we can have it all. Take it from them.*

I could see how I could do it. I could take it all.

The more I thought about it, the stronger that nagging feeling got, like I was missing something important. Glancing down at the folder again, I saw a picture of Ethan. He was at the same Christmas party, holding a glass to his lips, but his eyes were locked on something not in the frame. I lifted the picture of Savino and Toby and put it next to the one of Ethan.

"Ethan," I whispered as I realized how simple it was for me to figure this all out. I was not an idiot, but I was no genius either…at least, not in the same way Ethan was. No one, not even his wife, knew him like I did. Wyatt and I were twins. But Ethan and I were closer in some ways. I knew what he was thinking just by observing the way he held his glass or sat in his chair.

People thought I blindly followed him when I was younger however, that wasn't the case. Like when he first became the *Mani Di Forbice* by killing a priest who'd planned to sell out my parents in order to save himself from being exposed as a child molester. Ethan had grabbed on to my arm and told me not to go to that priest for confession. When I looked at him, I saw the warning, the raging storm that was coming and I simply said okay. I'd spent almost all of my life watching him carefully which is why I knew in my heart that if I could figure this out, if I could see the big picture… Ethan had most definitely seen it months ago.

"These were hard to get…" I stated to Jackal and she

nodded. "But not so hard my brother couldn't find out if he wanted too?"

Again, she nodded.

Toby was betraying us...and Ethan knew.

This whole time, he knew.

"Thank you, Jackal," I said to her, standing back on my feet as she stood up as well. "For reminding me I can't count on anyone."

She frowned at me as I reached into my jacket to pay her for the information she'd garnered. However, she put her hands up, shaking her head.

Rolling my eyes, I took out the monopoly money, making her frown, confused again. "I knew you'd try to reject it, so I had it wired directly into your account from a private account."

She made a face and I grinned, turning from her and walking out of the exhibit, trying my best to bite down on the rage threatening to break free from my lips.

Kill him.

Kill them all.

The words repeated in my mind as I exited out of the building through the security entrance.

***

The sun was just coming up by the time I got home and into my bedroom.

Toby was sitting on the edge of my bed and yawning. He glanced over at me, a happy grin on his lips. "I missed you. Where did you go?"

I stared at him. I wanted to grab anything I could get my hands on and bash his face in. I wanted to strangle him with my sheets. And I couldn't...not now.

"I went for a ride," I said, taking off my leather jacket and throwing it on the couch along with my jeans before walking to my bed.

"What did you need to think about?" he asked as I lay down on the bed.

"You."

At that, he turned back to me eyebrow raised, "Me?"

The secret to lying was the truth...telling people just sprinkle of the truth with fiction mixed in. "You hit me."

His mouth dropped open, "You hit me first! Twice!"

I had to force myself to grin at that even though the

very sight of him made me sick, "I didn't say I didn't deserve it. Nor did I say I was mad you did."

"So what were you thinking about me—?"

"You should have done it a long time ago," I told him seriously, "If you want to stand beside me, you can't always take my shit. I was thinking how if you fought me in private then maybe you wouldn't be so quick to try and speak for me in public or force my hand... It's good you're growing."

He snorted, laying back. "So you're saying all I have to do is take you in the woods—"

"No more woods, that was not comfortable," I cut in quickly. He rolled on top of me, grinning.

"I think we've *both* grown... Someone is a little affectionate this morning."

Rolling my eyes, I tried to push him off but he didn't budge, "Don't you have work to do? I'm still the boss and can sleep in for another half-hour."

"Five more minutes, ma'am." He smiled before kissing me.

Reach into the pillowcase, take the knife, slit his throat! the voice in my mind screamed, but instead I kissed him back, forcing myself to bear it for now.

I'd play along.

I'd let him and Savino think I was sitting in the palm of their hands. Then I'd get to Ethan.

DONATELLA - 14 DAYS AGO

"I know what you're up to, Savino," I said, sitting across from him at The Vocelli, one of his many restaurants throughout the city, Toby standing right behind me.

Savino ignored me, cutting into his duck and spreading it around the sauce on his plate, finally shoving it into his mouth, his tongue yapping like a dog.

"You can either work for me, or die trying to get a slice of what was never yours in the first place."

He snickered, licking his lips as he asked, "What's the difference between working for you and working for your brother?"

"For one, you aren't kissing the feet of the man who killed your daughter," I said coldly...so coldly that he seemed to freeze then glared up at me, nostrils flaring. I smirked, reaching for my knife and fork. "Don't get pissy with me; you're the one who asked a question you weren't ready to hear the answer to."

"Get the fuck out!"

"Why would I do that? I haven't even touched my steak," I asked him, stabbing the meat on my plate.

"I'm not asking you again!" he yelled and pointed his fork at me. "Take her out of here!"

I looked around the mostly empty restaurant at the ten...no, twelve men all around us, none of them moving. It took him a minute to realize that, too.

"Are you deaf!" he yelled, spitting duck out of his mouth.

But still they didn't move.

"That awkward moment when you thought you had bought my men, and they ending up giving that money straight to me," I said as if I were speaking to myself, lifting up my wine glass. All I had to do was look to one of them, the very same men he'd demanded drag me out of here, and each one of them lifted their guns, pointing them at Savino. He froze, staring at them blankly. "Don't feel bad..." I said, leaning back in my chair, bring the glass to my lips, "My family has always made being powerful look too easy. It makes people like you *think* you can be the same. Truth is many of them might even like you. Might even believe you and want to support you. But unfortunately, their fear of me...of the Callahan Family... outweighs everything else."

Well trained dogs never leave...not even if their owner abuses them.

Licking his lips again, he put his fork and knife down, leaning back as I did, folding his hands over each other as he gave me his attention. "If you were going to kill me, I'd already be dead."

"Who says you aren't in the process of dying now? I could have already poisoned your duck... It tasted off, didn't it?" I finished the rest of the wine in my glass, never taking my eyes off him. "My father always told me not to play with my food... But seeing the fear in your eyes right now makes me wonder just how much further I can push you."

Still he didn't reply but he did swallow slowly, the lump of his Adam's apple pressing against the collar of his shirt.

"Ms. Callahan—"

"Call me Donatella," I cut in, holding the glass closer to my face. "You and I are about become much closer."

"How so?"

At that, I stood up and Toby, who hadn't said word since arriving, pulled out my chair to make room for me to move. "I hold your life in my hands. How much closer can you and I possibly be?"

He opened to his mouth to speak, but I cut in once more.

"Your choices are to run to my brother, and he'll kill you most definitely; work for me and one day I might kill you anyway because I don't trust you; or third, you can try running away and you'll die by whoever Ethan or I send after you."

"All of those choices leave me dead—"

"So make me trust you Savino," I replied, already walking to the door.

"You didn't tell me what you wanted," he snapped at me.

At that, I paused, slowly turning back to him; "I thought it was obvious... I want what you wanted... The only difference is, I can get it. I rule Chicago and soon everyone will know it."

He didn't say anything, and I didn't wait to hear anything else. Toby held the door open for me as I walked outside.

"There is no coming back from this once you start,

Dona," he said gently, at the door.

Reaching up, I put my shades on; "Everything I am, everything I've gone through, has been for this one moment... Lamb to Leopard, Butterfly to Eagle, Golden Fish to White Shark. Once you've become something strong, why would you want to go back to being something weak?"

I could see it once he stepped in front me... The smallest niggle of fear in his dark eyes before it was quickly replaced with lust. If he only knew...leopards, eagles, and sharks all ambushed their prey. Then maybe...he'd be smart enough to run. Maybe he'd see me for what I was. What I was going to be...

The death of him.

FOUR

"And when her halo broke,

she carved the two halves into horns."

~ Jordan Sarah Weatherhead

DONATELLA - PRESENT

I hadn't told Wyatt everything.

It hadn't even been that long and yet, in a little over a month, I felt I liked I had aged years.

"Hell…" Wyatt whispered, stepping up beside me, facing the bloody carnage I'd left for all the world to see. I knew he was thinking of what to say, how to make light of this, but words failed him. I, on the other hand, was filled with words.

"It was so easy… All I had to do was convince them that Ethan wasn't for the Italians anymore. After he married an Irish wife, people were already thinking it. I stepped in to that gap, whispering how I'd take over, that I'd kill Ethan and make my twin brother a puppet for the Irish…then I'd rule Chicago. And they made me Don."

"What makes you think I'd just listen to you?" he tried to joke, and I looked over to him.

"What makes you think I would have given you a choice?" Or better yet, he wouldn't have done it just to fight me.

He sighed, shaking his head again, trying to find the

right words, but once again I beat him to it…slightly changing the topic.

"Do you remember Doval?" I asked him.

"Doval?" He turned to face me. A second later it was like a light bulb turned on in his head. "It was wolf-dog you took care of when one summer while we were in Ireland."

I nodded, "Only… I didn't know it was a wolf-dog."

"You thought it was Siberian Husky," Wyatt snickered and I elbowed him. Immediately, he put on a straight face, before adding, "He had Lyme disease, which then gave him severe kidney disease. At that point, there was nothing anyone could do to save him; you didn't lose hope, though."

He said that as if it were something to be proud of.

"I didn't lose hope because I was ignorant. I wanted him to live, so I didn't care what anyone said, which is why, when mom put him down, I vowed to get my revenge."

"You didn't speak to mom for a whole week after that," he reminded me, frowning, and I did too, mostly because she didn't try to speak to me either. "She was hurt."

So was I.

"Do you know what she told me before she killed him?"

He didn't answer... He just waited patiently as the clean-up crew took care of the bodies around us.

"Donatella," I said my name, just as gently and tenderly as she had said it, only this time in English, "you know no moderation, you hunger for everything, you are like chaos in a bottle, your love is like a Golden Fleece, and your rage Pandora's Box. You are like I was. I do not want you to change that. I want you to close your eyes, take a deep breath and think first. Have high expectations, do not doubt yourself and do not compromise. Be smarter and have more patience than everyone else. See the big picture and you will thrive."

"If anyone had a way with words..." Wyatt said, his eyebrows furrowed together and he still avoided looking at me.

"It was our mother," I finished for him. "I was so upset about Doval, I lashed out. I convinced myself that everyone was against me. That mom was always trying to break me. Teach me some stupid lesson. That she didn't want me to be happy because she wasn't happy when she was a kid. Doval was my breaking point. I had it all planned out. How I'd make her pay. Really pay. I think that's why dad finally me took me to the veterinarian,"

I swallowed the lump in my throat, clenching my jaw, "Did you know that some wolf-dogs become deranged in their final moments? The dog part of them goes away and the wolf takes over, fight-or-flight kicks in, and even if you'd taken care of them for years, even if you were the only person who'd ever loved them, out of fear and pain, they attack."

"He took you to see another wolf-dog?" Wyatt looked as if he'd figured out some great mystery.

"Usually the vets put down the sick wolf-dogs, but good old dad had arranged for them to hold off. He had them bring in a bench and sit it in front of the metal cage. He gave me half of his double sausages, double bacon, butter, white pudding, and brown sauce breakfast roll," I shook my head. My father, Liam, had a flare for the dramatic…and a good lunch. "He made a big show of it. He wanted the moment I realized how stupid I was to be forever etched into my mind. And so, I watched; this animal that looked so much like Doval, who had whined and whimpered in pain one moment and then bared its teeth to attack the next, and I realized my stupidity. The wolf-dog lunged at the cage, biting at the at the fence so hard that it was cutting its own gums. It didn't care; it just wanted to break through. It barked and howled, trying to claw at us. Dad made me sit there and watch it unravel for an hour; he'd eaten his sandwich and mine, before he got up and killed it."

He didn't need to tell me that my mother had killed Doval not because she was monster, but because she was a mother. She wasn't going to let my feelings for a dog stop her from doing what she needed to do to protect her family…me, her daughter. That was the big picture.

"I've been called a lot of things, *spoiled little rich girl, high-maintenance Barbie doll, shrill drama queen, immature, cynical bitch, over-the-top psychopath*—"

"By who?!" Wyatt snapped, his eyes directly on me.

Ignoring his question, I bent down to Toby's body, now in a black plastic body bag, the zipper stopping right at his Adam's apple.

"I am all of those things and much more, but what I am not is an idiot and nor am I blind. I couldn't betray my family," I said, speaking directly to Toby as I zipped it over his face and closed the bag.

"I didn't doubt you for a second," Wyatt said quickly.

Standing up back up straight and turning back to look at him earnestly, I told him the truth, "Wyatt, if I could do it, I would."

"Careful, Dona," Wyatt said, the corner of his lip turned up. "The longer you wear the mask, the more it merges with your face."

He thought I was joking. No. He knew me better than that. He just didn't want to take me seriously. He didn't want to think there could ever be a time where I would betray them. I could see it in his eyes, he was pleading with me to stop here. To walk back from the edge of the cliff.

So I swallowed, hoping that would stop the ache in my chest; I forced myself to smile, tilting my heading, and teased him instead. "Careful *little* brother, the monster isn't the mask; it's just you."

"For the hundredth millionth time, I am only one minute and ten seconds younger than you, Dona." He grinned, trying to reach over and lock my head in his arms. I gracefully ducked and walked forward, replying, "And for the hundredth millionth time, younger is still younger, Wyatt."

"Dona—"

I sighed loudly, whipping my head around to look back at him, "Can't you see I'm trying to make a dramatic exit here?"

"Then let me cue it up perfectly," Wyatt said in a brief moment of seriousness. "What happens now?"

"You say that as if I've done something. This part is just prologue."

The door shut once I sat inside of the car. And as Greyson, Ethan's former and my present bodyguard and chauffeur, drove away from them all, I wondered… What was going to happen to that part of me, that chaos in a bottle, that hunger in me, now that I have everything…

"You can't be everything you want to be!" Toby's voice came to mind once more.

I drowned him out with the memory of my mother.

"Have high expectations, do not doubt yourself and do not compromise," she said…and I wouldn't. I wouldn't

compromise my family for power.

"Greyson."

"Yes, ma'am?"

"Do you know of any good tattoo parlors?"

***

SMASH.

I sat up from my bed, pointing the gun directly in the face of… "Goddamn it, Helen! I could have killed you!"

"Don't worry, I'm used to it," she said, standing at the edge of my bed wearing a skin-tight leather Amazonian Wonder Woman costume, complete with gladiator sandals, armbands, gloves, and even the damn crown tucked under dark-brown curls. "I know! I look amazing! I would have killed it at Fall Con this year!"

Without a word to her as she sat down next to me, I flicked my fingers, glancing over to the digits that hovered over my beside table. I stared and stared before turning looking back to her.

"Helen… It's two in morning," I whispered.

"And it's seven in the morning in London," she went

on as if she did not see the problem here, taking her time to unzip her sandals and one by one take of her costume accessories. "Fall Con, starts at ten. All week I've been stuck in business meetings listening to old farts try to explain to me, *to me*, of all people, Helen B. Callahan,"

"B?" I paused as my brain slowly began to wake up. "You don't have a middle name…"

"Rub it in, why don't you," she pulled off her armbands and tossing them on the floor. "The B stands for badass. Helen Badass Callahan."

"If you have to tell people you're a badass, the chances are you aren't as badass as you might think."

"Man, you're cranky." She pouted, tossing her shin guards next.

"I should be! It's two in the morning!"

"Was it the same dream you were having? You looked sad."

"Get out."

"Where was I?" she went on. "Right, me, the genius computer scientist and programmer not genius in the '*oh, I'm being facetious type genius*,' but real '*I have certification genius*,' with cyber security of public-key cryptosystems.

One of them had the nerve to bring up the RSA algorithm! RSA? That came out in 1977, our parents weren't even alive! Grandma was probably just learning how to use a fork then!"

"You do realize I still have a gun in my hand, Helen, right?" I said it as if I were begging her, pleading for her to go to London or the moon, or anywhere else that was not my damn bedroom at two in the fucking morning.

"Yeah about that…" She grabbed the gun and quickly took it apart, putting it on my bedside table before getting up… Naked with the exception of her black short spandex shorts which were more like underwear. She looked amazing; every part of her was toned, her brown skin was flawless, not a single freckle or mismatched tone in sight. She walked…no, skipped into my closet. Grabbing my phone, I turned off all the lights she'd turned on.

"HEY!"

"Go to your own room!" Geez. The only person who could ever get away with this was Helen. My certificated genius, fast-talking, nauseatingly beautiful, computer nerd, comic, manga, anime, all things Netflix loving cousin, Helen. If your last name was Callahan, you were not normal. However, the least normal among us all was Helen. Because we were so close in age, and grew up surrounded by boys, we grew up as close as sisters. She was weird not because she was both a beauty and the geek but because she was like sunshine. Nothing really darkened her mood…and she had plenty to be depressed about. But nope, she went on as if she hardly noticed any of the negativity; it was fucking weird.

"Your bed is more comfortable," she yawned as she lifted my sheets up and hopped right in next to me.

"We have the same type of bed! Ah! You're cold, Helen!" I yelled, trying to kick her away.

But she curled up right beside me. "It's your fault!"

"How? How in the hell is me trying to sleep in my own damn bed the reason you are—"

"You killed Tobias," she whispered, and I went still… It was like I'd forgotten and then remembered all over again. I stared up at the wooden canopy of my bed. "I've been gone for only a month… I was supposed to just pop back into the city to say hi, yes I'm still alive if anyone was wondering before leaving again. I'd even gotten all dressed up, when I got word from Wyatt about what happened... I gave up Fall Con for you, Dona, you should feel honored."

Trying not to smile, I rolled to my side to face her, her big brown eyes staring directly into mine as she smiled back.

"Helen, I'm..."

"You killed Tobias."

I sighed; "Yes, I did."

"You liked Tobias."

"I like myself more."

"So, you feel nothing?" she asked me gently.

I thought for a moment and I even tried to feel something but the truth was, "No. It's—Tobias, was ..."

"Accessible," she tried to speak for me.

"Not what I needed," I corrected.

"Because he was going to betray Ethan?"

"No..." I yawned, not wanting to go on. "I actually enjoyed that he had the balls to do it."

"Ugh... Dona," she groaned, rolling on to her back. "Are we chastising him or defending him, I'm confused!"

"Certificated genius, right here," I joked.

"Shut up!"

"Ah!" She elbowed me right in my healing tattoo which her eyes immediately focused on.

"Oh shit, sorry! You got a tattoo? Without me? I want one!"

"You'd love it for about a week before complaining forever," I reminded her and she thought about it for a moment before nodding.

"That's true."

I laughed and so did she. We laughed until our sides hurt even though nothing was funny.

"We are chastising him," I finally answered her question, speaking much softer now. "Not for being calculating, or power hungry, not even for betraying Ethan…the family, but claiming to love me without knowing me…thinking I was simply okay with being his prize."

She yawned covering her mouth before saying; "But didn't you want to be Ethan? You know, the *Ceann na Conairte*… If so, you kinda missed your chance there."

"Be Ethan, no. Never." I snorted at that. "Be the *Ceann na Conairte*… I should be."

"There's never been a female *Ceann na*

Conairte...not even your mother took that title."

"Never does not mean impossible; it means not yet."

Now she snorted, a habit we both got from our Uncle Neal, "The line of succession is Ethan, Wyatt, Uncle Neal, cousin Sedric, then my dad, and my brother; you'd have to wipe out all the men in our family, and even then you would go from hell fucking never to maybe in your dreams... That is if Nari and I don't kill you for killing our dads and brothers, or you don't kill yourself for the same reason."

I froze, not moving as she spoke the reality I'd kept myself from facing, the reason I had to walk back the edge. The reason why I couldn't betray family even if I wanted to, because the only way I could be the *Ceann na Conairte* was if I killed them all. She figured it out. I figured it out. Ethan knew from the beginning...again. Which was why he'd felt so comfortable leaving me in charge.

"Dona?"

Focusing on her again, I could see the concern in her brown eyes... I didn't need or want her worry. So, a manufactured smile came on my face as I teased her back,

"I wouldn't have to kill Sedric or your brother Darcy, because the Irish would gladly make me *Ceann na Conairte* over an Asian or black kid any day."

"HEY!" she sat up like Dracula from the grave, "First! I'll have you know the Irish are way more tolerant people today and there is a huge growing population of black people in Ireland! Secondly, Irish guys *love* me. Third, Darcy and Sedric are *biracial* and I take offense on their behalf."

I rolled my eyes so hard I was shocked they didn't come out of my head. "We aren't talking about the Irish people; we are talking about the Irish mob - there is a difference. We aren't talking about the very best of us, now are we?"

"Says the sister of the head of the Irish mob," she muttered, falling back down on the pillows. "I'm just saying that...You love your family."

She said that as if she were silently begging me never to forget it. As if she still wasn't sure where the line between teasing and reality ended.

"Which is why I didn't betray anyone... Now shut up and sleep, goddamn it! And move your foot before I chop it off!"

She pretended to snore even though I knew she wasn't asleep. I left her alone and stared up at the ceiling of my room. I had arranged for a wakeup call to be sent at four, but it seemed like I wasn't going to get any sleep now anyway. When Helen's snoring become softer and deeper, I sat up, rubbing the back of my neck as I rose to my feet. I grabbed my cellphone as I walked into my bathroom, the lights turning on automatically.

Turning the faucet on, I splashed the water on my face, inhaling deeply and exhaling slowly before looking at my reflection the mirror. I vaguely took note that my dark hair was getting frizzy, that my ivory white skin looked a little dry. Yet my eyes, my green eyes, were the only thing that really captured my attention…maybe because they reminded me of my father's.

"If not for those eyes, I'd think your mother created you all by herself," he used to say to tease me. And when I'd say whatever smartass reply back, he'd laugh and say, *"You're my kid alright."*

I wish he knew how much strength his jokes gave me.

I wish he knew that each time I looked at myself in the mirror, I remembered... I am the daughter of Liam Alec Callahan, which meant one thing:

"I am a victim of nothing and no one," I said, standing up straighter. Taking the perfectly folded white towel from the basket beside me and drying my face, I pressed the green key on the touchscreen mounted on my bathroom wall.

"Good morning, ma'am." O'Phelan appeared on the screen, already dressed for the morning.

I smirked at him. "I'm now convinced you are a vampire, O'Phelan."

"I assure you, ma'am, I have enough gray hairs to prove I am not."

I smiled at that, placing the towel back on the counter. "The welcome home brunch in honor of Wyatt today; I do not need to remind you how important it is, do I?"

"No, ma'am." He lifted a notepad beside him. "I've already arranged for the yard to be prepared as per your direction by 7am this morning. The food will be out by 9:30. Guests arrive at ten."

"The clothes?"

"Arrived last night; they've been steamed and arranged. The maids will send them out by eight, along with further assistance for Mrs. Callahan, should she want it."

"Do not disappoint me today, O'Phelan." I was already dialing on my phone. "I'm every bit as meticulous as my grandmother."

"Which is why I sleep in this suit."

I paused, looking back at the small screen to see the corners of his lips turned up into a smile; "Two jokes before the sun is up, O'Phelan; you must be very sure everything today will proceed flawlessly. I guess time will tell."

"Would you like some assistance getting ready this morning?" He switched the subject seamlessly.

"No. Just take care of the others," I said, ending the feed and dialing my next victim as I pulled out the bath oils from the drawer under my sink.

"Who in the fuck—"

"Good morning, Greyson," I cut in before he dug himself into a very deep hole. There was ruffling and soft sigh on the other end...a female sigh. "I wasn't interrupting anything, was I?"

"No, ma'am—"

"Good. I'm hosting brunch this morning; I want all the most important family members, both Irish and Italian, to be here by ten am."

"Ahh..." He paused for moment before his voice became more serious...much more him. "Is the boss aware—"

"I. AM. AWARE," I cut him off before he could finish the thought. I walked over to my Le Grand Queen tub, made of exotic Caijou; it stood on four legs made from pure 24 karats and had features which made it worth over a million dollars. I turned on the faucet before continuing, "Ethan may be back in the city however, he hasn't officially told you or anyone else that I've stepped down. Which means when I tell you to do something, you do it without making me waste my breath."

"Of course—"

"Greyson," I said calmly, watching the tub fill. "Over the last few weeks I've come to think highly of you. However, you of all people should know that what I think of you means nothing if you cross the line with me. After all, I thought very highly of Tobias as well... Do you understand what I'm saying?"

"Yes, ma'am," he said quickly.

"So you're going to..."

"Bring the Irish and the Italians by ten."

I nodded, even though he couldn't see me, "And see, this is why you are the new go-between for the clan and the family. Congrats on your promotion."

Hanging up on him, I poured the oils into the water, watching for a moment as the steam rose before stripping down. I stepped in, not caring how hot the water was and rested back. In the water I lifted my arm and, sure enough, the water rolled over the clear breathable seal they'd put on my tattoo.

Lifting my phone again to let the rest of the family know... It rang over and over again before she finally answered.

"Donatella."

"Nari," I said back in the same tone.

"It's two in the morning."

"It's apparently seven in London." I smiled at that,

leaning back more, sinking into the water until only my head was above it.

"Are you in London?" she yawned.

"No."

"Then why should I care what time it is in London?"

"Good question; ask Helen. She's the one who woke me up, which means I can't sleep, and since I can't sleep, I thought I might as well wake everyone up early to get ready."

It took a moment of silence as she processed what I said. "Get ready for...?"

"Wyatt's welcome home brunch, *of course*," I said it bubbly and peppy, like a high school cheerleader during spirit week. "I've arranged everything; your clothes will be delivered to you as well as your daughters and Jason's. You're also going to call Darcy and Sedric and let them know they must be here, dressed, hungry, and with a smile on their faces by 9:45am."

"Sedric is out of town—"

"That's why I'm calling you now. You're his sister. You're both Callahans, I'm *sure* between the two of you, you can find a way to get him here by 9:45 right?"

She sighed, "Does this have something to do with Tobias?"

I forced myself to smile, even though I could feel myself getting annoyed every time someone brought up his name. As if Tobias was so important he'd affect what I would or would not do.

"Nari."

"Dona."

"Sedric and Darcy will be here at 9:45, correct?"

"Yes," she paused, "but why am I in charge of getting Darcy there as well, when Helen—"

"Thank you, Nari, see you all then." I hung up, dropping my phone to the side…sinking into the water and closing my eyes.

I didn't even bother calling Ethan or Wyatt; they should know by now not to fight me on these things and if they didn't… Well, that was too fucking bad.

We were doing this my way… There was no second option.

"What?" I said, answering my phone after the first ring only to hear Greyson's voice.

"Tobias gave a list to someone, we got him."

"Tell no one else yet. I'll be down in a moment," I replied, hanging up again.

It's true what they said about the wicked... There really wasn't any rest for us.

However, I started this and I was going to see it through to the end.

FIVE

"He offered me a gun, but I refused.
After all, you don't need a weapon when you were born one."
~ Blaise

DONATELLA

Putting my earrings on, I watched as my men beat into the face of the man in front of me. At this point, I couldn't even see the skin on his nose anymore.

"Is there any way we can speed this up?" I asked, glancing over to Greyson as he waited beside me. "He better actually know something and not be wasting my time."

We stood - well, I sat and Greyson stood - in the basement interrogation room of the mansion. The man currently being tortured for information was the last man Tobias had spoken to...and the man Tobias had most likely given orders to.

"Fuck you, CUNTS!" he screamed as they broke the last finger of his left hand. His right hand was already a deep purple color from all the broken bones.

Sighing, I rose from my chair and walked right to the edge of the pool of blood, not walking any closer until one of them put two thick red towels on the ground for me. I stepped on top of the towels as I stood in front of him, looking down at his bloody, oozing face.

"My brothers are home," I told him. "That means my time with you in this manmade hell is almost over. And true pain is coming for you. I'm trying to spare you from that. Tell me what I need to know and it will all be over—"

"Just like Toby?" He smiled with blood over his teeth. "You wrapped yourself around him, making him think you cared and then you killed him. He loved you and you killed him."

"Everyone keeps telling me that." I leaned forward. "But no one has asked me if I loved him. I didn't. I am not obligated to love someone just because they love me. He came to me, and he came to me weak. He stayed weak. He died weak! If a man wants my heart he's going to have to find it and then just take it because I don't offer it to anyone."

"Fuck you, you cold-hearted bitch and fuck the rest of your damn family. I hope you all burn."

Standing up straighter, I stretched out my hand; "I didn't want to have to change my dress today, but I guess I'm going to have to. Remember, Toby is dead; he lost, being loyal now is useless," I said as I pressed the trigger of the electric drill till it came alive, the blue light of thirty thousand volts rising like static waves from the drill bit. "When you're ready to give me names, just beg, alright? If not, we can bring out the maggots to clean way the dead flesh and start all over again.

"Have you ever felt that? Your own flesh being eating away as you live? I haven't, but I've seen it. The first time I nearly puked, the way she screamed. You have to hose them off once they get all the dead flesh too, because they can't stop, they just keep eating away, laying eggs and multiplying on you to grow and grow until they've eaten everything to the bone."

His chest was rising and falling quickly, only his left eye was open as he stared at the drill bit. "Why am I even bothering to explain? You'll see it up close and personal real soon."

I placed the drill right into his shoulder blade but before I could press the trigger again, he cried out, saying, "I'll tell you! I'll talk."

"I'm ready when you are." I smiled. Some men didn't care if you broke their bodies, they needed you to break their minds... The real weapon wasn't the drill; it was me. My words. Though, I was kind of disappointed he gave in so easily.

He must really hate bugs.

"Tobias had set up funds to send to..." I listened to him, with only half my attention. I knew full well that my job ended here. Greyson would apprise Ethan, and Ethan would take care of the rest himself.

As he spoke, I stared at the blood which could no longer be soaked up by the towels on the floor crawl towards me.

DONATELLA- 8 YEARS OLD

"How many people do you see?"

The painting was big. It was taller than me; it was taller than her. It took up almost all the space on the red walls, so no other paintings could be on the wall with it.

"Seven."

"Look closer, Dona."

I did. "There are seven."

"No, there aren't."

Frowning, I took a few steps back so I could see the whole painting. I squinted, tilted to my head to the side, but

I couldn't see the eighth face.

"Hmm." I heard her snicker in front of me.

"Mom!" I groaned, crossing my hands and staring at her back. "You're messing with me!"

Slowly she turned, her black hair falling over her shoulder and I saw her face, she was smiling; the way the light hit her brown eyes made it look they were sparkling. She reached out to me,

"Come, I'll show you."

Pouting, I took her hand, and it was so soft and warm. I grabbed her hand tightly, but she didn't mind, and she walked me to the painting. I watched the floor to make sure I didn't step on the back of her black dress.

"Here."

Looking up, I saw that she wasn't pointing to the painting, but the silver board beside it.

"Huh?"

She brought me in front of her, to stand directly in front of the board. She hunched down beside me and pointed to it.

"You didn't count Julia Rendell," she said.

"The painter?" I frowned again. "She's not in the

painting, though."

"Wrong again."

I sighed, I was tired of this. I wanted to go play with Wyatt and Ethan. "Mommy, I want to go play."

"Tell me why she's in the painting and you can. If not, you'll stay here until we go."

"I don't know! Ugh this is so not fair!" I snapped, pulling out of her arms and pushing her away.

"Are you yelling at me, Donatella?" she asked, crossing her arms. I looked away, frowning at the wooden floorboards. When I didn't say anything, she spoke again, "Fine, just stand there silently."

Her heels clicked against the wood as she left.

"Don't let her out," she said softly to the guard.

"MOM!" I yelled, but the doors closed behind her. I ran after her, but before I could reach her, both the doors shut in my face.

I pulled on the doors as hard as I could but they wouldn't open. "LET ME OUT!"

I banged.

I pulled.

I kicked.

But it didn't open. I could hear the music playing on the other side… Could they even hear me?

"Mommy, let me out please! Please!" Scared, I hit the door harder. I didn't want to, but I started to cry, angry, and dropped to the floor, my dress puffing up all around me. The tears came down so hard.

Wiping my face, I was just about to get up and try again when the doors burst open and…

"Daddy!" I cried, running to him and throwing my arms around his waist. He was hard, like hugging a rock, but I felt better. "Mommy wouldn't me come out."

Picking me up, he kissed the side of my head. "It's okay." He smelled like spices, it tickled my nose but I didn't let go; I held on to his neck tightly. "Do you want ice cream?"

I nodded against him.

"I'll deal with you all later," he hissed at the men at the door. When he turned to walk, I stuck my tongue out at them. I would have made a face but I saw her…

"Mommy," I called out softly.

She stood on the other side of the museum, next to the big white statues, Wyatt and Ethan stood next to her.

Ethan was pulling at his bowtie and Wyatt was talking really quickly...until he noticed Mommy wasn't listening. His brown eyes looked over at me. He made a face, and in my mind it was like he was asking, "What the heck happened? And why is your face so red?"

I would have made a face back, but the way Mommy was looking at me made me stop. She looked at me the same way she looked at the papers on her desk at work. Her smile was gone.

Mommy?

She looked away and back down at Wyatt, flicking his forehead, making him look away, too.

Her mouth moved and Ethan laughed...soon they were all laughing.

What was she saying?

I wanted to know...but we kept walking further and further away until we got outside and I couldn't see them anymore.

"Come on, princess," Daddy said, putting me in the back of the car.

"Are we going, Daddy?" I reached up for my seatbelt.

"Ice cream, remember?" He tapped my nose, smiling at me. "Two scoops or three?"

I grinned, lifting my fingers for him to see.

"Four? You sure you can handle it?"

I nodded, swinging my feet. "Of course, I can! I'm not a kid anymore, Dad!"

"Then four scoops it is." He laughed, sliding inside with me and nodding to the man in the front. "Drive."

He rested into the back of his brown seat, pulling out his phone from his jacket pocket. He dialed once then he waited as it rang and rang but there was no answer. Cracking his jaw to the side, he squeezed the phone tightly.

"Daddy?"

He blinked a few times and then looked down at me, putting his big hand on my head. "Don't be mad at Mommy, okay? Sometimes...sometimes she goes a little overboard. She loves you very much."

I looked down to my shoes again, nodding.

"Good, now wipe your face. You have a booger hanging from your nose, like Spiderman."

"Daddy!" I gasped, taking his handkerchief and covering my face, making him laugh.

"Tell me about school? You want to join the volleyball team?"

Somehow, I knew he was just trying to keep me talking because he couldn't reach Mommy...no because Mommy wouldn't answer. I knew that he was upset and didn't really want to get ice cream, but I talked anyway. I told him everything about everything. When I couldn't think of stuff to talk about, I talked about Ethan and Wyatt...until I ended falling asleep.

I hoped Mommy wasn't going to be mad.

DONATELLA- NOW

"Ma'am."

Looking up from the blood and at Greyson; "He's told us everything."

I nodded and got up, walking out of the room. But before the door closed, I gave only one order; "Kill him."

Walking on, I headed to the elevator. Of all the memories I had of my mother, why did that one come to mind? I hadn't even remembered it until this moment, nor could I remember what happened after.

After my dad took me out of the art gallery what happened? It felt like I blocked it out, but why? I couldn't remember why.

When the doors finally opened at the ground floor, O'Phelan was standing with a phone to his ear.

"Is everything ready?" I asked, fixing the watch on my wrist.

He muted the call and said, "Wyatt is being a little difficult."

"Of course, he is," I said, taking the phone from him and listening to Wyatt as he snapped over the line saying;

"Don't you know it's usually the messengers that die first? That's where the saying 'don't shoot the messenger,' comes from...the fact that they were often shot!"

SIX

"Just like our eyes, our hearts have
a way of adjusting to the dark."
~ Adam Stanley

WYATT

Metathesiophobia.

The fear of change.

There are many different names for the phobia of new things but *Metathesiophobia* was specifically about the ability to control one's environment and unwillingness to move, to progress or to change anything from routine. Children who moved a lot or parents who had lost their children often are diagnosed with this phobia, making them unable to change their kids' rooms after they died.

I was now beyond certain... No-one in my fucking family feared changing shit!

"I'm going to kill them," I muttered to myself, ripping the last goddamn cat poster from my wall and shoving it into the empty box before opening the door and throwing it out into the motherfucking bloody hall! "FUCK ALL OF YOU!" I yelled before slamming the door. I didn't give a shit if they were sleeping! If I couldn't fuckin' sleep, they shouldn't fuckin' sleep!

"Bunch of cunts..." I muttered, looking around my room, finally able to relax...when I saw it....one last item of cat paraphernalia - a pair of slippers by the dresser.

I balled my fist, trying to stay calm.

But I was at my limit.

Let us replay the last twelve hours, I thought. I had been in Boston, saving my shitty, stick-up-the-ass, know-it-all elder brother from bleeding out on the floor of what looked like a 1980s-porno set before going out and getting revenge on the man who had left him to bleed out on said porno set... Only to find out my fucking asshole of brother allowed himself and his wife to nearly die just to bring me back to Chicago... Where I had a gun pointed in my face by a rat-faced bastard who had the nerve to get his blood on my favorite pair of pure alligator-skin House of Testoni shoes after my twin sister shot him through the skull.

All of that I could take.

In fact, for my family...that was pretty much a normal Thursday.

Which is why I decided to rest. Simply go to my room, close my eyes, and mentally prepare myself for the long years of normal Callahan days that were to come now that I was back... I should have known. Why I let my guard down for even a second was beyond me... Everyone thought Ethan was nothing but a serious, cold, glaring, murdering, manipulating genius...he was...but above all that, he was my older brother. And like all older brother's, he missed no opportunity to fuck me with me.

Which is why when I walked into my room... Instead of seeing my room exactly as I'd left it, I walked into a fucking cat-lady's paradise.

Cat bedsheets.

Cat pillows.

Cat rug.

Cat bathmats.

And fucking...cat slippers!

Why?

Why?

Because first... I fucking hated cats.

Second... He wanted to call me pussy.

And third... He just wanted to torture me before I could sleep. This was the side of my shite-faced brother that no-one else saw.

"Oh...fuck you," I said once more, just in case I had the power to curse him, grabbing the damn slippers, marching to the windows and yanking them open before throwing the slippers towards the trees.

Taking a deep breath, I moved back to my empty bed, not at all caring about the sheets... I wasn't going to sleep in that damn cat nirvana, but I wasn't going to lose any more sleep trying to set up my room. There were people in this house for that, and they were going to do it once I woke up. *How very Callahan,* I thought, tossing my arms behind my back. But I was a Callahan... I didn't wake up to that fact only because of Ethan or what had happened in Boston. Ethan didn't force me to come back, he manipulated me into remembering who I was under the well-mannered mask I put on, the real reason I'd become a doctor... I enjoyed the feeling of having someone's life in my hands. They lived because of me...some died because of me...the rapists, child molesters, abusers, even one serial killer and the son of a dictator. Doctors weren't supposed to judge; they weren't supposed to care who their patients were... I didn't subscribe to that kind of bullshit. If a monster crossed my path, I'd hunt it down and kill it. I didn't think I was a hero. I didn't have some code. They disgusted me.

When I left Chicago, I couldn't see the difference

between my family and them. In all honesty, the line was slim. No one had ever raped or molested anyone…but had children died because of us? Yes. Did we harm others? Yes. But the difference was we didn't seek to. The blood on our hands came from those who sought to cut us first.

Seeing Ethan bleeding and Ivy weeping reminded me that I didn't need to be a doctor to have control over someone's life… As a Callahan, everyone else's life was already at our discretion. We had that type of power in our blood.

Rolling on to my side I closed my eyes for all of one moment when all of sudden—

KNOCK.

KNOCK.

Are you bloody shitting me?

KNOCK.

KNOCK.

"Sir—"

"If you knock on or open that door, I will throw you from my window, order someone to pick you up and throw out one more time, and you will then be buried with cat slippers on your feet… NOTHING ELSE, JUST CAT

SLIPPERS!"

I was going insane. I was back here not even a full day, and I was losing my mind.

I waited a moment, but luckily someone was still sane and left me the fuck alone—

RING!

My eyes snapped open and I rolled over, looking at my cellphone as it flashed on the bedside table. Doing my best to stay calm, I reached over and picked up, answering as un-murderous as possible.

"Dr. Callahan speaking," I said out of habit.

"Your sister requested that a maid deliver your clothes for the day—"

"As I have not yet slept, my day has not yet started. So tell my sister, O'Phelan, I am not in need of—"

"With all due respect, Sir," he cut me off, not sounding like he had any motherfucking respect, "your sister made it clear that this was non-negotiable. She said to tell you that if you refused to cooperate, she'd set your room on fire...*again*. She also said I should remind you that if you think of leaving, she will find you and set that place on fire, but only if Ethan does not find you first."

"Funny how you managed to say that so eloquently, without hesitation, and *with all due respect* to me," I sneered, gripping on to the phone tighter.

Unnerved, he replied, "I am simply the messenger, Sir."

"Don't you know it's usually the messengers that die first? That's where the saying 'don't shoot the messenger,' comes from...the fact they were *often* shot."

"So the warning is not for the messenger, but the person doing the shooting... After all, how well did it turn out for those that didn't have anyone to bring them important information?" He didn't say that...Dona did, suddenly appearing on the line.

"Sister dearest," I said sweetly.

"Yes, brother dear," she said, even more sweetly, her voice rising to an annoyingly high pitch.

"Do you know what I've been doing since I returned home?" I asked her, already getting up out of bed.

"De-catting your room while you cursed our brother?"

I bit my lip, nodding to myself before speaking, "Are you the perpetrator or the accomplice?"

"I'm the innocent bystander. After all, it's not my room…and I'm not a snitch."

Thou shall not murder thy siblings.

Thou shall not murder thy siblings.

Thou shall NOT murder thy siblings! But harm and maim should be allowed, right?

I had to repeat it three times as I reached the door, opening it to see a dark green, House of Kiton suit, a new pair of brown Calfskin Wingtip House of Testoni shoes to match the Rockefeller brown tie and dress shirt, along with a Jean Dunand Shabaka watch.

She's got to be kidding me? "Please explain to me what is so damn important that not only must I forsake sleep but I must also drape myself in over two-million-dollars' worth of clothing to attend?"

"Your welcome home party, of course," she replied without missing a beat.

"Oh, of course," I mocked, this time much more serious than I had been before… I paused for a moment, staring at the suit hanging outside my doorway. "Just whatever you're planning on using my return to cover up, *sister dearest*… Don't put me between you and Ethan."

I knew she was grinning on the other end of the phone as she said, "Is that physically or metaphorically?"

"Both."

"Brunch is at ten," she told me, changing the subject and adding, "and stop threatening the help. The last thing this family needs is rumors of you throwing maids out your window."

"You're sounding more and more like Nana by the minute."

"Fuck you and goodbye."

I smiled when she hung up and looked up, finally noticing the red haired, blue eyed maid standing and waiting patiently behind the trolley my clothes hung on.

"Can I bring them in, Sir?" she asked, and I moved aside allowing her to enter. I tilted my head to see her ass as she came in... She was slender, but the uniform made it hard to see her figure, her red hair stopping only a little bit past her shoulders.

"Do you need anything else, Sir?" she asked, turning around to face me.

Again, I looked her over, making sure she knew I was looking, before meeting her gaze; "Yes, I need a pretty maid; not too pretty, but pretty enough that she can hold my interest for short time; who simply wants have to fun and forget she's a maid for an hour...or two...but not lose her mind thinking it's more than what it is afterwards." I smirked at that, she swallowed. "If you know someone like that, please send her my way."

I opened the door for her to step out then waited for a moment before asking, "Aren't you leaving?"

"I...I know someone like that," she said quickly.

Closing the door, I turned back to her, walking up close and lifting her chin up so she could look me in the eyes.

"Are you sure you know someone like that? I hate women who lie, but I hate women who overestimate themselves even more," I whispered, placing my thumb on her bottom lip. "The last thing I want to do to an obsessive maid clinging on to me."

"You...won't have to... I'll...I'll be good."

The grin that passed my lips made her shiver, I saw it. Placing my hand on her shoulder, I leaned in, whispering directly into her ear, "Be good later, sweetheart, take me into your mouth and show me how bad you can be right now."

Gently, I pushed down on her shoulder and she got down onto her knees. As she grabbed hold of me, all I could think was...

It's good to be home.

ETHAN

Placing my hand on her cheek, I brushed back her blond hair, and she smiled, rolling to her side as she muttered, "Five more minutes."

"Five minutes for you is another five hours," I replied, lifting my hand from her.

She pouted, sticking her pink lip out and still not opening her eyes, "Five more hours then... It's not like I have job to get to; I married rich for a reason."

I couldn't help but smirk at that. "And here I thought it was my charm, good looks, and your desperate desire to get out prison."

She grinned, opening her blue eyes to look up at me. "The last one. And money helped, too."

"You're shameless." That was why I loved her... The

moment I thought it, I realized I still hadn't said it. I opened my mouth to speak, however she interrupted me before I could.

"I love you," she said, looking me in the eye...

Hearing those words from her made my heart ache and throat feel as if it were set on fire. Of course, she had to be the one to say it first. Shaking my head, I reached over to the bedside table and picked up her breakfast tray.

"This is very romantic," she grinned, sitting up. She was completely awake at the sight of food, forgetting her earlier words.

"This isn't from me," I said, watching as she drank the soup right out of the bowl. "It's from Dona. I've told you, I'm not romantic."

She paused, the bowl stopping right at her lips. "Donatella sent me breakfast in bed?"

"Yes," I said, lifting the tea bag out of her cup, "drink it, apparently it's a better alternative to the pills."

"Says Dona?"

"Says the nurse Dona hired for you," I said, taking the bowl from her hand and giving her the cup of tea instead. She took it but didn't drink it. "I know you don't like medicine, but at the very least—"

"It's not that," she interrupted, making a face I couldn't read. "First, you should be in bed, you were shot and almost died. Second, why is your sister giving me herbal tea and breakfast in bed...and a damn nurse?"

I sighed, shifting back to lean on the bedpost opposite her.

"First, I've had worse. Second, because she's...Dona." I snickered, making her frown more.

"Can I get a cheat sheet or instruction manual for your family?" she asked.

I thought of the simplest way to explain this to her, but I wasn't used to explaining anything to anyone for any reason. I simply did what I wanted, and everything fell into place soon or later. However, with her it was different... I *wanted* to walk through everything, step by step. I wanted to show her there was a method to the madness that was this family, even if it often didn't look like from the outside. But doing so dragged her further into the madness along with us.

"You're staring and not talking again," she said ironically as she stared back.

I glanced down at her food and the cup in her hand. "Let's compromise, you eat everything and listen to your nurse, and I'll explain what is happening, as well as answer any questions you might have."

"Deal. Win-win for me." She grinned, leaning back against her pillow and sipping from her cup. "Go on."

She's crazy.

"While we were in Boston, Donatella ran things here in Chicago—"

"Drug things," she interrupted, leaning forward eagerly.

I paused... In our family we made a rule to never speak of the business so blatantly, especially with people not part of the business. But as I looked at her, I remembered once again... I make the rules and break them at my own leisure.

"Yes," I answered blatantly in return, "Drug and family things. She figured out that the Mexican cartels are trying to cut us out of product and sell on their own. Savino Moretti, Klarissa's father, as well Tobias Valentino, one of my former men—"

"And Donatella's lover," once more she cut in,

opening the yogurt in her hands.

I clenched my jaw, not wanting to even think of my sister like that, so I went on. "One of my former men, made a deal with the cartels for power on the southern drug trades. However, knowing I wouldn't simply roll over, they decided to attack my family. They were the ones selling the bad drugs to the Finnegan brothers—"

"But you knew that before you went there and used it as a way to get Wyatt back," she replied, excited as she stuffed another spoonful in her mouth.

"Ivy, would you like to tell the story?"

With the spoon still her mouth, she shook her head but smiled. "Sorry, go ahead."

"They didn't know I knew. They thought I'd be distracted and tried to further cripple my family's influence back here in Chicago. After my mother's death, the Irish and the Italians haven't been…very close. They liked, trusted, and respect my father enough, and in honor of my mother, never stepped out of line. But when he passed and I took over, they were unsure of me…even more so now that I married you, a woman one hundred percent Irish-American."

"I think my great-great-great grandmother was Scottish, though."

The woman really can't help herself, I thought, ignoring her comment. "They managed to spread a few rumors, and on top of that framed an Irish boy for the death of Italian boy." Ivy opened her mouth to speak, but I gave her a look telling her that if she cut me off again I wasn't going to move on. Frowning, she stuffed a spoonful of yogurt into her mouth. "*However*, before the Italian boy was murdered, Donatella apparently made a big show of things. She managed to figure out something was off..." I still didn't know how. My best guess was Tobias must have slipped up, let his guard down somehow.

"And then she herself killed Savino as well Tobias at the airport," Ivy spoke again, and when I simply stared back at her, no longer speaking, she frowned so hard it looked like her lip was trying to escape off her face. "You weren't saying anything; I was just trying push the conversation along before you disappeared to the dark corners of your mind again."

"It's called thinking."

"You think too much," she muttered, leaning

forward to stick a few grapes into my mouth. "It can't be healthy."

"It's kept me alive this long," I replied before chewing.

"So, what's happening today?"

Today was Dona's victory party. "Dona is hosting what she claims is Wyatt's welcome home brunch. However, that's just a cover which serves multiple purposes. The first is to show all of us she succeeded in not only keeping peace in Chicago, but gained the respect of both the Irish and the Italians families. The second and most important purpose is to show the world we, the Callahans, are not only united and unbreakable, but also *both* Irish and Italian...hence her choice of attire," I said nodding over to the clothes which were displayed just at the corner of our bed. "Each one of us dressed in some color of either the Irish or Italian flags."

Myself in grey and Ivy in red.

"United, unbreakable, *both* Irish and Italian," she whispered to herself. "She's warning them...basically saying don't fuck with the Callahan family—"

"Us," I cut her off, just as she had done me. And

when her eyes met mine, I reminded her. "You are Ivy Callahan."

My wife.

"Don't fuck with *us.*" She smiled, but it was only for an instant, before she looked back to the clothes.

"I know you're tired but—"

"I'm not tired," she said quickly, finally looking away from the clothes to me. "Your sister scares me a little."

"That's the reaction most people have when they get to know her. She prefers it that way."

"This will sound awful and selfish," she said slowly, and I nodded for her to continue. "After hearing about your mother from you and others and then getting her letter, I was a little relieved she wasn't here because I knew she'd think I wasn't good enough, and be the type of monster-in-law you see in movies."

It was a selfish thing to say, but I didn't fault her for her honesty. I didn't really think I could fault her for anything today.

Bloody shite... I sound like my father.

"But," she went on, "after yesterday, I'm sure your

mother would have been easier to deal with."

No, she wouldn't have been. "Why do you think so?"

She sat up straighter on the bed as she spoke, "Yesterday, the look in her eyes... I didn't get it then, but it hit me just now. She killed her lover... She did it without hesitation, without shedding a single tear. She did it...because she is used to sacrificing for this family. It's second nature to her...so when I tried to step in front her, she put me in place... She was telling me I hadn't sacrificed enough, I hadn't suffered enough to stand in front of her and demand anything. I feel like I have to prove myself to her, get her respect...me, of all people! And I generally don't give a shit about what other people think of me; isn't that scary?"

"Terrifying." I smirked, watching as she went back to eating happily, but not telling her the real reason Dona was terrifying... How this celebration wasn't just a warning to outsiders but to the rest of the family as well.

Today we'd wear what she wanted us to wear.

Eat what she wanted us to eat.

Say what she wanted us to say.

Because her message was clear... *In an instant, if she*

wanted to, she could destroy us all.

If she tried to fight for the control, I'd kill her. It would shatter me; I'd hate myself, I'd hate everything and everyone and she'd haunt me to the grave, but at the end of the day I'd still kill her. At the airport, just in case, I'd had sniper waiting... I had forced myself to prepare to for the slim chance she wasn't rational anymore. That she didn't see the big picture and that she would force me to kill her. And had I done it, Wyatt...if he didn't try to kill me in return...might have lost his mind... The whole family would have fallen faster than a stack of cards built on strings.

Growing up, I saw the family business like a chess match, and when Donatella came back from boarding school, I knew right then... If she couldn't play the game, she'd take the players as hostages...take *me* as her hostage.

I ruled this family, this city, with a gun to my head.

She couldn't shoot because we were family, and she loved this family...but her hunger for power wouldn't let her put down the gun either...I couldn't make her...not without...without chopping off her damn hand.

So she and I were at an impasse.

"Why are you smiling?" Ivy's eyebrows furrowed together as she tried to read my expression, even though I hadn't even realized I was smiling until she pointed it out.

"My greatest enemy…is my greatest weapon."

"Huh?"

I shook my head, closing my eyes, resting against the bedpost… Donatella's ambition, her desire to rule, forced her to protect the family. There was no point making her drop the gun, I was more than satisfied being her hostage. After all, I was only a hostage when no one else was around… When someone came close, she was my own personal body guard.

And now she knew it, too…

If she took over the family, she'd destroy it, and if she destroyed it, how she could rule it?

It's why she punched me. Why she was so upset…she knew she couldn't win.

But it wasn't a draw. I wasn't satisfied with sharing victory.

Wyatt and Dona had fallen perfectly into place. That was my doing.

Checkmate.

SEVEN

"She's an old soul

whose heart speaks

an all but forgotten language."

~J.M. Storm

HELEN

"Show me a strong woman and I'll show you the scars on her soul that made her so," I whispered to myself, peeking through the dark violet blinds of my bedroom window. I stared down at the horde of people, young and old, who now covered the lawn behind the mansion, and out of them all, Dona stuck out like an orange in a field of apples, which wasn't anything new.

In fact, none of this was new; parties like this were commonplace. However, it was the first time that neither my mother, Cora, nor my grandmother, Evelyn, were the ones organizing it. Dona had everything planned and set up to perfection...and she was radiant as she greeted people as they arrived, dressed in a beautiful, fitted orange cocktail dress, her black hair pulled back into a French braid.

"They even have the kids kissing the ring now," Darcy snickered, coming over to me with a drink in his brown hand, using his free one to open the curtains further. He was dressed in a burgundy jacket and ripped jeans.

"Dona will have you kissing the grass soon if she sees you only wearing the jacket she sent you," I snapped, looking him over.

He rolled his eyes. "How do you know she sent me the jacket?"

"Because I've seen those jeans enough times to know I hate them passionately. Dad gave you that watch and mom, the shirt…like a year ago."

"I'm sorry, I didn't know clothes have expiration dates on them," he mocked me before lifting the glass to his lips. However, I took it right out of his hands. "Helen—"

"Go change into the clothes she gave you," I said seriously.

Annoyed, he glanced over to me, cracking his jaw to the side. "Helen, I'm not a child! However, I am starting to get really fucking annoyed with having to put my life on hold for this family—"

"Your family," I corrected him, staring directly into his hazel eyes as they glared into mine.

Standing up to his full height, which was much more than a few inches taller than me, he said, "You don't need to remind me. I know who my family is!"

"Then you should have worn the damn clothes!"

"AH JESUS!" he groaned. "They are just clothes, Helen! If Dona or Ethan or Wyatt tells me to shit in the corner, are you going to walk me to the fucking corner? Are we their family or their slaves!"

Without hesitation, I punched him right in the gut and instinctually he bent over, his hands going to his stomach.

"U—!"

I wrapped my arms around him, hugging tightly. "Darcy, I'm not trying to pick a fight; I'm trying to keep you safe, stop making that harder for me, please."

He froze for a moment, not really sure what to do. Letting go of him, I backed up and flicked his forehead.

"Ouch! Stop hitting me!" he snapped, backing further out of my hands. "Right now, I need someone to keep me safe from you. Christ, what's up with you today?"

"Did you hear about what happened while Dona was running Chicago?"

He nodded, still rubbing his stomach. "A little - something about Boston and Ethan getting hurt or something."

"Dona almost killed Ethan." It wasn't lie… It wasn't the whole truth, either.

Again, he paused, his lips a hard line as he stared at me. "What do you mean? She wouldn't—"

"Not because she doesn't want to," I admitted. "She realized if she killed Ethan she'd start a war and end up killing this whole family. No matter how badly she wants to be in control, she still loves this family…but one day she could stop caring. She's a ticking time bomb and today is only adding more pressure."

"What?" he asked, and I nodded back to the scene outside my window. He stepped forward again, moving the curtains aside to see. "She's the center of attention—"

"Wait for it." I told him. And we didn't have to wait long.

Everyone stopped, everyone looked away from her, everyone's smiles and greetings turned directly to Ethan, who walked out dressed in a fitted grey suit, Ivy on his arm dressed in a beautiful red dress. Both of them looked as if they had walked off the stage at New York Fashion Week: beautiful, strong…and in love, like they hadn't been through hell. Ivy never let go of Ethan's arm, even as others came up to them. Ethan even grinned as if the party was for him.

It was. He had won, like always.

"Just like that," I said softly, my eyes shifting to Donatella, who stood by, smiling as her brother and sister-in-law made their way towards her, even though I could see her doing her best to fight her true feelings. "The ring is no longer on Dona's hand. She's just reverted back to sister of Ethan again. Everything she's done, everything she will do… The credit will always be given to Ethan. She's knows that, but on the same day she's reminded of it, do you annoy her further by not listening to her? It's not just clothes, it's respect. She asked you to wear something, you wear it because you respect her. Give that to her before she lets her rage out on you."

He rolled his eyes and nodded without saying a word and turned to leave… He made it a few feet before rushing back and punching me right in the side.

"Ugh…" I bit my teeth together while he just grinned.

"I was just treating you equal to any other guy." He grinned from ear to ear and when he did, he looked so much like dad.

"You little shite..." I kicked off my heels but stopped when he opened the door, nearly colliding into Wyatt.

"Well, if it isn't the little shite that cost me ten grand," Wyatt snapped at Darcy, locking him under his armpit. "You lost to the Wizards? The fucking Wizards? Who takes a three pointer with thirty seconds on the shot clock, and two guards on him?"

"You only bet ten grand on me?" Darcy tried elbowing him to get free. "Since when did you become a such a cheapskate!"

Wyatt let him go, eyeing him down with a deep scowl on his face. "I earned that ten grand on my own—"

"Yeah, yeah... Sure. Fine, Doc, why don't we go to the courts right now—"

"How about you both get downstairs? We're late," I jumped in, and they both looked at me in surprise, as if they had forgotten I'd been standing right there.

Walking over to Wyatt, I gave him a one arm hug, swallowing the lump in my throat and smiling as I said, "Welcome back."

He hugged back, sighing in relief, "Finally, someone

in this family welcomes me back normally; I was about to lose all hope!"

"Shouldn't have left in the first place. Who has a mid-life crisis in their early twenties?" Darcy muttered as headed back to his room.

Wyatt let go of me, turning to yell, "People who are prone to dying early!"

I tried to make my escape, walking forward without either of them when Wyatt walked over, putting his hands my shoulders.

"Are you gonna be my wing-woman, dear ol' cousin?" He beamed.

"To what end? Bringing them or keeping them away?" Rolling my eyes, I tried to lift his hands off my shoulder but he kept them on me.

He brought his face close to mine and looked like a child on Christmas morning as he replied, "Both?"

"I'm going to need a whore swatter," I muttered to myself, pushing him away for real this time and walking on my own.

"Helen, I'm shocked," he gasped dramatically, "Just because a woman enjoys to get—"

"Not them," I said, getting on the elevator turning back to him to say, "You."

He just grinned, getting in the elevator beside me, fixing his tie and standing straighter when the doors closed.

"To the mouth of hell we go," he whispered, all traces of humor gone from his voice.

He was only at the mouth, and here I was, swimming in the stomach of it.

"You look nice by the way," he said quickly, before walking out when the doors opened and I couldn't help but think again, *Show me a strong woman and I'll show you the scars on her soul that made her so.*

EIGHT

"The only people for me are the mad ones,
the ones who are mad to live,
mad to talk,
mad to be saved,
desirous of everything at the same time,
the ones that never yawn or say a commonplace thing,
but burn, burn, burn
like fabulous yellow roman candles exploding like spiders
across the stars
and in the middle you see the blue center-light pop and
everybody"
~Jack Kerouac

DONATELLA

Just like that, after everything I'd done, I'd been regulated to the sidelines. I'd been pushed to the corner; watching my brother and Ivy, a woman who had only been in this family for a few weeks and barely had a backbone, become the center of attention and appreciation. Watching as all the people who were so polite and uptight with me, relax around Ethan. Yes, relax, after all he was a man, don or not, they could relate to him.

I could feel the rage rising within me.

The anger.

The flames.

He did nothing! I did this! *Only because he let you do it.* The moment the thought entered my mind it was as if someone had dumped water on me extinguishing the flames, and I felt powerless, trapped in a cycle of rage as I watched the family gathered around Ethan and Ivy the more, and numbness at knowing Ethan put me in the position.

You should have killed him. The darkest voice in my mind whispered.

"You have three options," a deep voice I didn't recognize in an accent I couldn't place spoke beside me, "option one, you make a huge scene and get all the attention back on you; option two, you continue to stand here in silent rage with that manufactured smile plastered on your face."

"I thought you said three?" I replied, not even bothering to look back at him.

"I did, however it's the most painful option for someone like you."

Someone like me? I was not in the mood to be polite, nor was I in the mood to deal with another man who thought he knew me and deserved my attention. I was just going to tune him out when he said, "Your mother was an only child. So, from day one she had all the power coming to her. But you... You were never meant to be the *Ceann na Conairte*, as you people call it, because if you were, you'd be an only child too. You should know this. In fact, I'm sure you do know this, so why you keep running headfirst into the wall like a bloody idiot is beyond me...unless you enjoy the pain."

I felt myself shaking, the blood in my veins boiling

to the point where I burned from the inside out again. Swallowing the saliva in my mouth, I stood straighter, turning to him, but he didn't turn to me. He was taller, around Ethan's height, his hair a dirty brown-blonde, dressed in dark jeans and a white button-down shirt, the sleeves were rolled up at the wrist.

"You seem very interested in my family—"

"Only because you and your family make it a point to make people interested," he cut me off before bending down to grab the ball that rolled to his feet. He smiled as he handed it to the little girl who took it from him, before rising back up. "The whole point of these little celebrations is to make sure people talk correct? Keep the Callahan family saga going. It's a little irrational to get upset with people for doing what you ask them to do."

"Irrational?" I gasped out. "Do I look like an irrational person to you?"

He snickered and, for the first time, glanced over to me, his gray eyes studying me before looking away. "If insanity could personify itself, it would choose to be you, Donatella Callahan; the woman who loved her mother but hated her mother so much she wanted to become just like her mother by killing her mother's children. By God, you are the Greek tragedy Sophocles forgot to write..."

The glass in my hand shattered; the pain, the blood—*my* blood—which dripped off my hand didn't faze me in the slightest. I couldn't stop myself, before I knew it, my bloody hand was gripping on to his white shirt, pulling him closer to my face, and I was pressing my gun to his forehead. "Now that you've gotten my attention, would you like to repeat that AFTER I blow your fucking brains out of you head, that's if you even have any!"

His gray eyes looked down at me, disappointed. "There you go, running head first into that wall again—"

I moved the gun to his eyes, not liking how they looked at me. "Are you asking to die today?"

"No, I'm asking if you are tired of option one."

I didn't understand what he meant for second before I remembered what he said earlier...*making a scene.*

"Calm down!" Wyatt yelled right into my ear, which was impossible since he was over by Ethan and Ivy. However, when I looked over my shoulder, he was right beside me, staring at me with wide eyes. Over his shoulder, I saw everyone... Everyone's attention was on me. And not the attention I wanted, not the attention I'd planned; there wasn't respect or fear, it was like…like I looked at wolf-dogs. When I finally saw Ethan, he…he was furious.

Letting go of the stranger's shirt and stepping back, I tried to figure out a way to gracefully get out of this. But I couldn't think. If I ran, it would look like I really was insane. As my arms slowly began to drop to my sides, a hand reached out and touched mine briefly, taking the gun from me. I looked up at Wyatt, thinking it was him, but he backed away as a fist collided with his nose. I didn't have time to process how I ended up in another man's arms… All I knew was that my gun was now pointed at my skull. Everyone's expression had changed to concern. Ethan's rage changed to panic as he stepped closer, the men beside him all reaching for their weapons.

"I wouldn't if I was you," the man holding me hostage said to one of the guards. I wasn't sure who the idiot was that charged at him from behind, but even I could hear his lead feet as he tried to sneak up on madman who held a gun to my head.

He turned quickly, spinning me with him while tightening his grip on me. Just like that, he fired twice at the fucking guard's feet. "I told you no, didn't I?"

Using that moment, I stepped on his foot, elbowed his rib, and butted my head back into his nose. When his gripped loosened, but not as much as I'd hoped, I twisted out of his hands and jumped up, locking my legs around his neck. I brought him down to the grass hard. I tried to hold him there, but he broke out of my headlock and twisted my arm back to pin me under him, bringing the gun to my head.

"And just like that, the student has become the master," he said loudly. But I had no idea what the fuck he was talking about. He just kept talking, saying "To think you, the Queen of Beata Veronica Negroni da Binasco School for Girls, of all people would let your guard down. You've lost your edge, Donny."

Donny? I wanted to cringe, instead I kicked him right in the balls and punched him in the throat, forcing him to roll over before punching him again. He dodged, locking my arms.

"I should have shot you back when I had a chance..." He squeezed a little tighter.

What the hell is he talking about?

I didn't get a chance to think much longer, due to his headbutt.

"You were a shitty fighter back then, and you're still one now," he added, smiling, as I glared at him.

BANG!

We both stopped at the gunfire, and he even had the nerve to check the gun in his hand. Realizing it wasn't him, we both looked up to the voice above us.

"Are you two finished or would you like to keep acting like high-school children?" Ethan asked, staring down at us angrily.

Inhaling through his nose and rolling his eyes, he pretended to be in pain... "Seems we're going to have to call it a draw, *Donny*."

"Or..."

"Donatella," Ethan's voice hissed above me.

Letting each other go, we both rose to our feet.

"Sister dearest?" Ethan said, rage dripping out of his unnaturally calm tone. "Who is this?"

That's what I wanted to know! But I couldn't say it, not with so much attention on us. We'd look like fools if they found out I just fought—and didn't a kill—some random madman who somehow got past our security and gained entrance into our home. It was then that I remembered what he'd said.

The Queen of Beata Veronica Negroni da Binasco School for Girls.

"Dona," Ethan repeated slowly.

"An old annoyance," I answered, staring at the strange man with grey eyes.

He frowned, rubbing his wrist. "*Donny*, just because I rejected you back then doesn't me—"

"You rejected me?" I gasped in disbelief. He really was out of his fucking mind, and I wanted to die.

"That's how I remember it—"

"Obviously you need to get your head checked, then!"

"Really, is that why you pulled a gun on me a decade later? If you rejected me, shouldn't I be the one angry?"

I stared at him in utter confusion. The only word I could think of saying was "Huh?"

I didn't know him! What the fuck was he talking about?

"Luckily our brother is a doctor, he can check if you

are both alright," Ethan said with that fake politeness in his voice again.

"If they are, I'm going to make sure they aren't," Wyatt muttered, now off the ground. He wiped the blood from his nose, his hair a disheveled mess as he glared at the man beside me. I wondered how badly I must look now.

To make it worse, Mr. Crazy leaned forward and pet his shoulder saying, "Sorry *mon amie*, I didn't see you there. You alright?"

Both Ethan and Wyatt glanced down at his hand, then back at him at the same time, their expressions the same. I wanted to laugh; I wanted to laugh hard because sometimes it's like they were the twins between us.

When they both glanced to me again, at the same time, I shook my head and walked around them, knowing full well everyone else was unsure of whether to continue having a good time or be concerned.

"I'm so sorry about that, childhood friends just know how to get under your skin. Please enjoy the rest of brunch." I smiled at them and they relaxed, allowing me to calmly walk back into the house.

I knew I couldn't escape. Ethan would follow and

most likely Wyatt, but I wanted to understand who that other man was. I went to Beata Veronica Negroni da Binasco School for Girls, but my father told people I went to another school to make sure no one knew where I was. The only people who knew were my father and my grandmother.

I stared down at the gun still in my hand… I'd lost it. My temper had gotten the best of me many times, but never like that, never publicly.

Walking straight into the Ethan's study, I picked the phone off the receiver but then the wooden doors opened and my brother walked in, along with the man in question, my bloody hand print still on his white shirt.

"Who are you?" I snapped.

Wyatt closed the door behind them and leaned against it, a knife his hand. He spun it carefully, the tip of the blade pressing in his finger as he waited. Ethan came forward, sitting on the edge of his desk, and took a gun out from his jacket. "You should answer her question quickly because I don't have any. I know you aren't Irish or Italian and so you were not invited to my house—"

"That's where you're wrong," the man before us

said casually as he took a seat on the couch before resting his feet on the coffee table.

"I'm never wrong," Ethan shot back.

He grinned from ear to ear. "I'm sure your grandmother would beg to differ, wouldn't you Evelyn?"

I wasn't sure who he was speaking to until he took his phone out of his pocket before placing it on the coffee table.

"I would," a familiar voice said over the speaker and, just like that, Ethan, Wyatt, and I stood a little straighter. "Last time I checked, Ethan, the house belonged to me, unless you've written me off for dead."

"I—"

"Welcome back home Wyatt, I wish I could have been there to see you."

Wyatt came closer. "Nana, I—"

"But then again you shouldn't have ever left home to begin with. You have a lot to make up for. I hope you don't think you can just come back and get everything handed to you?"

"I—"

"But most of all, I'm disappointed in you, Donatella,"

she continued and I felt my hands sting like she hit me with a switch, something she often did when I was younger. "So much has happened since I left Chicago and you, my sweet granddaughter, never once thought to call me? You are that big of a woman now you can't ask me for advice or help? You know everything? You can do it all by yourselves, right? Am I already dead to you?"

"Nana," all three of us said at the same.

"I may not be in Chicago, but know this: long before any of you were even a twinkle in your father's eyes, before your father was even the head of this family, there was me. Me. I buried my father, my husband, and my son! Don't you ever make me hear that any of you were on the verge of dying, Ethan. Or betraying this family, Donatella. Or forgetting who you are, Wyatt. Or so help me God, I'll show you how small you all are when compared to me. Am I understood?"

None of us said anything. If we even thought to, our father might rise from the grave just to smack the shit out of us all.

"I take it back Evelyn, you are bona fide gangster," the stranger on our couch snickered, tossing Ethan's cashews into his mouth, happily.

I cracked my jaw to the side and speak sweetly into the phone, “Nana, who is this strange person, why is he in our home, and can I kill him now?”

“You’re asking questions instead of apologizing?” she questioned back and I bit my lip. “You’re too big to apologize now? And at family gathering. How could you? Have you lost your mind?”

Strike one, I thought, handing the phone to Wyatt. He looked at me like I was mad as I pushed to the phone to him. He gritted his teeth at me before taking the phone.

“Nana,” Wyatt said with full charm, “I’m so sorry I haven’t been able to call; I’ve been so busy! I saved Ethan’s life and then there was—”

“And yet you still found time to play around with the maids? How many times have I told you the women in the house are not your toys?!”

Wyatt closed his mouth, shaking his head as he tossed the phone to Ethan who caught it gently. *Strike two.*

“Grandmother,” he said casually, “how are you?”

“You would know if you called,” she shot back.

Ethan nodded. “I would know, however I told you I

wouldn't be able to get in touch for a while."

Foul.

"You told me you'd call before you left Boston because you needed some information. Where are you currently?"

Ethan made face. "Chicago, but I no longer needed the information. The plan changed so I thought I'd allow you to get some more rest."

Foul two.

"Aren't you the same one who tells me not to rest too much or I'll end up dead? Honestly Ethan, I'm hurt; you're usually on top of things like this. I was even more hurt after what happened to you and Ivy."

He paused, watching as the stranger moved from the couch over to the globe, lifting it up and pulling out a Scotch for himself. He glanced around inside in search of something, until he finally looked over to us, displeased. "Where's the ice?"

"Why would there be ice in a globe?" Wyatt asked, annoyed.

"Why would there be Scotch in a globe but no brandy?" he questioned back in the same annoyed voice.

"Obviously, it's not a globe, it's a bar. A bar stocked by someone with poor taste or who likes to force other people to drink bad whiskey. Either way, I'm trying not to complain about that and accept what I'm given. However, it's quite difficult to do when there isn't any ice…in a bar."

I felt my eyebrow twitch and looked over to Ethan, praying he'd toss him out the window.

"Gabriel, how many times must I tell you, scotch does not need ice?" Our grandmother asked over the phone.

He frowned, pouring the glass for himself. "I'm not sure how many time you *must* tell me. But I'm sure you'll tell me a million times more, seeing as you're planning on living forever and I plan on drinking my scotch with ice for as long as people keep offering it to me."

"No one has offered you anything." Ethan still managed to say calmly and the man, Gabriel, I could only assume, looked back to him.

"I know, it was rude of you, which is why I helped myself and didn't make a scene about it. But if you'd prefer I point out all the shortcomings in your hospitality, that can be done."

What the hell? Where was I? When did I go to the Twilight Zone?

Ethan lifted the phone back up to his lips. "Grandmother, once again, who is this person and how important is he to you?"

"His name is Gabriel, and he'll be staying at the mansion for a short while. I've already let the staff know to prepare his room."

"Thank you, Evelyn," Gabriel said, walking in front of Ethan and taking the phone from his hand. "You're so sweet to me... If only you were fifty years younger."

"Ugh," Wyatt cringed, turning away.

"Not even then. Do your best not to get yourself killed by my grandchildren—"

"So we can kill him?" I asked her and he glanced up, glaring at me.

"Goodbye Evelyn. Rest easy; I'm sure your grandchildren know how to behave around a guest," he said, not waiting for a response before hanging up on her. "That's how you feel after I saved you?"

"You saved me? From what?"

"You seem to have selective memory disorder," he

snapped back at me. "You went mad, shattered a glass with your hand and then grabbed my shirt, only to pull a gun on me…and your doctor was no help. Shouldn't you be worried about her hand, not your nose?" He directed that comment at Wyatt. "She is your sister, isn't she?"

The moment he brought it up, it was like he kicked down the door to the pain I'd blocked out. I looked to my hand, which was still bleeding, small shards of glass embedded in it. Wyatt moved quickly, taking the glass of scotch from Gabriel and pouring it on my hand before taking a napkin to tie around the wound.

I jumped as it burned, looking back into the grey eyes now watching us.

"Gabriel what?"

"Excuse me?" he asked.

"What is your last name?"

"I don't have one." He grinned, rising to his feet as he added. "Think of me like a Greek God, here to see how the tragedy will unfold."

He winked at me before walking to the door, but before he could leave, Ethan called out to him saying, "God, man or monster, if you *ever* lay a hand or pull a gun on anyone in my family again, I'll drown you in warm scotch myself."

This was the moment where most people knew to step back from Ethan Gabriel, however, simply looked amused, "So you're a Shakespeare man… Good to know."

Just like that he left, and when the door closed behind him, Ethan said to me directly, "What did he say to you before? It's not like you to lose your cool in public like that."

I didn't answer, so Wyatt spoke up, "Obviously he wanted to get under our skin. Whatever he's up to… I don't trust him, even if Nana does."

"Obviously," Ethan muttered, walking back over to his bar. "Any man who drinks scotch must be mental."

Wyatt snickered, checking over my hand, but I didn't say anything. I wasn't sure what was going through my grandmother's half-burnt mind, but something told me this *Gabriel* was much more dangerous than he seemed. How else could he so easily stand up not only to me, and my brothers, but also to my grandmother; he was either accustomed to being in the company of monsters or he was one himself. And it had to be the latter because no one was as bad as my family; Gabriel just didn't know it yet. He was ignorant and I'd enlighten him.

"You don't think Nana would be pissed enough to make us live with a serial killer, do you?" I asked them, partially joking, but neither of them laughed.

"Kill him and apologize later," Wyatt suggested to Ethan.

Ethan shook his head, "We don't kill blindly, brother. We find out who he is, and his connection to Grandmother...then we kill him."

Our family didn't do well with outsiders for a reason.

They ruined everything.

GABRIEL

"How was day one?"

"She pulled a gun on me, and I think bruised two of my ribs," I said as I came out of the shower, using the towel to dry my hair. Noticing the red marks from her legs on my neck. "All of that happened after she shattered a champagne glass with her bare hands... So, not as bad as I was expecting."

"Why? Because she didn't shoot you?"

"Exactly," I answered, cleaning the steam off the glass in order to see my reflection. "From here on out, any day she doesn't shoot me, I consider a win."

"That's a low bar."

"And yet it's still higher than where your son started off," I said, lifting the phone off the counter and closer to my lips, "A bullet through the thigh, correct?"

"He at least kissed her before she shot him," she corrected me.

"I'm sure you were proud, Evelyn," I said coldly. "But I've already spent the last month waiting on the sidelines. I'm done waiting; I'm taking what was promised to me."

"Nothing was promised to you but an opportunity. My granddaughter will make you work for the rest." She hung up on me, and I couldn't help but grin. The old woman had bite to her, even when half-dead on bed a thousand miles away.

From what I could see, all the Callahan women were the same: beautiful and dangerous. However, Donatella... I couldn't help but grin as I placed my hand on my chin. I loved a woman who could fight back both physically and mentally, who wasn't afraid of a little pain, but best of all, she was awe-inspiringly beautiful. When I'd held her to me, I felt the curves of her body, the warmth of her skin, how she smelled like Mediterranean lilies... If I had kissed her, we'd make a scene in a very different sort of way.

The day isn't over yet...

NINE

"You either like me or you don't.
It took me twenty-something years to learn how to love myself,
I don't have that kinda time to convince somebody else."
~ Daniel Franzese

DONATELLA

I hadn't straightened my hair in a while so when I finally let it down, it was a thick mess of curls. I would have just left it up until I could get it done professionally tomorrow, however, tonight was our first family dinner in a long time. That, plus we had a guest.

"I never thought I'd see the day you were worried about what to wear..."

Looking up from my mirror to the door; there stood Nari, in skinny pink trousers and a deep blue V-neck blouse, a single gold bar necklace around her neck. Beside her, dressed in a yellow and white above-the-knee floral print dress was Helen, who frowned while looking me up and down.

"Are you trying to look nice for Gabriel?" Helen asked.

"I don't *try* to look nice, I do that naturally," I corrected her, looking back to the mirror and brushing my hair. "Looking nice isn't my goal; I need a look that will make him want to approach me."

"You want to seduce him?" Nari questioned, coming

up beside me, her pale face appearing in the reflection of my mirror. "Isn't it a little soon after—"

"He's here for a reason," I snapped at her, cutting her off before she crossed the line. "And I'm positive it isn't a good one. The faster I can get rid of him, the faster we can avoid the shit-storm that's coming after him."

"But didn't grandma invite him to stay?" Helen came over to the mirror with a few dresses, holding them up to my body. When she found one she liked, she held it in front me before looking and saying, "He can't be that dangerous if she—"

"Maybe he has something on her?"

"Dona," Nari scoffed in disbelief, reminding me of Tobias when I'd told him something was off with Marco's death. Taking the dress from Helen's hand, I turned to face Nari and looked deep into her brown eyes.

"Are you laughing at me?" I asked her.

Nari lifted a brow and stood straighter. "No, I just find it hard to believe—"

"That's your first mistake," I replied coldly. "Nothing should be too hard for you to believe by now."

"If there is anyone you can trust, it is Evelyn," she

replied.

I stepped closer, so close I could feel her breath, "Me. Myself. And I. That's how far my circle of trust goes. I'm almost one hundred percent certain my grandmother wouldn't do anything to harm us. However, I'm also certain she's hiding something...when she left here she was on the edge of death and not a word since then. Now, all of a sudden, a man shows up in our house at her request! Why? No answer. Who is he? No answer. What is he doing here? Again, no answer. And I'm supposed to be alright with that? Fuck no. My instincts tell me this is bigger than she's explaining. How big, I'm not sure. Which is what I plan on finding out... That is, if you are done laughing at me?"

She smiled and nodded, "I apologize if I insulted you, cousin."

"You're forgiven, cousin," I smiled back.

"I'll see you downstairs."

"Of course," I said with the same politeness and she turned to leave without another word. I turned back to the mirror only to see Helen's brown eyes glaring at me. "Yes?"

"I don't know what he said to make you so upset this morning," she said walking over to hand me another outfit. "But it isn't her fault which means she didn't deserve that bullshit."

"Perfect, thank you," I said, taking the black satin wrap from her hands, ignoring her comment as I held the clothes up. "Black really is my color."

She didn't say anything more, knowing I wasn't going to talk about it. Instead she just picked up her small purse and walked out the door. When it closed, I inhaled deeply, tilting my head to the ceiling. It was so easy for them to see me as the villain, the raging bitch.

"You were never meant to be the Ceann na Conairte."

"So why do you keep running head first into the wall?"

"You enjoy the pain."

His words felt like ants on my skin, crawling all over me and each time I tried to brush them off, they came back. The whole day, all I could think of was him. O'Phelan had let us know he'd gone to sleep; apparently, he was jetlagged. That, plus his odd accent, made it clear he wasn't from America and had only come here recently. Ethan hadn't been able to get any information on him. Nor could Helen or even Jackal, which was unheard of. Perhaps my grandmother was hiding who he really was, making him even more dangerous.

He knew everything about us.

He was under my grandmother's protection.

And we knew nothing about him...*for now,* I reminded myself. I stripped down, changing into the satin romper, the shorts stopping mid-thigh; it was casual enough that it looked like I didn't put effort in, but sexy enough to catch his attention...once I had that, I'd see if he "enjoyed the pain".

Not wasting any time my bed spun around, I grabbed my favorite pair of black heels with gold straps, before heading back to the bathroom. I skipped make-up completely and only put on lip balm. *I couldn't make it too obvious.*

Pulling my hair back into a messy ponytail, I only stopped to pick up my cellphone before exiting my room. Just as I stepped out, so did he, dressed in an oversized gray sweater and gray gym shorts that stopped at his knees. He wore vintage round-framed glasses and carried a red book, which he didn't look up from, as he walked to the elevator. I watched him, stunned, as he waited quietly, getting in when the doors opened. When it began to close, he finally looked up at me.

"You're a little overdressed, don't you think?" Just like that, the doors closed and I had no words. Well, that was lie. I had words. Three of them actually.

"Go fuck yourself."

GABRIEL

Lifting my glasses up, I pinched the bridge of my nose, trying to get the image of her out of my head. Her legs were so bloody long, and that outfit! If it could even be considered an outfit and not just a fucking too-thin robe... I could easily see all the lines of her body.

Well, at least you know you're attracted to her, I thought, trying to be rational. Lust was good thing. Lust was a good starting point...however, it was just *my* starting point. I didn't get that feeling from her yet; all I got was rage. I could work with rage; it was just a step ahead of passion. She needed to be reigned in a little. I'd been warned about her. How Donatella Callahan was like a siren, her beauty so enchanting she drew men in and pulled them to the deep before they'd even realized. I'm sure men before me, lesser men, easily walked into her trap, the thought of being with her was worth the risk of death. I, on the other hand, wasn't a lesser man nor were her looks worth losing everything I was fighting for. I needed her to get what I wanted; what she looked like was irrelevant...*but fuck me,* she wasn't holding back.

"It's just the first day," I whispered to myself, stepping off the elevator. I glanced back down at the book I could no longer concentrate on reading. Part of me wanted to try and see how she'd try to trap me in her web, to play her game, but I just didn't have time for that.

Work first, play later.

"Good evening, Sir," the old butler said to me when I reached the dining room. Looking up from the book, I nodded back, thanking him before heading inside.

There, seated at the head of the table, was just one of my many obstacles. Dressed in a dark three-piece suit with a black tie, a glass of ice-less scotch in his hand, was none other than Ethan Callahan himself. His green eyes, like hers, looked me up and down.

"You're a little underdressed, don't you think?" Her

soft, yet steady voice questioned from behind me.

I glanced around the table. To the left of her eldest brother was his blonde haired, blue-eyed wife dressed in white, who stood staring as she sipped on a juice box. Next to her was an African-American woman with curly brown hair and standing beside her, an Asian-American woman with shoulder-length black hair. Wyatt, obstacle number two, was dressed in the same suit from this morning, though his jacket was gone. He took a bite of his bread, not taking his eyes off me.

"Please sit," Ethan said, nodding over to the spot beside Donatella.

"O'Phelan," he called when I took my seat. The butler came over to me carrying a bowl of thick, rich soup with bread on the side. "I hope you aren't allergic to anything?"

I smirked, shaking my head and placing my book on the table to look to him. "I'm not, thank you for your concern."

"This is my wife, Ivy, and my cousins, Helen and Nari." He looked to them all. "But I'm sure you already knew that."

"Did I?" I pretended to be oblivious before looking over to his wife. "How did a beautiful girl like you end up with a man like him?"

"Evelyn didn't happen to break you out a prison, did she?" she asked instead.

All of them, with the exception of Ethan, shook their head. "Why? Does she bring inmates home often?"

"Inmate 974024-041, nice to meet you," Ivy laughed to herself.

"And here I thought being drop-dead gorgeous wasn't a federal offence," I replied, winking at her.

"It's not; but running over a dancer while drunk is," Donatella cut in before Ivy could speak again, casually tearing the bread and dipping it into her soup.

"Ivy," I frowned, still giving her all of my attention, "say it ain't so."

"It's so," she replied, less ecstatic than before, her eyes on Donatella who refused to pay attention to her. "It wasn't me though. I was innocent."

"*Was* being the key word." Donatella mumbled softly under her breath.

Glancing to the other two women across from me, I

asked, "Are you all also married to wrongly convicted felons?"

"Single," Helen said.

"He's a—"

"None of your business," Wyatt cut them off, glaring over at me, "Why the hell should we explain ourselves or our family to a stranger?"

"Simply making conversation," I said, tearing my bread and dipping it into the dish. "Or do you all prefer your dinners to be hostile?"

"You are free to leave," Ethan stated, leaning back into his chair. "If we happen to be too hostile for your liking."

This family had walls almost as high as mine around them. To my great joy, a silence fell over the dining room. I tried to pretend I didn't notice their eyes on me, but it was like walking into a den of lions in the middle of night. Reaching for my book, I lifted it back up to read as I ate quietly among them, more aware of Donatella than I'd like. It was very easy to spot women who were trouble; women who would only complicate your life. It was clear Donatella was that type of woman. It wasn't her family, it was her personality; from what I could tell and what I'd heard... She was like a ticking time bomb ready to go off at any moment.

Evelyn had only given me two pieces of advice: defuse her as quickly as possible and never let her think she controls you. The old woman looked genuinely concerned her granddaughter might kill me.

"Hmh," I snickered to myself at that, causing her to stiffen beside me.

"Ethan," she spoke softly, with that horrid fake smile back on her pretty pink lips, not at all like the laugh she'd allowed herself this morning.

"Yes?" he asked.

She looked over to him, "I've been thinking of stabbing him with my salad fork for the last ten minutes. Please tell me who he is and when he can leave?"

I grinned. "How could he tell you something he doesn't know."

"Why don't I know?" Ethan questioned and didn't look at me, focusing only on Donatella.

"If you want a straight answer *Donny*, you should go to the source."

"Donny?" She whipped her head back to me so

quickly, I'm sure she'd hurt herself. "My name is Donatella, and why would I trust a word that comes out of your ugly mouth?"

I laughed. "Ugly? I've had numerous women use a *plethora* of adjectives to describe my mouth, however, ugly was never one of them."

"Why don't you find those 'numerous' women and leave us the fuck alone?" she snapped.

"I was leaving you alone when you threatened me with silverware. So, once again, you're annoyed because of your own actions."

"You little piece of shit—"

"Are you still bitter because I called you an idiot for wanting to usurp your brother?" I said loudly and happily. "Resorting to name-calling is a bit petty, don't you think?"

She gripped her fork so tight I was sure it would bend.

"Shut. Your. Mouth." She hissed through her teeth.

"Or you'll what—"

Before I could finish speaking she brought the fork down *hard* right beside my arm; I could even feel the silver graze my skin. "Or I won't miss next time."

She trembled, breathing through her nose like a bull ready to run me down. Reaching over her hand, I freed my sweater from her wrath. "Why is the truth so hard for you to hear—"

"Why do you keep speaking to me as if I know you?!" she snapped at me. "You make it seem as if we're close but we aren't! I'm sure I've never been so fucking annoyed to meet anyone as I have today. So I doubt we've met before!"

"Let me understand, you believe the manner in which I'm speaking to you now is the way people who are close speak with one another?" I asked, genuinely surprised by that. "The more we speak, the more I wonder about your mental stability."

Once again, she lifted her fork, but before she could stab me, I grabbed the knife, blocking it, the silver clashing with each other.

"That's the third time you've insulted me today—"

"It's a shame you can't read my mind." I winked at her, still having to put force behind the knife to keep her at bay. "You'd know how badly I'd prefer not to have a raging homicidal madwoman screaming in my ear, but an agreement is an agreement."

Her eyes were like liquid green fire. The more I stared, the hotter I felt; it was like looking down a volcano.

"What agreement?" Ethan asked and for a brief I'd forgotten he, along with the rest of the family, was still here.

Defuse her, I remembered. I'd hope to not have to go this far, to start with this lie, but it seemed none of them were going to give me the space I needed. *Very well then.*

"The verbal one your parents made with mine before they all died," I lied. It wasn't a total lie but it was close enough. At the mention of her parents, she seemed to snap out of her rage, pulling back slowly as her brother pushed forward with his questions.

"And that is?"

Looking directly at her, I said one word, "Marriage."

Wyatt choked on the bread he was eating, coughing so hard his face turned red. The butler came forward with water, but Wyatt merely turned to me. "Marriage? What marriage?"

"My marriage to your temperamental, impulsive, screaming banshee of a sister, Donatella Aviela Callahan."

Her face was void of any emotion, even anger. She just shook her head. “You’re lying.”

“If I was, why would your grandmother push herself to call and make sure I was not only welcomed, but also in the room right next to you?”

She got up, her fist balled at her sides. “Who are you to marry me?”

“Wrong question.” I pushed my chair back, rising to my feet. “You should be asking why only you? Your parents had three children, why did they only bother to arrange a marriage for you?”

She froze; her green eyes wide as she looked through me, not at me.

“I don’t know.” She didn’t answer. Rising behind her like a beast, Wyatt stood glaring at me as if he wanted to gut me alive. “I don’t know. I don’t fucking care. My parents are dead. Their opinion and wishes are irrelevant now. However, if they were here, they’d skin you alive for speaking to my sister this way. Good thing I’m alive and I’m good with knives.”

“Skin away then,” I said, tossing him my knife which he caught with ease. “When you’re done, I’ll still be here.

Your sister will still be here and so will the agreement between us."

She stood up, standing between the two of us but facing me. She wasn't as enraged as she'd been before; now she was calm, too calm given the current situation. "There is no agreement. I'm twenty-six years old. I'll pick who I marry, not my parents. Not my grandmother."

"Yes," I nodded to her, speaking just as calmly. "How did that work out for the last man you picked?"

She inhaled through her nose but still managed to keep it together; "Let's break the agreement so you can go back to hell now."

"Fine by me, so long as you understand that it's you who is breaking the agreement."

"I—"

"Stop." Ethan cut in, proving he was much smarter than I gave him credit for. "What happens if she breaks the agreement?"

"I don't care what happens!" She snapped at him. "It's my life, don't you—"

"All agreements have some type of collateral. He wants you to break the agreement, Donatella. Which means whatever he gets for you breaking it is worth more than having you. You are the only sister to the *Ceann na Conairte*, the daughter of a former governor, and business mogul. On top of that, you're beautiful… What man in his right mind would turn that down just because he dislikes your temperament?" Mr. Know It All questioned, making them turn to look at me like prey they couldn't wait to tear apart.

Bravo Ethan.

"Well?" Wyatt asked, waiting while Dona did her best not to scream.

"Italy," I answered, looking from her to her brother as he sat comfortably at the head of the table. "All the drug routes in Italy; that's what I get."

"Ha." Ethan laughed in shock. "Bullshit. My family would never give up our home—"

"Which is how they were sure that your sister would end up marrying me," I said, taking off my glasses and picking up my book. "But, like she said, she's old enough to decide who she marries, and I'll support whatever she chooses. Thank you for dinner."

I knew I wasn't going to make it to the door. This

family could never let anyone else have the last word.

"What happens if *you* were to break the agreement?"

So, I repeated what her brother had said; "You are the only sister to the *Ceann na Conairte,* the daughter of a former governor, and business mogul. On top of that, you're beautiful… What man in his right mind would turn that down just because he dislikes your temperament?"

The look on their faces was magnificent.

On this side of the world the Callahan's were the most powerful family, without a doubt, but they were extremely ignorant if they believed there weren't other powerful families out there.

Opening the book in my hand, I read on from where I'd stopped… *Beowulf* was such a classic; *"The dragon began to belch out flames and burn bright homesteads; there was a hot glow that scared everyone, for the vile sky-winger would leave nothing alive in his wake."*

TEN

"Vipera in veprecula est.

(There is a viper in the bush.)"

~Unknown

ETHAN

"You're calling again so soon; I truly feel loved," my grandmother said on the phone.

"I'm not sure love is the right word," I replied, looking up at Dona who stared blankly at the phone in my hand, her head bobbing slowly... I wasn't a doctor, but the doctor beside her seemed to worry she was going into shock.

"Love is always the right word." She giggled. With my eyebrow raised, I looked over at Wyatt, who leaned forward grinning.

"Nana, are you high?" he asked.

"As a fucking kite," she replied. "I knew it. The hospitals have all the good shit."

Wyatt laughed outright at her response and so did she. The only one who didn't laugh was Dona. I was used to her snapping and I was used to her being cold...but this was neither. She was just numb, and I hated being witness to it.

"Grandmother, this Gabriel apparently believes that our parents arranged a marriage between him and

Donatella."

"He believes that..." she hiccupped. "Excuse me, because it's true."

"Twenty-six years of living with you, eighteen years with father, and not once did I hear about an arranged marriage for anyone."

"Why would anyone tell you? It has nothing to do with you."

"Me," Donatella whispered. "It's about me so why didn't anyone tell me?"

The smile on Wyatt's face fell at hearing how hurt she was. Hurting Dona wasn't easy, but when accomplished, it made everyone else hurt right along with her.

"If you don't want to marry him dear, then don't marry him—"

"Then he gets the routes in Italy?" I questioned, wanting to see if he really was telling the truth.

"Oh right," she said as if it was an afterthought and not our family heritage. My mother's home, everything she'd built with her own hands! "If Dona doesn't want to marry him, then he gets to control the drug flow of Italy.

Meaning nothing gets in or out with—"

"I understand the meaning!" I snapped at her and Wyatt cringed, shaking his head. Why I suffered to bring him back, I couldn't remember at the moment.

"Did you just raise your voice at me?" she asked softly.

Rubbing the side of my head, I inhaled slowly. "Nana, I don't understand why my mother or father would ever promise something like that to a stranger. It would be like Father giving away Ireland, it doesn't make sense."

"It doesn't make sense because you are forgetting who your mother was—"

"I'll never forget that," I replied without hesitation.

"Then you know your mother would put everything on the line for only one reason—"

"Her children," Wyatt answered, not being helpful at all. "If it came down to the whole world or us, she'd choose us."

"Exactly. See, this is why you were her favorite."

He beamed like a pet waiting to get his reward. What made him our mother's favorite? Apparently of us three, Wyatt was the only one to ever say *mama* and since then he'd been crowned her favorite. So now, due to Wyatt's big head, our mother's grudge against Dona and I for calling out to our father first, was cemented for all eternity. Our mother had been so petty...like her daughter.

"No." Dona shook her head, sitting up straight. Her eyes refocusing on us. "I'm sure *Melody* would risk it all for us...but only if it was the last option. And only if our lives were at stake... My life isn't at stake, so why put everyone at risk? Because she's sure she won't lose a fucking thing... She's sure I'll go along with it."

She laughed bitterly, shaking her head as she looked up at ceiling. "Even from the grave she's still trying to make me do things her way."

"Dona...sweetheart."

"Nana, get some rest; I'll call you later," she said, hanging up my phone and dropping it back on the desk. She rose to her feet.

"What are you going to do?" I asked her.

Holding on to the doorknob for a moment, she hung her head. "I don't—I'll come up with something."

Just like that she was gone.

She was going to say she didn't know. She doesn't

know how to fight… She needed help but she wasn't going to ask…stubborn and full of pride to the end.

"Did you really not know?"

I glanced over to Wyatt who was leaning forward and now looked ready to shoot me, all humor gone from his voice.

"What?"

"Did you sell off our sister so you didn't have to worry about her?" he asked, grinding his jaw, his eyes furious. "So, you didn't have to worry she'd betray you?"

"You heard grandmother—"

"I've seen and heard grandmother lie on your behalf before! How the fuck do I know you weren't the one that brought Gabriel here? You told him what to say and had Nana vouch for him. I'm sure you'd even convince Uncle Neal and Declan just so your bloody plan could come together."

I watched him clench his fist to stop himself from trembling with rage.

"She's my sister—"

"Which is why I'm sure you didn't kill her. Instead, you picked some random douchebag to marry her off to!"

At that moment, I wanted to smack him. "Get out Wyatt!"

"I swear to God, if you are behind this—"

I rose to my feet, the only thing between us my desk. And even that wasn't going to be enough to stop me from beating his ass. Calming myself down, I walked around the desk to stand in front of him. "Let's say you are correct, little brother. You're not, but let's say you're right and I am selling our sister. What makes you think you have any power to stop me? Your army is my army. The last I checked, most of them still think you're nothing but a scared little bitch who ran from his responsibilities. To them you are just a spoiled little playboy, the little prince who can only talk like this to me because we're blood and *I* allow it."

I reached over to fix his tie and dust the shoulders of his suit before adding, "You can swear to whichever God you like, little brother. But swearing is nothing without power, so you better get your own before running your month."

He glared at me, before reaching for my wrist and gripping it tightly. "Careful what you ask for, big brother.

You know better than I; fortune, in this family, is on the side of the second son…and you've already been at death's door once. And this *scared little bitch* saved your life. Know this—you *don't* want to piss me off, because I don't need an army. I just need to step back and watch you take all the bullets. Then people will know I stood in your shadow for twenty-six years; not because I was afraid, but because I enjoy the shield… From there I'll rise just like Grandfather. The second son. His elder brother ruled for a while too…yet who remembers his name?"

Like Dona, Wyatt had a talent for knowing exactly what to say to get on my last damn nerve.

"Are you going to release my wrist or am I going to have to break your hand?" I asked him patiently. He did, stepping back and heading towards the doors. Just as he opened it, I called out to him once more. "Welcome home, little brother."

He flipped me off as he walked out, and when the door closed I moved back to sit in my chair. Hearing a small click behind me from the secret door of the bookcase, I turned around to see her frowning as she stepped closer to me.

"Eavesdropping now?" I asked her as she came forward to sit on the edge of my desk. "I would have told you later, Ivy."

"I know," she said, brushing her blonde hair behind her hair. "I just happened to be walking by."

My eyebrow rose at that. She just so happened to be walking by in the secret passage route through the mansion? "Would you like time to think of a better lie?"

"No, I'm just going to change the subject." She tried to smile but that worried frown on her face was still there. "What did Wyatt mean by you both knowing fortune favors the second son?"

"My grandfather and my father were not supposed to be *Ceann na Conairte*. They were the seconds sons, meaning they had elder brothers who were supposed to take over. My grandfather's elder brother - Uncle Declan's father, Killian - was murdered, so my father's brother stepped back and allowed my father to take over."

"So, it's a curse—"

"Two hardly constitutes a curse," I cut her off quickly. I'd heard more than a few whispers about the Callahan curse and I preferred not to hear them from her.

"And even if it were, don't you think I'd be well prepared for it?"

She rolled her eyes; "Of course... What's your plan? I mean you brought him back, so obviously you aren't going to kill him."

"Obviously." She spoke of killing Wyatt so easily, as if the thought had just crossed her mind.

"So..." she pressed.

"*Audentes fortuna iuvat and omnia vincit amor.*" She waited, annoyed that she couldn't understand. "Fortune favors the bold and love conquers all..."

"I don't get it."

"Don't worry, you will," I said, taking her hand and gently pulling her to sit on my lap.

She brushed my hair back softly; "This Gabriel guy, what are you going to do about him? I'm surprised you didn't kill him for talking to you like that."

Inhaling, I placed my hands on her waist; "I can't kill him."

"You? The great Ethan Callahan, *can't* kill someone?" She gasped, leaning in to place kisses on my eyebrow and down the side of my face. "And here I thought you were all powerful."

"I am," I replied. Seeing her like this made me smile slightly.

"But?"

Closing my eyes, I enjoyed her lips as they sucked on my neck, "But so are the people who created me."

She paused in her actions, sadly, and I felt her sit up. I opened my eyes to find her staring down at me. "You aren't killing him because of your parents?"

I nodded; "I became who I am by watching my parents. They were always plotting, building the foundations for plans that were months, sometimes years, in the making. Of all the men in the world, they chose this Gabriel. For my mother to do that, to accept that, and for my father to agree to it… It means they weighed all the options, and decided he was it."

"It for what?"

Good question. "Knowing my father, he'd want Donatella to be happy and to live as comfortably as possible. Something she could do on her own, but I still think he wouldn't have agreed if Gabriel didn't have wealth of his own. But my mother…"

"She wouldn't want Dona to be happy?" She pouted. "I didn't know her personally, but from her letter I could tell she loved all of you a lot."

My mother's love was different, though. "My mother..." I paused, not sure how to explain it. "Her love was in the future."

"Huh?" She made one of her many faces at me.

I nodded again, feeling a bitter ache and not wanting to speak on it, but forcing myself to continue. "My mother loved us beyond our present selves. Sometimes we'd get so angry at her while growing up, not understanding why she'd push us so hard, and then something would happen and we could handle it because of how she had pushed us. She didn't always give us what we wanted but she always gave us what we needed...The problem is she gave it to us before we realized we needed it. All three of us have these moments..." I paused again, unsure why my throat burned as much as it did. Why speaking about my mother bother me like this?

"We've had these moments when... It's like we realize we can do or we're doing something because our mother showed us how when we were younger. Back then when we didn't understand, we fought her, Donatella especially... She thought Mom loved her less. Now, as adults, we see just how much our mother loved us, how far she went for us... But it's too late to thank her. We can't show her we are grateful."

I sighed, sitting up and brushing the side of my nose. Focusing back on her as she looked at me gently, her hands on the side of my face. "So, to answer your question, she chose Gabriel because she believes he's the best way for Dona to get whatever it is she truly wants. I trust my mother. That's why he isn't dead. That's why I'm going to step back from this and let it play out between them. Whether Dona likes it or not."

"I don't know if you are bad brother but you are a good son...and a better husband," she whispered, and before I could think her lips were on mine; and just like that all of me relaxed, wrapping my arms around her as she moaned into my mouth...

Day by day, Ivy was becoming my biggest weakness.

It made me wonder about Dona and Wyatt. They were romantics at heart, and like myself, whoever they fell for would be their weakness. Neither of them knew it yet, though. How could they?

As much as I distrusted this *Gabriel,* I knew he didn't want Italy. He wanted her; why else would he try so hard to push her buttons, to get in her face and challenge her, make her only see him?

"Ah..." I pulled back when she licked the part of my lip she had bitten hard.

Grabbing the sides of my face she forced me to look at her; "You're thinking, and not about me. Stop it!"

"Yes, Mrs. Callahan." I grinned, giving her my full attention.

ELEVEN

"The wolves should be fed and the sheep kept safe."

~ Leo Tolstoy

DONATELLA

I had that feeling again. That feeling that something was off. That I was missing important pieces of the puzzle in front of me. Gabriel had been in our home for three days now and had barely spoken to me or my family. He left during the day an Ethan and I both had people tail him; a fact he must have been aware of that but didn't seem to faze him. It was where he was going that bothered me. He'd gone to the OC on the first day and volunteered from morning until closing. The staff said he hadn't made any calls nor disappeared during that time. They all gushed about how kind and funny he was, and how the elders all liked him. The second day he'd gone to Morning Glory Hospital and volunteered there, reading fairytales to the younger kids, then playing Mahjong and Boggle with the elderly. The third day was the worst. He went out running and then sat on the grass, leaning against a tree and reading for the entire day.

None of it made any bloody sense.

If he wanted me, he'd try to make that clear.

If he didn't want me and wanted Italy, he would

have tried to provoke me and force me to break the agreement. But he wasn't doing either of those. He was simply...doing nothing. For a man to come into our home, to have the backing of my grandmother, and the word of my parents but to simply do nothing didn't add up. This was why I knew something was wrong; I just wasn't sure where to start looking.

"Ma'am, we're here," the driver informed me. I looked over to the restaurant on my right, the name Melody's Garden etched into the glass. The valet opened my door quickly for me to step out.

"Welcome, Ms. Callahan," The freckle-faced man said, pointing me forward as I took off my sunglasses.

This is going to be fun, I thought sarcastically, walking through the wooden doors as they opened for me. Once inside, as always, it felt as if I'd been transported to Verona, one of my mother's favorite cites in Italy. The walls that led to the dining hall were made of brick that had been imported from the city itself. The end of the hall was so bright, it looked as if you were walking into the light at the end of life. I could hear their soft voices as they laughed and giggled, which died down when I reached the light at the end. As always, I found myself unable to look away from the glass dome above, where all you could see was the bright blue sky. Centered in the middle of the dining room was a saltwater Roman-style fountain. Apparently, the statue of a woman pouring water from a jug was meant to look like my mother...but I couldn't see it. All around the restaurant were perfectly trimmed and managed bushes.

Inhaling, I smiled; "Good morning, ladies."

"Good morning, Donatella," they all said it, which was kind of funny. They sounded like school children and I was their teacher... No, not funny—pitiful for them. They were all much older, much more important in the public eye at least; one of them being the governor's wife and another the mayor's, and yet even they had to come for the monthly Callahan Foundation meeting.

"You look beautiful, as always." The governor's wife came up to me first, as usual. Her brown hair cropped short at her shoulders. She came up first as a way to define the order of importance to the other ladies and I didn't stop her.

"Thank you, Brigitte..." I reached out to take her hand when she offered it, but she paused... No, not just her, but all of them looked around me.

Turning around, I watched as Ivy came in, dressed in a tight pale pink dress and a white jacket that hung on her shoulders. Her golden blonde hair over one of her shoulders in soft waves, she tucked her beige clutch under her arm, taking off her sunglasses and smiling at the ladies assembled.

"Morning ladies," she said and even though no one replied, she confidently made her way towards me.

"Dona, you left without me! I know you hate being late but honestly… I'm hurt." She laughed, grabbing on to my arm. I stared at her, unsure of what to stay. No…that was a lie. I wanted to tell her to let fucking go of me before I kicked her to moon. "Can you do me a favor?" she had the nerve to ask.

"Can you tell them to step back?" She nodded at the guards behind her… One of them being Greyson himself. He nodded to me but then focused on Ivy. She whispered, "Ethan is strict about making sure I'm protected. However, you don't have guards so obviously I don't need one either."

No. She needed them.

She needed them to protect her from me.

"Ivy, welcome!" Nari came to her rescue, hugging gently and kissing her cheeks. "I'm so glad you could make it today. We thought you were still resting."

"Do I really need that much rest from my honeymoon?" Ivy laughed, letting me go and taking Nari's hand. "Actually, I take that back."

A few of the other women laughed, and as if she didn't see me, Brigitte stepped before me to Ivy offering her hand.

"Mrs. Callahan, I'm so happy we can finally meet."

"Brigitte Orton." Ivy took her hand and shook it. "I've heard so much about you from Dona. Thank you for your donation last month; who knew we'd end up needing it and so much more for the hospital? How's your husband? Ethan was saying we were all going to have dinner sometime soon."

"I will only agree if you and Ethan allow us to host you both at the governor's mansion." Brigitte smiled brushing her hair behind her ear.

"I'll see when Ethan has time."

"Well, I'm hurt." Fatimah Gupta, the mayor's wife,

came forward. "Where is my invitation?"

"Mrs. Gupta, how are you?" Ivy asked, offering her hand. One by one, it went on like this, the crowd around her growing and growing, and pushing me farther and farther out. I felt the lump in my throat growing.

"Ethan!" I was going to kill him. This place was mine. He knew that. Mother had left it to me, and grandmother had taken care of it until I took over four years ago. For four fucking years I had built this! Why the bloody fucking hell was I feeling excluded? Why the hell was she here?

"Breathe, Dona," Helen whispered, suddenly appearing beside me. "You can't leave but—"

"Why would I leave!" I hissed at her under my breath. "The foundation is mine."

She squeezed my arm, her brown eyes piercing into mine; "The Callahan Foundation belongs to the next Mrs. Callahan. That isn't you, Dona; it's Ivy. You know that. Everybody knows that. So, act like you know, and don't get angry."

I stared at her in disbelief and then a small, short laugh escaped from my lips. Reaching up to her arm, I pushed her hands off of me.

"I do not need you to tell me how to act or what to feel. I'll handle this the same way I've handled everything else…in my own way," I said to her, turning and walking towards the front of the hall to the first table which sat in front like a high table allowing us to see everyone. It was the table for the Callahan women, as well as the governor's and mayor's wife and any other government and business wives. A hierarchy of sorts. I picked up the microphone, swallowing my rage as I spoke to them gently.

"Ladies, ladies, I'm sure you'd all love to have lunch or dinner with Ivy and my brother, but please let us not forget why we are here. The Callahan Foundation is here to help this city and our great state; it is not simply our tea hour. Ivy," I called out to her and she turned slightly to me. I pulled out a chair for her, saying, "Please sit so we can get started."

"Of course, forgive me." She laughed, walking towards the table, however she didn't sit at the chair I pulled out for her. She instead sat in the polished brass and red velvet Chiavari chair…the chair that had once been my mother's. All chairs were red velvet for these meetings.

However, that chair, my mother's chair, was slightly bigger. It was placed at the head of the table and had her initials carved into the arm.

I wanted to slap the fuck out of her, but instead pretended I didn't notice where she sat. I looked over to Helen and Nari; "Please, come sit."

They both smiled and nodded moving to sit at the tables, followed by Brigitte and Fatimah. Only once they and everyone else was seated did I turned my attention to my dear, sweet sister-in-law.

"Ivy, everyone is so glad you are here. Me especially. For the last four years I've run The Callahan Foundation hoping and knowing one day I'd past to reins over. I'm grateful it's to someone like you who truly understand how it must be for the most unfortunate of us all. To suffer as you have suffered for seven long years in Ricker Hill. Losing your ability to even get an education, beaten almost daily, drugged far too often, and only God and you know what else must have happened to you. On top of that, to be born into such poverty, without a mother, and to rise so high is such an inspiration to me and all the women of this foundation. I'm confident that my mother would be proud knowing you're now in charge of one of her most beloved organizations." Turning from her to address the rest of the women, "Ladies, as Jane Austen once said, 'Marriage is indeed a maneuvering business.' To my sister-in-law, Ivy Callahan, our new master strategist. Listen well, I'm sure she has much to share."

I smiled, handing her the microphone. The look in her eyes one of anger. I knew her well enough by now to know she'd be able to handle this job, but also knew everyone else well enough to know that they'd make it as hard as possible. And what's more, every word I had just said would be used in the future as a weapon against her. Their words wouldn't hurt; what would hurt was trying to fill that chair and not make a fool out of herself, Ethan, and our entire family every time she sat there. The weight of that would hurt for a while and she'd get used to it, but for now... I just wanted her to squirm.

"Thank you, Dona," she said softly, her voice cracking slightly. "You always have such a way with words. I missed the last meeting sadly, but I did hear we were discussing budget increases—"

"Mrs. Callahan." Brigitte, who actually hated our

family, spoke up as she often did because she was an attention whore. "In the last email sent out we were discussing planning events to raise the city's spirits after that awful attack."

"Oh," Ivy replied, thinking for a moment. "Did anyone have any ideas?"

I snickered to myself because she'd just unleashed one hell of a can of worms.

"I was thinking a city fair in Donald Park." Fatimah sat up and quickly said, "It would be perfect with the weather we've been having—"

"We can't always have these events in Chicago. We should spend a little time outside the city—"

"But the bombing happened within the city," another woman spoke out. "Of course, we'll need to lift the city's spirits first."

"Yes, but other cities have had hard years, too—"

"There's a big difference between a hard year and a city bombing."

One by one, they all started to speak, all of them trying to get their voices heard, and their ideas made with Callahan backing to boost themselves. They were like hungry piranhas that would bite almost anything, even their own in order to get more. Each and every one of them were greedy, power-hungry bitches. They didn't give a flying fuck about helping anyone but themselves. I knew this because I was like them...only I knew how to rule over people like that and keep them and their greed in line. I'd honed that skill my entire life and Ivy thought she could waltz in here and just take over. She'd most likely learned how to fight dirty in prison, but anyone could fight dirty. A real queen knew how to fight clean, to hold order with grace. Ivy was beautiful, maybe smart, but she didn't have that grace.

Imagine their reactions when they realize she doesn't even know the difference between her forks. Snickering, I lifted my glass of water, bringing it to my lips and drinking as they all yelled over each other.

"She's family," Nari whispered to me, as if telling me to do something.

"She came because she wanted to take her place; let her take it and see how well she fits," I replied, looking to Ivy just as she glanced over at me.

"Donatella, what is your idea? I'm sure you had

something in mind what with how quickly you came here this morning?" Ivy asked me.

"Me?" I said in surprise and frowning as I shook my head, "I'm just here for the food. You should try the cheese rolls; they are to die for." I smiled, waving over the waiter and ordering without paying any of them any mind.

Squirm Ivy, squirm.

IVY

"Your sister is a bitch!" I yelled at him, taking off my heels and tossing them into the corner of my closet. "Actually, they're all bitches! You put me in charge of a foundation of bitches! Why?"

Ethan sighed, taking off his watch and placing it on the bedside table; "Because that's your role as my wife."

"Ethan, I'm not good at stuff like that! And Donatella knows it; that's why she dragged me front and center and left me to deal with those...harpies!" I was angry. I never thought I'd miss prison so damn much. At least in prison no one sugarcoated shit. If people hated you, they didn't hide their knives. They came for you. But in this organization, everyone was two-faced. I could see it so clearly, they were only speaking and smiling to me because I was *Mrs. Callahan*, but in reality, they just wanted something for themselves. I wanted to call them out for their fakeness, but that would only make me look weird.

"I don't want to do this," I told him. "I'm a science and math person, Ethan. If you want me to do something…then…then let me help with the drugs—"

"Stop!" he snapped, turning to glare into my eyes. "Ivy, we all have roles. You may not like it. You may not like those women. My mother hated those women, too. But she understood what you need to understand. Those women are married to important people. Those women hear important things, sometimes without even realizing it. So, when they go out to brag, and I assure you they will brag, they'll drop breadcrumbs about people and the power they have. You're there to see what drops. You are there to make sure they know that our eyes and our pockets are endless. You don't have to like them. But you must make sure they respect and fear you."

"How, Ethan?! How?"

"I don't know! It's your job to figure out!" He groaned rubbing the side of his head. "You've gotten your vengeance. You can't keep being Ivy O'Davoren. You must be Ivy Callahan. Who Ivy Callahan is up to you but know that it's also a reflection of me and our family."

"So now you're telling me I need to change?" I didn't want to change. And I wasn't going to.

"No," he said placing his hands on my face. "I don't want you to change. I'm not telling you to change. I'm telling you that you're going to have to do what we all do in this family, and that is to pick a mask to wear for the world and only take it off when you're with me."

It was only when he'd said it that I remembered how Dona sucked in her anger. I knew going there would piss her off, yet I didn't notice anything off about her... She even seemed happy. How long ago had she picked her mask?

"Okay." I nodded. "Don't get angry if I mess this up. I'm not as good at this as the rest of you yet."

"Don't worry, I'll always clean up your mess." He kissed my forehead.

I didn't like how he said it, but I understood and it

made me feel better. Frowning still, I muttered, “I still want to play whack-a-mole with those women’s heads though.”

“Maybe one day you will.”

“Just remember, all of those women, all their power… It can be replaced, and replaced by your word. Speak to them like that. You’re the one who holds their lives in your hand. You don’t have to kill them, but you can squeeze.”

Next time…at the next meeting I’d show them all.

DONATELLA

“O’Phelan, I want anything that will go with a glass of Rosé,” I said as I sat in the empty dining room. It was well past dinner and I’d come home this late for one reason…to be alone. I kicked off my heels, leaning back in my seat, and relaxing when all of sudden the door opened.

“Good evening, big brother. How was your day?” I smiled, crossing my legs in his chair at the head of the table.

“Quite interesting, thanks to the list of traitors you were able to get me,” he said walking up the opposite end of the table.

"You're welcome; what are sisters for?" I shrugged, resting my chin on my palm. "Did you come down just to tell me that?"

"No," He replied, picking up one of the knives from the table settings. "How was your day, little sister?"

"A few hiccups here and there but nothing I couldn't handle, of course."

He nodded, spinning the knife in his hands. "Was one of the hiccups my wife, and did it you handle it by dragging her past through the mud?"

"I didn't say anything you couldn't read on Wikipedia," I replied, sitting up straight as he moved closer to me. "Why, was she hurt?"

"Would you like her to be hurt?"

I snickered. "I'd be disappointed if she were hurt so easily. It would mean she was weak and you were stupid enough to marry weak, and arrogant enough to think she could so easily replace me."

"Dona," he said my name through clenched teeth, gripping the knife in his hands. "She is family; you do not embarrass—"

"YOU EMBARRASSED ME!" I hollered, slamming my fist on the table and rising to my feet. "Without warning, once again big brother you put your wife in my face! Four years I've run that foundation! Mom's foundation. Four fucking years of being judge, jury, and executioner; it has been ME who has told you when we needed a new governor, which judges might be in debt or having an affair. ME who sat and listened to those women bitch and moan just so you could hold an axe over them all. For years I did that for you, big brother. And you didn't have the decency to tell me you were sending her!"

"I did tell you! What do you think the fucking wedding meant?" he snapped back. "She is my wife!"

"Which is why she let her take over today," a new voice chimed in.

Looking over to the side door that led to the kitchen, I watched as Gabriel came forward; a plate in one hand and bottle of Rosé in the other with a towel over his shoulder. He placed the plate in front of me and then lifted the bottle to pour as he spoke. "Ivy is your wife; she has the right to be at the head of the foundation. Your sister respected that. She stepped back, allowed her to take over and your wife stumbled. That isn't Dona's fault. No matter what Donatella said, Ivy was going to stumble because she is a baby wolf left alone in the forest. If her teeth aren't sharp enough, that isn't Donatella's fault. If a child falls, don't blame the floor; blame the parent who put her there, wouldn't you say?"

I cracked my jaw to the side; "This isn't about you. I don't need you to back me up—"

"I wasn't backing you up," he said, handing me the wine glass. "I was simply telling the facts as they are, knowing your brother is a reasonable man and will see the truth himself."

Ethan stared at him bored, before asking, "How much of our time do you plan on wasting, Mr. Gabriel with no last name?"

"For as long as it takes for your sister to marry me." Gabriel smiled and for the first time she noticed he had a dimple in one of his cheeks. Taking the towel off his shoulder, he cleaned his hands.

"You might be here until kingdom come," I muttered.

"That's fine, I've only learned two of your favorite

dishes today, anyway. Chef Carluccio isn't the most patient teacher I've ever had," he replied, shifting his gaze to me.

I looked down at the food in front of me and sure enough it was one of my favorite dishes. Salmon with sunflower-dill pesto sauce and a small side of avocado and shrimp spicy Gazpacho. I felt my mouth water involuntarily.

"Do you mind?" Gabriel asked Ethan. "She hasn't had dinner yet."

Coldly, Ethan looked to me. "Ever since Ivy came, you've been acting erratically, I hope this soon-to-be-dead loon isn't going to add to that."

"So far it's just you who's been making me act erratically; making me wonder if you're actually my brother still? Making me wish I did pull that trigger. You just met her, and now it's my fault whenever I stand my ground in my own goddamn home. If you were going to treat me like this Ethan, you shouldn't have pretended to give a fuck about me at all. Pick your wife, I'll pick myself. You're as useless to me now as father was to all of us back then."

He stared me and I saw his eye widen just a little

bit. I hoped I hadn't imagine the hurt in his eyes, I hoped I had stabbed something of merit under that suit of armor but I wasn't sure. He simply tossed the knife back on the table, allowing it to hit the glass before stabbing me with his words. "And you, Donatella, are still that selfish little girl who can't recognize the reality of the world around her."

"Goodnight Ethan," I replied, picking up the Gazpacho, taking a spoonful into my mouth.

Ethan didn't say anything else before turning around and walking out the doors from which he had come. And I wanted to relax but I looked over to see Gabriel staring at me while drinking a glass of the wine he had brought.

"Can I help you?"

"Is it good?" he asked and nodded to the bowl in my hand, waiting eagerly for my reply. It was then I remembered he was the one who had made it.

"What is this?" I asked.

He frowned. "Avocado and shrimp—"

"No." I chuckled, not meaning to. "Why are you making me food? Is this a ploy to get me to like you?"

"Kind of," he admitted but didn't seem sure himself. "You don't seem like the kind of woman who'd go to anyone's arms to cry or complain about your problems. You just want to force them down and bottle it up. Food helps the pain go down."

I paused, swallowing the food in my mouth. Going over his words in my mind, I said, "This is your way of comforting me?"

He nodded. "You don't have to talk about it—"

"I have nothing to talk about," I replied, taking another bite.

"Okay," he replied, reaching behind him and I tensed. He raised his eyebrow then lifted the book for me for to see. "It's just a book."

"Why my parents would have engaged me to a book nerd like you is still beyond me." I shook my head.

"Says the novelist," he muttered flipping to a page of his book. I tilted my head to the side to see what he was reading, praying it wasn't my book. And thankfully it wasn't. It was Leo Tolstoy's *War and Peace.*

He didn't say anything more and neither did I.

I simply ate.

And he simply read beside me.

I hated to admit it, but I enjoyed it. It was like being alone and not being alone at the same time...which meant... *I needed to get rid of him.*

He was getting too close and too comfortable with me.

I glanced at him from the corner of my eye and wondered *how?*

TWELVE

"I'm a kind person, I'm kind to everyone,

but if you are unkind to me,

then kindness is not what you'll remember me for."

~Al Capone

GABRIEL

Death had a smell.

It wasn't the type of smell that brought vultures.

It was the type only certain living people could smell. People who'd come close to losing their lives one too many times, who'd been living on the edge of death's door. I was one of those people. When death tried to come for me, the air around me would become still, the hair on my arms would rise, and I could smell the scent of peach and vinegar, just like I had last night. At first everything had seemed fine. But then she looked at me from the corner of her eye and I knew... Death was going to try to take me again.

I had to applaud her.

The ability to call forth death was something all men secretly wanted. That's why Americans were so damned attached to their second amendment. *The right of the people to keep and bear arms, shall not be infringed.* It was merely eloquent words for pure savagery. It shouldn't have been called the right to bear arms; it should have been called the right to call death upon thy enemies. No matter how innocent a person was, no matter much good they did, there was still a black blemish in their hearts; the place where they caged their savagery, unleashing it on those who could hurt them. Guns made it easy. Easy to give the gift of death to those one came up against...so easy that they could detach themselves from how vicious they were being. The simple pull of a trigger and death came and went.

No. I didn't want to be detached.

I didn't want death to come and go with a single finger.

My whole body needed to be steeped in it because when my enemies...or in this case my fiancée, sent death after me... Death would join my side.

I made space for it.

I decisively walked into backyard, and kept walking into the woods, pretending to read the book in my hand. Over the last four days, I had known they had men watching me, tailing after me. So, if she'd sent them to kill me, they'd do it now.

Why?

Why was she doing it?

In a way, it actually made sense; she was scared. No one was on her side. Not the way she wanted it. They were all pushing her into a corner, starving her of respect and consideration. They didn't mean to. They didn't understand, when you are born with fire in you, when you wanted to rise but reality kept weighing you down. Like being a bird with broken wings staring up at the sky through which you were meant to soar. The sight was maddening. I understood her madness. Because I had the same madness in me as me as well. It was why I was here.

I was running out of time.

But I still knew to be patient.

What was worth having was worth waiting for. Worth fighting and killing for.

Snap. I paused in the middle of the trail, which was covered in leaves still green and blades of grass.

Closing the book, I looked up to see six of the men surrounding me on all sides with guns in their hands.

Looking over them all, I asked one question, "Are we doing this like men or like bitches?"

They glanced over at each other before snickering; one of them stood up straighter and dropped his gun to the side.

Hubris was a sin for a reason…and they were going to learn that today.

DONATELLA

I was just about to take a bite of my French toast when all of sudden the doors burst open, and Helen gasped.

"Oh my God!"

Gazing through the door, I flinched at the sight of him. His light grey shirt was covered in blood and some even sprayed across his white face. In his right hand was a pair of dismembered hands, hog-tied together with shoelaces and dripping blood. Gabriel breathed in deeply as he walked around the table towards me. Wyatt got up but Ethan held out a hand for him to stop, his green eyes glancing at me. His eyes asked a clear question: what did I do?

Ignoring them all, I took a bite of my food. The only bite I'd get seeing as how Gabriel decided to drop a pair of hands on top of my plate as if they were toppings. He pushed his face directly next to mine.

"I got your gifts," he said, brushing the side of my face, but I pulled my head away.

"I have no idea what you're talking about. Did something happen?" I asked, turning to look him in the eye.

His gray eyes shifted back and forth, making it seem like he was reading my eyes; "If it wasn't you, I can't forgive this. I'll think it only could have been your elder brother. How else could six men jump me on his property? I don't want to think it's your elder brother because that means he just declared war against me at the same time he's trying to prevent a war in the south, keep you from killing his wife, as well keeping the Irish and Italians from feuding once again."

He stood up straighter. "You must really enjoy juggling, Ethan."

Ethan's eyebrow twitched slightly and he glared at me before looking back up at Gabriel. "I'm not sure what happened to you Gabriel, however once I find out, they will suffer the consequences. You are a guest here, under our family's *word* of protection. Anyone who respects me would never do such a stupid thing."

The second part of his words were obviously directed at me. Reaching for my water, I drank, looking at none of them.

"No need, they aren't capable of suffering now anyway," Gabriel replied, picking the hands off my plate and tossing them to one of the guards standing off to the side. "My apologies, Donatella. It seems I falsely accused you."

"Apology accepted." I smiled, rising to my feet. "I've lost my appetite though; please excuse me."

Stepping around him, I walked out the door quickly. My jaw set angrily, I marched up the stairs and into the elevator. But instead of going up to my room I went down, needing to scan my palm and my eye before the doors opened. When they did, I saw the dozen men who were meant to be watching the damned security cameras.

"WHAT THE FUCK HAPPENED?" I hollered at them.

"Ma'am—"

"Don't talk! Show me the motherfucking feed," I said to them, marching up to the screen. I could hear fingers typing away on the keyboards before finally seeing Gabriel on the screen in a stainless V-neck shirt and jeans.

I watched as he walked down the path before suddenly stopping to close his book and look up. The men were then around him. However, he said something and instead of shooting, one of them dropped his gun to charge him... The idiot only ended up being tossed and flipped over on his back; Gabriel twisted both of his assailant's arms behind his back until they broke and fell lifelessly on the dirt.

After the second assailant squared off with him they all charged, and I watched as Gabriel used one man as a shield to take bullets before using another man as a weapon to kill both. He broke the necks of the rest. When he was done and his attackers lay broken like discarded toys, Gabriel looked directly at the camera, reached into his boot, and retrieved a knife. He then bent down on one knee like hunter with his prize, and began to cut.

"Is this how you were all trained?" I asked softly, standing up straighter. "You were given an order and instead of doing what was asked, you allowed yourselves to be provoked into a fight and lost?"

"Ma'am—"

"DO I HAVE TO DO EVERYTHING MY GODDAMN

SELF!" I screamed, turning around on them. Inhaling slowly, I nodded. "Forgive me. I was mistaken to think I could count on you all."

I laughed bitterly and they had the nerve to hang their heads. The elevator doors opened for Ethan, in all his mighty glory, to come forth. But I didn't stop speaking. "I forgot you aren't my men but my brother's. So, my orders can be handled carelessly like this. My future can be dropped and kicked to the side so you can all compare dick sizes and protect your useless pride. A man can walk in here and demand I marry him and you..." I laughed. Shook my head. "And you all can just look away. Fine. Keep looking down..." I said looking directly at my brother as he stared back. "When you look up at me again I might be burning this place to the ground and dragging you sorry bastards straight to hell with me."

Ethan didn't stop me as I walked towards the door, proving he was just as smart as everyone thought. In this state, I would've tried to kill him this time for sure.

ETHAN

I watched the feed, asking, "What were her orders?"

"To kill him and make it look like suicide," one of them answered.

"Who picked these men?" I asked, still watching.

"I did, Sir." Boyle, who had been working as a house guard for almost six years, stepped forward. Short hair cut in a standard ex-military buzz cut.

"Follow my sister's orders."

"Kill him tonight, Sir?"

I looked away from the screen and looked to him. "Not him. You."

"Sir—"

"A mistake of this magnitude needs to be made up for somehow," I replied, fully turning to him and pointing to the screen. "They are all dead so they can't pay for it. You picked them so you will pay. My sister wanted death by suicide... You will give her what she wants. In doing so, you will remind the rest of these men that the next time they are given an order and fail to complete it because they've decided to take it upon themselves, as my sister said, to *compare dick sizes and protect your unless pride*, you'll all remember you are gambling with your own lives as well."

"Sir—"

"Boyle, you can die her way or mine. Believe me, her way is kinder," I said, turning from him and moving to the elevator. "Drink bleach if you must, I don't care, but you better be dead when I check in again."

Stepping inside, the silence was heavy. I'm sure all the men liked Boyle but they weren't here to make friends or take it upon themselves to deal with situations as they pleased. They were meant to be robots; when they were given orders, those orders needed to be completed as instructed. If not... They were broken and I needed to get new ones.

"Oh, Dona." I exhaled when the doors closed.

I thought the ticking would stop, that the bomb in her had at least been partially defused...but apparently it had only quickened.

She really did have the power to bring this all crashing down and she couldn't be fucking rational anymore because of Gabriel. He'd either drive her to destroy us all or maybe...hopefully...redirect the blast somewhere else.

I didn't like either option.

It left my choices up to a man I knew nothing about.

If she had killed him...it might have been better.

At least my hands would be cleansed of it.

GABRIEL

I could have taken a longer shower, I thought as I sat on the edge sofa waiting, twisting the knife in my hands around slowly as I stared at the ceiling...finding it kind of odd that there was a ceiling fan in any room in a mansion so modern as this. Everything else was automatic; even the curtains closed themselves in the evening if you left them.

"I never thought I'd need a lock for my room." I heard her voice as she came inside.

Glancing over to her, I smiled. She was beautiful in dangerous sort of way, glaring at me with those fearsome green eyes. "You shouldn't have been so upset. You aren't the first woman to fail to kill me."

"So, this happens often to you."

"It's a tragedy really. Being as handsome as I am yet surrounded by women who prefer power instead."

"Power instead?" she replied. "You speak as if you

are better than having power. What can you do that my gaining power can't?"

"I can keep you warm at night?"

"I'm rich. I can afford a blanket made with the fur of polar bears to keep me warm."

"Witty conversation?"

"The voices in my head provide me with more than enough of that," she replied and I laughed at that. She was funny…good. I might count on that humor in the future.

The way she stared at me sent shivers down my spine. How could any man not want to tame such a fearsome beauty? To have this…her, that fire on their side?

"Stop fighting me Donatella and you'll—"

"Can't you see?" She smiled up at me as she spoke. "All I know is fighting, Gabriel. And it's a shame, because if you weren't here trying to force my hand, I'd actually find you attractive. I'd be turned on by how well you fight. And how fearless you are. But you are here trying to force my hand, so I will fight you until you give me a reason not to. I'll fight you in every way I know how and with everything I have. Because you aren't being honest with me. You're hiding something very big…no, not hiding—you're waiting. Like a wolf under the cover of darkness, I feel you watching and waiting to strike at me."

I wanted to touch her. It was as if she were fire drawing me closer to her brightness, but I could only get so far before she burned me.

"You're right," I whispered in the space between us. "But I'm not waiting to strike just you; I'm coming for everyone," I replied, lifting her chin and kissing her lips hard, only to be slapped across the face with such force that my lip cut on my tooth. Licking the corner my mouth, I told the truth, "The kiss was worth it."

"Fuck you."

"I want you to give me a time and a date," I replied.

She was breathing hard and for a quick second, there was lust in her at last, but she'd pushed it down and grabbed the handle of her door to open it. "Don't push your luck anymore tonight."

"It wasn't luck that I had tonight, but skill," I said, walking to edge of her door. "Have you ever seen a wolf-dog as they die?"

She flinched, her whole body freezing, her eyes going wide as she stared at me. I went on as if I didn't notice.

"In those final moments, the pain becomes so bad, the dog part of them dies, and all that's left is the wounded wolf. The wolf knows to fight to their final breath. It doesn't care who or what, it could even be another wolf-dog, their own pup, and it will still claw and bite and rip them apart. No more friends or foes... It's blind to everything else but its own survival... You remind me of a dying wolf-dog, Donatella. And its shame because you don't have to die."

I stepped out of the room, but she continued stand in the doorway; unblinking and staring at the space in which I had once stood. Frozen.

"I look forward to tomorrow's battle. If everything goes as planned, I'll be able to explain what it is I'm waiting for."

She slammed the door closed.

Till tomorrow then.

DONATELLA

Sitting in front of the mirror, I couldn't get Gabriel's words out of my ears. They just kept replaying on a loop in my mind.

You remind me of dying wolf-dog, Donatella.

You remind me of dying wolf-dog, Donatella.

A...dying wolf-dog, Donatella—

"I'm not dying," I said to my reflection. Reaching up I felt the burning in my throat...unsure of where the pain was coming from.

"I'm not dying."

THIRTEEN

"The Devil is real and he's not some little red man with horns and a tail. He can be beautiful because he's a fallen angel and he used to be God's favorite."

~ Leah (American Horror Story)

DONATELLA

He was the Devil.

And this was Karma.

I had killed Tobias and so now I had…Satan. I was sure of his identity now. How else could one man walk into this family and make a mess of things so quickly? He caused chaos and destruction whenever he opened his mouth. What was worse, I wasn't sure how to escape this yet… And just like always, it seemed I'd been left on my own to deal with the aftermath of someone else's shit.

Satan had decided to marry me.

Of course, this was the type of life I had.

I really am a Greek tragedy in the making.

"Should I gouge out my eyes?" I whispered softly to myself as I floated in the water of the pool.

And Satan replied, "Seeing as you are already in water, why don't you stick with Shakespeare and drown yourself?"

Opening my eyes and allowing my legs to drop down as I stood, I looked to where he was now sitting; in my white pool chair, drinking my smoothie, while once again reading the same book from lunch.

"And you're here, why?"

"Here in this house? Or here at the pool?" he questioned, not bothering to look at me…even though I was half naked in the water…that was new.

"The pool," I said swimming to the edge and rising from the water.

"Can't a man visit his fiancée as she swims?" he questioned.

The word fiancée from his lips was worse than a thousand nails on a thousand chalkboards. *He wants to fight, Dona!* I reminded myself and I wondered if salt wouldn't keep him away, then maybe sugar would.

"You're absolutely right," I said sweetly, walking up to him and at the tone in my voice he made a face before glancing up. The moment he did, he couldn't look away; his eyes following the beads of water as they slid down the space between my breasts and past my stomach, not stopping until they disappeared into the waistband of my black bikini bottoms. I walked over, sat beside him on my chair, and leaned forward while brushing my hair to the side, "Forgive me *sweetheart* for being so harsh. Can you hand me a towel?"

"You're free to get it yourself, *my love*," he replied just as kindly, shifting to the side for me to take the towel that was right beside his waist. "Your poor nipples look like bullets."

Gritting my teeth, I reached over carefully to take the towel, my eyes never leaving his and his gray eyes never leaving mine. He seemed completely amused. The longer he stared, the more annoyed I became. I even thought about strangling him with the damn towel, but resisted and wrapped it around myself instead.

"Gabriel?"

"Yes, Donatella?" He nodded, closing his book.

"I'm a very reasonable person, you seem like you are capable of being reasonable too—"

"I'm not though," he said, sitting up. "I'm wrathful, demanding, and vindictive. I'm only reasonable when it comes to things which benefit me. So, *Donatella*, what is it you need my reason for?"

Punch him! Beat his insolent ass into the next century! Not only did this cunt interrupt me, he had the nerve to challenge me even when I was trying to be nice.

Inhaling, I went on as if he hadn't said anything, "My brothers will never let you take Italy."

"I guess we're getting married then."

My fist clenched so tightly I could feel my nails digging into my palm but I smiled. "Perhaps you have not noticed but I'm temperamental, prone to violence, and hostile to authority... I doubt you want a wife like that."

He snickered, nodding in agreement before saying; "I'm sure you'll change; after all, look how sweet you are right now, dear."

"Or you could find another wife."

He sat up and grabbed my chin. "I could but I doubt she'd come with the same fearsome attitude, and round, slap-able ass, so pick a date and a nice dress."

He brushed me off and got up.

At that point, I'd lost all my patience. I took off my towel to swing it at his head, but he dodged and grabbed on to it, pulling me close. In retaliation, I kicked right into his chest and he stumbled back, only slipping slightly before regaining his footing.

"I tried being nice—"

"Was that you being nice?" he laughed, tossing his

book onto the pool chair. "I thought you were constipated—"

My fist hit his jaw and caused his head to twist to the side for a second.

"I'm sorry, you were saying?" I told him while lifting my fist up.

He licked his lip, just like last night, and glared at me, not saying a word. Before I knew what he was planning, he bent down and pulled on the towel I didn't realize I was standing on, sending me on the ground…hard.

"Fuck—uh!" I screamed out as he grabbed on to my ankle and dragged me until I felt my body hit the water. Bubbles and water rising around me, I opened my eyes, and tried to swim up but before I could, my back was slammed against the wall of the pool, and his hand was wrapped around my neck. My eyes went wide as I stared at him calmly pinning me underwater against the wall.

Let GO! I mentally screamed at him, trying to push his arms away. But he didn't budge and the more I struggled, the more my vision began to tunnel…stupidly forgetting that the more energy I used, the harder it was for me to hold my breath. So, I tried to calm down, but it was too late, my lungs were already burning as I hadn't breathed when he threw me in. Reaching up, I grabbed his wrist and dug my nails in as hard as I could, but he stared at me emotionlessly...coldly, not even caring as I drew blood.

There was a sensation I hadn't felt in a long time...fear. It creeped on me as the pain in my lungs got even worse.

Dona, I made you, and I made you strong, beautiful, and fearless. My mother's voice came into the back of my mind.

And then my father's voice, *I could give away everything I owned, Dona, and even then, it wouldn't come close to equaling you. You are worth the world, princess.*

In that moment, I could focus on him, the man in front of me, and I let go of his wrist, smiling at him sincerely before opening my mouth and inhaling... And a split second before everything went dark, I saw the shock and panic that came over his eyes, forcing him to let me go.

I win. I thought happily.

GABRIEL

She was bloody insane!

Completely mental!

"Come on." I pinched her nose before breathing into her mouth and placing my hands over her chest. "You'd really rather die? Is that what you're saying? COME ON!"

"WHAT THE FUCK ARE YOU DOING!"

BANG.

That was all I heard. It felt like my arm was on fire, and I was on my back beside the pool, the back of my head hitting the ground so hard my ears started to ring. When I opened them again, it was none other than the elder standing over me, rage in his eyes, a gun smoking in his hand.

Did he fucking shoot me? I thought, and got my answer when I tried to sit up and he stepped on my shoulder. No, the bullet had only grazed my arm but it still hurt like a fucking bitch.

"Ugh!" I bit my teeth when together he stepped harder.

"I gave you the benefit of the doubt for my grandmother's sake," he spoke above me. "But it seems that was mistake on my part."

There was no saving myself from this apparently, so I tried to ignore the pain and looked up at him calmly.

"Is she alright?" I asked.

He pulled back the hammer of the gun; "What right do you have to ask?"

"She's my fiancée."

"And when did it become acceptable to try and kill the person you are engaged to?"

"Didn't your mother shoot your father when they were engaged?" I asked, more than ready for him to get off my shoulder.

"Ethan." I heard her voice call out to him and only then did I take a breath of relief. The voice was faint, but it was her.

He moved off me and grabbed on to my shoulder. Blood now covered the whole left side of me when I sat up. It wasn't just Ethan; Wyatt was bent in front Dona and checking her pulse. Helen, her cousin, wrapping a towel around her, and Ivy, standing by the door. And most notably, at least twelve guards now in the pool.

"I wouldn't move if I was you." *Make that thirteen guards,* I thought, feeling the gun at the back of my head.

Well, this is a bloody mess, isn't it?

Ethan reached out to help her up, but her legs wobbled and she tried to push him off. There was something odd about it...however Ethan just grabbed on to her, lifting her up. Wyatt stood up in place for a moment before looking to me, and I was sure as anything else in this world, he was thinking of a way to get rid of me.

"Lock him in his room," Ethan said as they all moved to leave.

All of them were looking forward but her. Donatella, looking over Ethan's shoulder, grinned brightly at me and winked... And the moment Ivy looked to her, Dona's expression changed to pain...the witch.

She wasn't trying to die. She was trying make sure I did! In the back of my mind I could see her laughing like the little madwoman she was...

This isn't over, sweetheart.

"Get up!" they yelled, pulling me to my feet.

"Gentle, I bruise easily," I joked. Apparently, they didn't find it funny...and whatever they then hit me with made everything dark.

***

"Fuckin' shit," I hissed when I woke up. I wasn't sure what hurt more, my head or my arm. When I reached up to touch my arm, I felt the bandages wrapped around it and was thankful they at least had the common sense not to let me bleed on the floor.

"You awake, sweetheart?" The madwoman asked softly, and when I opened my eyes, I realized I was not on my bed, but on the floor. I rolled over and saw her sitting on the vintage chaise by the window. She was dressed in a short navy dress, her smooth thighs tucked underneath her as she happily ate her vanilla ice-cream from a crystal bowl. She grinned, the small spoon on her lips. "You should go back to sleep, you're much safer there."

"You knew your brothers would save you, which is why you inhaled the water," I groaned, sitting up, "But for a brief moment you were scared, weren't you?"

"I'm a Callahan, I don't—"

"Bullshit," I cut her off. "For a brief moment, you thought I was going to kill you, and you got scared."

Her green eyes narrowed on me as she sucked on

her spoon, which left me both turned on and annoyed. "Was that brief moment worth you now being chained to a bed post?"

"Chained?" I questioned, glancing around. Sure enough, like a bloody prisoner, these people had me chained to the bed. I reached for it and then looked back at her. "What 90's prison did you all steal this from?"

"That's your reply? You think you're in a position to be witty?"

I nodded, leaning back on the bed. "If you all were going to kill me; I'd be dead already. But seeing as you have treated my wounds and given me at least some type of drug, I'm not going to die."

"Don't rush to assume...both of my brothers are fond of torture," she reminded me.

"So am I, and even if you want to keep your prisoner alive, you don't take care of him this well. So, my love, try again." I winked at her. Her jaw cracked the side, and she put her ice-cream to the side. Rising from the chaise, her bare feet on the wooden floor, she walked over to me and knelt right in front me. "Careful... I could try to kill you again. You've been here for a less than a week and in that time, you've been shot, punched, mobbed, and threatened…and still you don't seem in the least bit worried about your life. Either you're insane or whatever your family used to get my parents to agree to our marriage is much more important than I thought."

I leaned forward and whispered, "Both."

She was calm now, calmer than I'd ever seen her, and I wasn't sure if it was because she planned on stabbing me to death with a spoon or she was really trying to think.

"Who are you?" she pressed. "More importantly, what mafia family are you linked too?"

"Are you asking or your brother?"

She leaned in closed to my face and said, "Both."

"And here I thought you were trying to oust your brothers. First you use them to get to me, and now you are in here trying to get information for them."

She didn't flinch, just stared me down like a wolf. Her eyes were mesmerizing, I didn't want to look away.

It's the drugs, I tried to lie to myself.

"I use a lot of people," she finally spoke again. "Using people doesn't make you weak, it doesn't mean I can't fight on my own; it means I'm so strong I don't need to. The reason I want to take power from my brothers is because I already have the power. Ethan and Wyatt, no matter what they may say or do, will have my back. I know it."

"Sounds like you're trying to convince yourself, which is why you keep fighting with your brothers so openly," I pushed back.

"I want everyone to know. I want to publicly wear that crown. I want to see people have no choice but to bow down to me nowhere I go," she admitted, rising and taking her ice-cream before heading back out the door. "Which is why I can't marry someone I don't know, someone who is weak and can't protect themselves from my own brothers."

"Then who will you marry?" I asked her.

"None of your—"

"You are temperamental, prone to violence, and hostile to authority," I repeated her words to her, "on top of that, your family is feared, and you killed your last lover. Who would be insane enough to marry you? Who can even make it on to your list to be considered? What you want most is strength and power."

"If no one comes, I'll stay single—"

"And wither from the vixen every man wants to the old maid no one wanted. When you walk by they won't speak in fear but laugh in judgement. It's not fair really; a man can stay single all his life and no one would question him. But a single woman, no matter who you are, no matter what you are worth, or how much you accomplish, people will still consider you a failure."

"You really think I care—"

"Not just them," I cut her off. "I'm sure your brothers will have kids, and you'll drop in importance even more, their kids will think something is wrong with you. Hell, with that temper of yours they may even fear you, crazy Aunt Dona. Ethan and Wyatt, to save their own, will start keeping you away. They'll lock you up somewhere where the only power you will have is over peas and mashed potatoes—"

She threw crystal bowl right beside my head and it shattered, cold chunks of ice-cream splattering on my face. Reaching up, I wiped some off my cheek with my thumb and tasted it. "There you are, love. I was beginning to worry the water had short-circuited your rage," I said, my grin wide as I looked into the fire within her eyes.

"You are dead-set on pissing me off!"

"Only because I prefer that to your fake Stepford-wife smile," I snapped back. She froze, as if that wasn't what she expected to hear. "You have a temper, a tendency to break things due to that temper, and you are not above physical violence. I'm well aware, Donatella. I've seen it up close and personal for days now. But guess what? I'm neither shocked by it nor am I afraid of it. I. Am. Not. Afraid. Of. You. Or. Your. Bloody. Brothers! If I need to throw you back into the pool and hold you down until you calm down, I will. Though I might have to find a method which you won't use to your advantage to harm yourself first."

"Why in the fuck would you—"

"Because I want you," I told her truthfully. She looked a mixture of confused and scared. Why, I didn't know. "I want to marry you. I have my reasons. I'll use you at times. But I'll be honest about it. Just like you can use me to avoid becoming a prisoner in this mansion, to escape your fate if you remain here forever, single and with only a fraction of the power you crave."

"You really are insane—"

"Marry me, and you'll have everything you want. Power, respect, public acknowledgement...and affection. You'll be the most important person to me, my family, and millions of people."

She paused. "And how is that?"

"You'd like me to explain how affection works?" I teased, knowing full well she didn't care about that.

She crossed her arms, waiting.

"Do you really think your parents would marry you off to someone who they didn't think was worthy—"

"My father would never have thought you were worthy."

"Like most fathers. However, even he must have known you'd be safer with me."

She chuckled at that. "Safe with you? You're chained to a bed at the mercy of my family."

"Wrong." I shook my head, taking the chain off my ankle. Her eyebrow rose as I stood on my feet. "The Callahan family is at the mercy of me. Ethan wants to know who I am and he wants me out of his house, yet here I am. Wyatt wishes to kill me, but he can't. You want me to break the agreement, but I won't. You all are waiting for me to give you information...waiting to see if killing me will cause unforeseen damage to you all. The same question is going through all of your minds... Why me?"

"We'll find out who you are—"

"Or you could agree and I could just tell you," I said, stepping up to her. "I could tell you, and once you know, you'll regret fighting so hard."

"Take another step, and you'll regret not dying."

I paused and then took another step, and her nose flared. Smiling, I stopped, not pushing my luck any further. "If you won't agree yet, at least stop fighting long enough for me to show you..."

"You started the fight."

"All I did was tell you the truth." Boldly, I stepped forward, and she pulled a gun from some hiding spot, I didn't know where, and held it in front of me.

This damn family and bullets.

I didn't say anything; I just stared her down.

"Winning me over will be harder than trying to stop my brothers from killing you."

She put the gun down and left, slamming the door behind her.

“The sweetest honey is always at the top of the tallest tree,” I whispered to myself before gripping on to my shoulder. “Bloody fucking Jesus…” It burned like fire.

Grumpily, I moved over to the side of my bed, taking out my cell from the drawer and dialing. She answered on the first ring…

“Have you lost your damn mind?”

“I’m the victim here, Evelyn. I was shot.” I pouted.

“I couldn’t care less! And good for them for shooting you! Going around talking about Liam getting shot, you earned yourself a damn bullet,” she snapped and I rolled my eyes, laying on the bed.

“Other than that small hiccup, I’ve finally gotten her to warm up to me.”

“What?” She paused her anger. “How?

“A few truths….and couple lies.”

DONATELLA

“Well?” Ethan asked me as I came into to the study where he and Wyatt were both waiting for me.

I said nothing as I took Wyatt's glass of whiskey and sat down.

Wyatt sighed and turned to Ethan. "Let's get rid of him and whatever happens—"

"He's the devil," I said, mostly to myself but loud enough for them to hear.

"What?" Ethan asked me.

I snickered and drank, not breathing until I finished. The whiskey burned my throat as it went down. "He's convinced me to do something crazy...something I might regret."

"What?"

"Give him chance." How the hell did that happen?

"How the hell did that happen?" Wyatt questioned, reading my mind.

Handing over the empty glass, I stood up, facing Ethan; "Leave him alone. I'll handle it from now."

"That's what you've been doing! Dona, he tried to kill you—"

"No, he didn't." He was afraid when I almost died. Looking to Wyatt, I hugged him. I didn't have a reason; I just did it and let him go. Looking to Ethan, I said, "Let him do what he came here to do and we will see what happens."

"*We* will see?" he questioned. "So, you'll marry him?"

"Worst comes to worse, I'll marry him, fulfill the contract, and then kill him. At least then I'm a widow and not a spinster," I joked but neither of them laughed.

"Since when do you care about being a spinster?" Wyatt asked, brows bunched together, completely lost.

I understood why. I'd never thought about it. It had never crossed my mind. Until the Devil whispered into my ear. Now, the more I looked at them, the less I saw my brothers as my brothers and the more I saw them as men. Men who would have their own families. In the back of my mind, I'd known that would come but right now it was all I could see... It was all that was going through my mind.

What happened when they both had their own families?

What would people say of me?

At my age, my mother had already married and had Ethan. I told myself that I shouldn't care. Screw what other people thought. A much bigger part of me remembered the fact that this whole family was built on what people thought of us. We were perfect on the outside, so why wouldn't I get married? I tried picturing myself single for the rest of my life, and I remembered my parents together. I tried thinking of a man to stand beside me, and I didn't have one...with the exception of this stranger. And all I knew about him was that he had balls to not only speak back to me but fight back.

My mind was a mess. I felt myself being pulled in ten different directions and the more I thought, the less I wanted to.

"Dona?"

"Huh?"

"Are you sure you're alright?" Ethan asked me seriously.

I laughed. "Why? Because I said I'd give him a chance?"

"Yes," Wyatt said, as if it were the obvious answer.

"You're free to give him a hard time; I'm not going to go crawl into his arms. I'm going to find out why out of all the men in the world they picked him..."

At least he's sexy... Whoa, where did that come from?

"Okay." Ethan nodded at me but I couldn't read the expression on his face.

"Okay, then." I nodded back... I was going to date the devil.

Date?

Urgh, oh Lord help me, I thought as I left the room for the second time today. This time I went straight to my room, wishing I hadn't when I saw Helen on my bed.

"Please go; my head is mess and I have no idea what is going on," I whined, walking over to my bed and falling on top of it. I grabbed my pillow and put it over my head.

"Gabriel?"

"Don't say his name!" I held up my hand to stop her. "Just hearing about him right now gives me a migraine. He's just...ugh! What is his problem? A rational person would be running yet there he is, saying he could give me everything! How? Where? When? He pops out of nowhere and says he wants to marry me? Me! Does he not know I'm not the marrying type? I'll fight him every day of his life and he'll go bald from pulling out his hair. We might go bald from pulling out each other's hair. On top of that, he has no boundaries. He's just in my face pretending to be

Casanova... What if he tries to be romantic now? I don't do well with romantic. I'd tell him to ask Toby but... You know he's dead. Which should be his clue to run away! Why is he not running away!"

"Donatella, look at me."

"Why?" I lifted the pillow off my face to look at her. She grinned so wide I thought her face would crack. "What?"

"You were rambling."

"What?"

"You were rambling!"

"I don't ramble!"

"You just did. Since we were little, this is the most normal you've been...ever. You're like a regular girl."

"Fuckin' shite." I stared at her in horror and not even jokingly, I blessed myself with the sign of the cross. Because of him, *Gabriel*, the book nerd devil... I had Shakespeare on my mind. Specifically, The Tempest: Act 1, Scene 2, Line 215: *Hell is empty, and all the devils are here.*

FOURTEEN

"Here's all you have to know about men and women:

Women are crazy,

men are stupid.

And the main reason women are crazy

is that men are stupid."

~ George Carlin

HELEN

Was I supposed to be annoyed or happy that he never changed? I wasn't sure, and the more I stared at the text message on my phone, the more confused I became.

Dona was usually a light sleeper; however, her mind must have overworked itself, explaining the almost comatose state she was in. Rising from the bed, I changed into jeans and one of her shirts, before leaving her room. Part of me felt like I was sneaking around, afraid my father would catch me and wonder what the heck I was doing out bed so early in the morning... But the much more rational part of me knew I was old enough, and free enough, to move about the house however I chose. It still felt weird though. It must have been the goody-two-shoes in me.

Stepping into the elevator, I leaned back against the wall and closed my eyes, nearly drifting back to sleep. Had it not been for the chime as the elevator doors opened, I would have crashed. Walking forward into the kitchen, there he was, making damn waffles.

"How many do you want?" he asked as he carefully took his seventh waffle out of the iron and reached for more batter.

"Wyatt, can't you think of healthier foods to make when you're annoyed?" I asked, moving to sit at the kitchen island in front of him.

"*Nope*," he answered, setting a plate of three waffles topped with bananas and chocolate chips in front me.

"Where's the chocolate syrup?"

"I was making it healthier," he mocked me as he poured syrup over his own stack of waffles.

"If you're determined to make me fat, you should commit to it."

"No one's forcing you to eat."

"Fine, I'll go—"

"Here," he snapped, drowning my waffles in brown, sugary, artery-clogging syrup. "Happy?"

"Over the moon!" I grinned, cutting into the waffles and stuffing my face. "So, what are you upset about?"

"I'm not upset," he said as he rammed a forkful of waffles into his mouth.

"Okay," I nodded, knowing he'd spill soon enough. Since we were young, whenever he'd felt bad or annoyed, he'd come to the kitchen for chocolate and banana waffles.

"Who do you think this Gabriel guy is?"

"An arranged fiancé for Dona," I answered. He exhaled through his nose, chewing angrily. "Not the guy you wanted?"

"I don't like him. I don't trust him. He's a stranger who knows too much about us—"

"Us or Dona."

"Dona is us and he knows too much. He acts as if he's already family!"

"I mean, seeing as how your parents gave him their word, it looks like—" "Why are you being difficult?"

I coughed, almost choking on a piece of banana. "I'm being difficult? Me?!"

"Yes, you!" He pointed his fork at me. "You should be saying let's hack into whatever mumbo-jumbo zeros and ones computer system to find out the truth!"

"First, mumbo-jumbo is a phrase used to describe a meaningless language; hacking into multiple agencies, departments, and/or personal databases is simply called a background search."

"There you are, being difficult!" He groaned, waving

his fork at me.

Smacking his hand away, I held my fork out to him. "I'd rather be difficult than be a sourpuss just because your sister might be engaged."

"This!" He shook his head in confusion. "Why is everyone so okay with this idea that he's legitimately engaged to Dona? We don't know him. He could be a serial killer."

"If he's one, you're are too; so, Dona will be fine," I answered. He glared at me and I glared right back.

"Dona is my sister."

"Dona could be his wife."

"Could...could," he replied angrily. "As in, not yet. So why the fuck is he on such goddamn high horse?"

"It's a very strong possibility..." I drifted off when his eyes met mine, this time stuffing more of my waffles into my mouth and telling him to do the same. "Eat or they'll get soggy."

He pouted like a child before eating. He only managed two large bites before his head snapped up again. "He tried to kill her."

"No, he didn't."

His Italian side came out as he dropped his fork and started to talk much more passionately, his hands moving with each word. "Are you kidding me? He flung her into the water and held her under. It was only when she lost consciousness that he took her out. It was your body chain she wore that alerted us she was in distress and your cameras that let us zoom in, only to see him trying to kill her!"

"Dona hit him."

"So, what?" he snapped. "He can't handle being hit—"

"Donatella is abusive!" I snapped at him and he paused like he wasn't expecting me to respond and I went on because I wasn't in the mood to hear him yell at me. "She is physically and verbally abusive...to everyone! It's not her fault. In fact, everyone in this family is abusive to some degree. But Dona... She's harsh and she became that way in order to protect herself from all the people constantly trying to worm their way into this family. If she wasn't harsh, people would walk all over her. It's how she protects herself. How we all protect ourselves. A man who is cold-hearted is seen as sexy and mysterious, but as a female you're just seen as bitch. Imagine what would have happened if Dona had warmed up and been forgiving to Tobias? He'd have become even more bold. Men want us to be soft and kind and gentle. But she's a Callahan; anything soft, kind or gentle in her was buried long ago!"

"What does any of that have to do with the man that almost killed her!" he yelled at me.

Urgh, he was so dumb!

"He's the first person that fought back!" I hollered back at him. "For once, someone who wasn't family stood up to her. He's the first one who said I can take the abuse and I will dish it back. And why? Because he's not afraid of her or you or Ethan. He acted without giving a damn about who she is, other than female. He wasn't trying to kill her. He was showing her that she couldn't bully him like she does everyone else...at least not without getting herself hurt. Tobias betrayed the family because he wanted to be on the same level as Dona. He wanted her respect... and years later, he still couldn't get it. Gabriel earned it in a day. There is something different about him. He's not like the others. He can actually stand toe to toe with her. Ethan sees it, I see it, and so does Dona. Dona, for the first time ever, is excited, Wyatt. She doesn't know she's excited yet but if you saw her tonight, you'd know she was. Finally, someone is in front of her, ready for anything she might dish out. Everyone needs a rival or balance. A positive to her negative. I'm excited for her... I'm excited to see what's under those ten layers of rock and ice around her heart; why aren't you?"

He hung his head, giving up. He kept eating, completely silent as he leaned against the kitchen island. He didn't say anything, and neither did I as I reached for the orange juice on the counter, quietly waiting for him to process what I had said.

"We know nothing about him. Why didn't anything come up on Ethan's background check?"

I shrugged. "I'm guessing grandmother had my father or someone else to wipe his records..."

"I know you. You could put it together, if you wanted." His eyes looked like he was begging...and I almost caved.

"I could." I nodded slowly. "But I don't want to."

"Helen..."

"Wyatt... In normal relationships, you don't know

everything about the other person before you start dating them."

"Which is why normal people end up hurt."

"And know-it-alls end up alone," I countered.

"Better to be alone than hurt."

"Says who?"

He shrugged. "Me."

"You're wrong." He hadn't been hurt in that way, so he had no right to talk. "When you're hurt, it means you had reason to smile and laugh before. Being alone is like sitting in darkness; there is nothing to look back on or hope for."

He flinched and made a face at me. "Stop talking like you speak from experience."

I did.

"Stop being worrying about Dona. She'll handle whatever comes her way; just let her be a woman. Let her explore this. Let her, for once, not worry about mafia this or that, and just care about looking pretty and watching a cheesy movie with a man she might be developing feelings for."

"You have this all set up in your head; maybe you're

the one who hid all his information." He eyed me carefully until I leaned over and smacked him. "Ouch! Just kidding."

"Promise me you'll stay out of it."

"Nope." He grinned, getting up and moving to the big fridge.

"Man, I'm glad you aren't my brother. You'd think Dona was your daughter; not your sister with the way you're trying to hold on to her."

"What are you talking about?" He laughed as he pulled out some chocolate ice-cream. "Any guy you bring home will have it just as bad; you're basically my second sister."

There was that stab to my chest again.

Shoving more food into my mouth, I tried to suffocate my desire to scream at him with the waffles.

"Slow down; I'll make more," he said, refilling my glass. "Least I can do for your cousinly therapy sessions."

I hated him.

"Seriously though, Helen, I appreciate it," he said, patting me on my head.

I really hated him.

"But you aren't allowed to get married for at least

two years while I get over this Dona nonsense, you hear me?" He smiled genuinely, like a kid.

And all I could do was smack his hand away and flip him off, causing him to laugh.

I fuckin' hated him…

Liar.

WYATT

Get over this Dona nonsense?

Impossible.

How do you get over losing a part of you?

Losing… That's what it felt like. Like I was losing touch with her. She didn't even seem to remember I was near her anymore. Every time I looked, her mind was on Gabriel and it was starting to piss me off.

I shared with one person and that was my sister; but I didn't share my sister.

I wanted him gone. But… Did she?

FIFTEEN

"I am the guardian of power, not its owner."

~ Vicente Fox

HELEN

"Cain, check to see if the ADSL signal is connecting to the SAAS." I didn't get a reply. "Cain?"

Slowly, I slid from under the panel in the wall, only to see grey eyes staring directly at me, causing me to jump so that I narrowly avoided hitting my head.

"Hi—"

"Jesus, Mary mother of Joseph!" I screamed, sliding out further, ready to smack the hell out of him. He just laughed.

"I think you got that phrase a little mixed up."

"Gabriel! How did you get in here?" I snapped, trying to rise. He offered me his hand and I stared at for a long moment before taking it. He pulled me to stand.

"I walked through the door," he answered, looking around at the grey and white pixelated walls around us. Each pixel fell like square rain drops on the wall. Slowly, he took in each and every corner of room. He was dressed in all black; a casual top and jeans, a leather wrist band. His blond-brown hair was still a little wet. "It's like something out of a science fiction novel," he added.

"You shouldn't have been able to just walk in here," I said, taking a step away from him towards the intercom? "Cain, how is he inside?"

"Who is Cain—?"

"Systems operations back online. Please repeat question?" Cain's voice finally replied.

"Cain is AI?" Gabriel grinned, nodding to himself as he walked slowly up to the walls of the room.

"Cain, there is an intruder."

"Scanning." The room flashed. "No intruder found."

"What?" I asked, staring wide-eyed at the man before me. There was no way in hell he could mask himself in here. "Identify occupants."

"Helen Badass Callahan and Gabriel, found," Cain answered.

I wanted to groan when Gabriel turned around and looked at me, a wide grin on his lips. "Don't."

He raised his hands up in defense. "I didn't say anything."

Moving to the glass table in the center of room, I opened my laptop and tried to figure out why he was identified. The only way that could happen was if someone put him in the system...my system.

"Evelyn told me about this, but I didn't believe it," he said, still in awe. For the second time, I paused, looking at him.

"My grandmother couldn't have given you access—"

"She said she'd make her son do it."

"Dad," I sneered through clenched teeth. I knew someone had been in the system! I'd spent few days trying to rewire the whole system, thinking someone had hacked me and it was my own father! Taking the tie out of my hair, I tossed it on the table and scratched the side of my head.

"What does Cain stand for?"

"Callahan Active-Matrix Information Networking System," I replied, taking a seat in the white curved hourglass chair behind me.

"Evelyn said it allows you to find people anywhere in the world?"

Ethan was going to be pissed once he learned Gabriel had been in here. He might even end up killing him. Cain was a secret we didn't even talk about within the family, despite the fact that we all knew it existed.

"Not exactly," I answered. "It allows us to use facial recognition and cross-reference it with security cameras all around the world."

But that was just the tip of the iceberg.

Gabriel glanced over his shoulder at me. "Isn't that the same thing?"

"No, it isn't. If you go underground and off the grid, we'll only know the last place—none of that is important right now. Why are you here? Why did my father give you access to this? And most importantly, is he the reason we can't find out who the hell you are?"

"They weren't joking around when they say crime has become organized," he replied, ignoring me. "Who would have thought the Mafia would become the eye in the sky like this—"

"Gabriel, I'm not one for violence, but I can call some people who are."

"Helen," he sighed like he was exhausted then walked around the table, leaning on one of the chairs. "I come in peace, I swear."

"Liar." I knew that much for fact. "People who come in peace don't come near our family. If you are here, it means you are here for war. But war with who?"

"Cain, can I see a map of Europe?" he asked and just like that, the pixels came together to form the map he'd asked for.

"You're at war with Europe?" I asked, watching him as he looked over the map without answering. "You're truly pushing your luck. Ethan is going to kill you for being in here, and maybe even my father and grandmother for granting you access. It's only for family—"

"I'll just have to make sure I become family, then." he smiled and I could see the small dimple in his cheek. It was chilling, the way he smiled; he looked so innocent and so sweet. You'd never think he was the same man who'd dropped a pair of severed hands on Donatella's plate. "That's the real reason I'm here, anyway."

"Here in the mansion or here in this room?" I questioned.

"Both," he replied, looking around the room. "But before I get to my main point, I want know...would you build this...another Cain—?"

"No," I replied.

"Why?"

"One, I don't think you have the funds for it."

He frowned at that. "Whatever the price is, I can pay it, I assure you."

"Two, it took my father and I years to build Cain. It's a two people, no, a two *genius* job. He has carpal tunnel in his hand from coding so much. I'm not going to put him through that."

"Surely someone else—"

"Three, I only work with people I absolutely trust. Four, Ethan wouldn't like it or allow it. Five, yes, I care what Ethan allows or not. Six, your family don't need your own if you can just use this one."

"Fine, I'll ask again later." He snickered, taking a seat in the chair beside me. "Now to the most important reason I came…Donatella."

"I'm not involved—"

"She's your best friend, isn't she?" he asked and I really wanted to know just how much Evelyn had told him. He knew way too much about us all. No wonder he unnerved Dona so much. It was like he'd studied up on each and every one of us and knew just how and when to approach.

He was dangerous.

But to who?

"What about Dona?" I asked, making sure to hit the record button on the side of my computer.

"I want to take her on a date."

"Excuse me?" Well, I wasn't expecting that. He was in a room where I could literally pull up information on anyone he wanted, and he wanted to ask me about dating Dona?

"What is her dream date?" he asked seriously but gently, those eyes of his eyes warm and kind and caring. It was so hard for me to merge the two sides of him I'd been witness to: the cold-blooded murderer and the guy simply asking about a girl he wanted take out.

"Her dream date?"

He nodded. "I'm sure she doesn't talk about that stuff now, but you've know her your whole life. You must remember her wanting to do one thing if she hadn't been born a Callahan. Something she wanted to do but couldn't."

"I'll answer your question, if you answer mine," I replied.

"Ask anything but who I am and what I'm doing." He

nodded and I wanted to kick him over the head. Those were the two most important questions yet he was deflecting from both of them; who could he be that was so bad, even with this family, that everything about him was shrouded in secrecy? Not only that... Why were our parents helping him so much?

"Helen?"

"Cain, what is Gabriel's cell phone number?"

"Only known number...737-8141."

Taking out my phone, I texted him what he needed to know.

"Is there a reason you didn't just ask me?" Gabriel leered, taking out his phone but not reading the message.

"Yes," I said, leaning back and crossing my legs. "You enjoy fucking with us like this. But the difference between me and everyone else I don't like getting involved in those games. I trust the people who helped you get in here well enough to know that whatever we get out of you down the track must be worth the provocation right now. You and I will revisit this conversation when all of our cards are on the table."

He rose to his feet, amused. "If only everyone else

was like you, we could get to the good part of this story so much quicker."

"Of course, they can't be like me; I'm the black sheep of the family." I winked at him.

He laughed and nodded. "Thank you, Helen. I owe you one. When my cards are on the table, I'll pay my due."

I didn't say anything else as I watched him walk to the only part of the wall not pixelated, pressing his hand on the door which opened to let him out.

"Session saved," Cain said.

"Send it to Ethan, then call my father."

"Session sent. Calling Declan Callahan."

I listened to it ring twice before he answered, "Hi Melon; your mom and I were just talking about you."

"Daddy…" I spun around in my chair, looking up at the ceiling, "You're in trouble."

"Story of my life," he snickered. "What have I done now?"

"Gabriel?"

He didn't reply.

"Sweetheart?" My mother came on the line.

"Did Dad just palm me off to you—?"

"Forget about that. How's Gabriel? Does Donatella like him?"

These people had no shame. "Well, she sent six men to kill him."

"You ladies are dead-set on being alone, aren't you?"

I stopped spinning at that and sat up. "Mother, there better not be any random men ready to claim they're engaged—"

"I'd kill him!" I heard my father yell in the background.

"So, you're still there?!"

I might have been the black sheep, but the wolves loved me and because of that love I built Cain *alone* to make sure they were always the hunters and never the hunted. It was the one thing I could do for them, seeing as how I didn't get any blood on my hands. I wasn't a fighter like Donatella. I wasn't determined to prove myself like Nari. I was the guardian.

Gabriel didn't need to know that, though.

SIXTEEN

"Because there was a hunger in me to see everything and do everything. I wanted to be everyone I saw. I wasn't enough for me. Can you understand that?"

~ Sidney Sheldon

DONATELLA

"Is Ivy coming today, Donatella?" Brigitte, the governor's wife, asked as we walked through the high-school building - another Callahan foundation chore.

"Am I not enough company, Brigitte?" I asked her, looking up at the wall of the self-portraits the senior class had drawn and displayed. They were all terribly bad; many of them looking as if they hadn't even tried. With the expectation of one who hadn't focused on realism, instead drawing a self-portrait of themselves in Cubism, only partially in color.

"Ms. Callahan?"

I looked back over my shoulder to the small group of women around me. Principal Pomar, a thin Hispanic woman who wore glasses I didn't think she needed, hurried to my side.

"Do you like them? Our seniors worked really hard on them this year."

I pointed to the only one that caught my attention. "Who did this one?"

The woman frowned then took a deep breath,

shaking her head and fingering the fake pearls around her neck. "Penélope Muñoz who is, as you can see, a troubled girl. I told the art director to take down but he insisted it would add contrast—"

"I've heard that name." Fatimah Gupta came forward and leaned in, whispering, "Is she the pregnant one? Her mother came down here once, correct?"

The principal cringed but nodded, glancing around before saying, "We're a Catholic school, we didn't want her to abort it. We told her to stay home till after the baby was born, then restart. However, her mother came here and made quite a fuss. We just left her to herself; she's only making it harder for her daughter. I feel for the mother though, she's a single mother what else—"

"Where is this Penélope?" I asked, interrupting their need for useless gossip.

She had to think before looking down at her watch. "I believe it's lunch period for most of her grade."

"Brilliant, we'll get to see the cafeteria as well. I'd love to see how that healthy choice initiative your husband signed is working, Fatimah," I said, looking to Principal Pomar and waiting. She looked to rest of them and I wondered why; they weren't the largest donors to the school. I was. "Is there a problem?"

"Of course not, right this way. We've just had the whole kitchen menu..."

I stopped paying attention at that point as we walked through the hall. Each of the monthly meetings for The Callahan Foundation served a dual purpose, as we also discussed our family business, charity which didn't benefit us had a very clear objective. Nari, Helen, and I often went to different schools, parks, hospitals, and various other organizations for the public to, as my cousin Darcy would say, "toss gold coins."

I'm sure Ivy, once she got settled, would pick her charities to shower money on as well. The objective was to make people feel grateful to us, or at the very least, not detest us. People had tendency to hate the rich, especially the generational rich, and that hate turned to violence if they suffered long. It was what brought about the Reign of Terror.

To prevent anarchy, toss gold. My aunt Cora had taught us that when we were young, and we all still lived by it now.

"Here we are," Principal Pomar said as we stood at the upper level, looking down at the students who all laughed, ate, and drank among themselves.

I wondered how it was possible for high school to never change. Even at my boarding school for girls it had been the same. Everyone broke into cliques; the pretty and popular, then the anti-popular kids who thought they were so cool because they smoked cheap cigarettes and listened to older music. Then of course, there were the traditional athletes, nerds, and the geeks. Yes, those were separate groups. I knew, thanks to Helen, that nerds were intelligent and industrious, while geeks, apparently, were random people who cared immensely about random things no one else gave two shits about. Penélope Muñoz was not among any of them. She sat all the way at the back with her nose in a book, eating a homemade sandwich. I knew it was her right away; her stomach was a dead giveaway.

"I'll be right back," I said to them, walking to the side steps.

"Ms. Callahan?" They called after me but I ignored them and walked down by myself.

It didn't take long for the boys to notice and stop

talking to gawk. I wanted to smack a few of the jocks who thought it was funny to flex and blow kisses at me.

"Isn't that Donatella Callahan?" a girl to the right of me whispered. "She's so freaking pretty."

"With that much money, we could all be pretty," another of them mumbled and I wanted to stop and tell her not enough money in the world could change her ugly little mouth. I restrained myself, knowing her greedy parents would claim I'd bullied her and caused mental distress in hopes of getting a pay day.

Instead of replying, I ignored them, allowing them to talk and think what they wanted. Their lives were going to be insignificant to me, as always.

Knock. Knock. I beat my knuckles in front of her brown paper lunch bag. With mustard on the side of her lips, Penélope stared at me wide-eyed.

"Can I sit?"

Frowning, she took out her earbuds. "I guess I don't own the table."

As I sat across from her, she sat up a little straighter.

"I saw your drawing." She didn't seem to hear me; she was too focused on everyone else.

"On second thought, maybe you shouldn't sit here. Everyone is staring at you," she quietly spoke, then leaned in.

"Are you sure it's not the mustard on your chin they're staring at?" I asked her and she rushed for a napkin, wiping her face.

"Of freaking course." She laughed sadly to herself. Dropping the napkin on the table before looking to me. "Let me guess, you're one of those PTA moms who want to help me make the right choice?"

"I should smack you across the face. Do I look old enough to be the mother of a high-school student?"

She tilted her head to the side. "Honestly, I can't tell anymore with the Botox they keep injecting into their faces. But I'll give you the benefit of the doubt since your face still moves when you talk."

I laughed. Like actually laughed. "You remind me of a less pretty, more pitiful, underprivileged, poor version of me."

"Fuck you. Is that supposed to be a compliment?" She made a face. "That's horrible."

I shrugged smiling. "I said it because I was sure you

could take it. Besides, any version of me is better than a version of anyone else."

"Wowww." Her mouth made an O and again, she tilted her head to the side. "How does your neck support such a big ego?"

"I do a couple chin tucks each morning and I'm good to go," I said, showing her.

She tried not to laugh but couldn't help herself. Shaking her head at me, she said, "Fine. I don't mind being a less pretty, more pitiful, underprivileged, poor version of you."

"Penélope," I huffed and exhaled loudly. "Just when I was starting to like you."

"What?"

"You should mind. Who wants to be a less pretty, more pitiful, underprivileged, poor version of me?"

She looked at me like I had lost my mind. "You just said that's better than being everyone else!"

"Exactly!" I said in the same whiny tone as her. "You're already better than everyone else. You should strive for more, not just settle. I saw your self-portrait and thought... This girl is ahead of her time."

"The ones displayed in the hall? You liked that?" she asked in disbelief.

I nodded. "I love art. But I love artists more, despite the fact I can't draw to save my life. Everyone probably sees that drawing and thinks you're weird, right?"

"I mean, it isn't the only reason, but it didn't help my popularity," she said a little less cheery than before.

"High school popularity is shit and I say that as someone who has always been popular."

"So, you don't know what it's like to be on the outside, then. To always be out in the cold," she muttered before drinking her milk.

"I didn't say that." I rested my cheek on my palm. "And you also don't know what it's like to be on the inside. They're not any happier. In fact, they're so terrified of being out in the cold that they're willing to bend, deform themselves, inject Botox into their faces, cut away pieces of themselves just to stay popular. What they don't realize is that those pieces they are cutting away are important."

"What are you, a walking, talking self-help book?" She tried to laugh this time, but it didn't come out the way she wanted, so she just hung her head.

"If you mean myself... Yeah most of the time." I nodded. "But today I decided to share my almighty greatness with you, poor child. Think of me as your one-time fairy godmother."

That did make her laugh. "One time?"

"Make one wish. Please don't wish for something small and useless, I'll be insulted. I'm too rich for small wishes."

"Why?" she asked me, carefully, and I liked her even more for doing so.

"Because when asked to draw a self- portrait, you didn't draw yourself one dimensional. You said, I am many things which make the whole; I am pieces put together in strange angles and I cannot choose just one for anyone."

"I could just like cubism," she muttered, before sucking on her straw, and we gave each other a look before laughing. "Fine one wish, and prepare yourself, I make big wishes."

"Bring it." I waved her on.

"I'm not kidding. I'm going to come off like a total parasite, trying to take everything I can—"

"Good on you." I nodded to her. "Now you sound

even more like me."

"Don't say I didn't warn you," she muttered, sitting up and rolling her sleeves. She was so funny.

"Well, I don't have all day—"

"Make me rich," she cut me off. "Make me so rich, they have to respect me. So that they can't abuse my mom and the teachers can't look down on me."

I smiled from ear to ear, leaning in close to her. "If I give you this, you aren't going to go crazy, lose your personality, and try to become one of the popular girls, are you?"

She waved her hand over her stomach. "It's kinda hard to be a cheer girl with a belly."

"Fine. I'll trust you." I nodded, getting back up. "Keep drawing. Your stuff is going to be worth a lot. I'll buy the self-portrait for one-five."

"$1,500 is a little steep for a high-school painting—"

"$1,500? I've spent more on shoes. Try one point five million."

Her mouth dropped open. "You lie."

"Always, but not about this. Enjoy your last shitty

sandwich and watch how the popular ones are the first to swarm to new fires."

I turned around, ready to make my great exit; happy with completing my good deed of the year when I saw him. Dressed in head to toe black, standing at the front of the cafeteria, and grinning at me proudly.

In the next meeting, we are definitely discussing the school's damn security system.

GABRIEL

"How did you get in here?" she hissed once she'd gotten close enough. I looked her over; covering my mouth as my eyes drank in her curvy hips under the tight, high-waisted yellow skirt which stopped just a little below her lacy crop top, showing a small sliver of her mid-section. "My eyes are up here." She snapped her fingers at me.

"I'm not looking for your eyes," I said, finally looking back at her. "Though they are beautiful, as always. I'm trying to figure out how you got in here."

"Excuse me?"

I waved my hands over her outfit. "I know you enjoy being every man's fantasy, but this a little much, don't you think? They're teenagers; you aren't playing fair."

She raised her hand as if she were about to smack me, but I quickly side-stepped her, looking to the women who now stood behind her. "Ladies, please excuse us, but Ms. Callahan has another engagement this afternoon and we must leave now if we hope to be on time."

"Ma'am," I turned back to Dona, waving her towards the door. She gave me a look that was more than annoyed… Which I had to admit hurt, seeing as how I'd just witnessed her true smile.

"Ladies." She faced them, speaking politely. "I'm sorry, I must go. Principal Pomar, someone will collect Penélope's drawing later."

"You're buying it?" The woman's eyes almost fell out of her damn head.

Donatella simply nodded, looking over at her shoulder at the girl she'd spoken to. Other students were now gathering around her. "I have feeling that girl is going to be a great artist one day. I'm surprised someone as *sophisticated* as you didn't know her talent. For shame. I guess it's true... Somethings you can't buy, or teach. You're either born with it or not."

When I wasn't on the other end of her attacks, I had to admit that the way Donatella made words into weapons was masterful. Without another word, she spun around gracefully and walked out.

"Ladies." I nodded to them once more, hurrying to catch up. I matched her pace to reach her easily. Noticing one of the girls in the hallway taking a photo with her phone, I winked at her, and they all gasped and giggled, nearly falling over themselves.

"A little much, don't you think? They're teenagers, you aren't playing fair," Donatella mocked me as we reached front glass doors, which slid open.

"You know, I like this side of you," I said, walking down the stairs.

"What side of me?"

"The playful one. You were even, dare I say it," I gasped placing my hand over my mouth, "nice."

"Give me the keys. I'll go by myself."

"What keys?" I asked, placing my hands in my pockets.

At the bottom step, she paused and shook her head. "I'm not playing this game with you; where is the car?"

"What car?"

She nodded to herself, lifting her phone and starting to dial. "Yes, I'm finished. I need a car—"

She was cut off by the sound of the helicopter as it flew overhead before landing on the grassy field to our right.

"Option one, you wait out here for your car. There's traffic, so it will take at least twenty minutes for the car to get here. Option two, you go inside and wait with the woman you politely berated—"

I didn't even need to finish. Dona was already walking towards the helicopter. I grinned again, catching up and walking in pace with her.

When the door slid open - because I was born a gentleman - I placed my hands on her ass, *helping* her inside before getting in myself.

As I sat beside her, she said, "I'm going to kill you later."

"I'm ready when you are," I replied, taking a set of headphones, carefully brushing the loose strands of hair out of the way before putting them over her ears. She didn't even pretend not to glare at my face as I did.

When I was done and had put my own headphones on, she crossed her arms and legs and looked out the at the city below us. The noise from the chopper made it far too difficult for us to talk, but that was fine. We had time for that.

Step one: Get her to give me the smallest of chances; even if the door to her heart opened a millimeter, it was still an opening I could work with.

Step two: Get her to invite me in.

Step three: Stay there at all cost.

I was currently on step two. Step one took much longer than I'd anticipated. Step two required even more patience and a man proficient in seduction.

Luckily, I was such a man. Normally the secret to the art of seduction called for one thing—knowledge. Knowing exactly what it was the other person craved and giving it to them in small doses until they became addicted. However, with Donatella, I was sure it would take more than that. I needed to make sure she was always on her toes, that she never knew what to expect. I needed to frustrate, anger, excited, confuse, and amaze her. I needed to give her everything. I needed to *be* everything.

It sounded daunting, exhausting, for most men at least.

However, I was not most men. Since I was a child, I'd been taught and trained to be best at everything. So, I was willing to do almost anything even if it meant crawling to her cousin and begging for a clue. I was sure she'd do it, with a little convincing and I was right. What didn't expect was her answer.

Her text simply said, "Donatella is greedy in the same way all women are greedy. Her dream date is every cheesy thing you've seen in movies and read in books. She wants to have every experience."

The answer was both helpful and completely useless.

She'd basically told me *anything is fine* in the most eloquent way possible. Meaning I was left to think of something on my own. Fortunately, there was no shortage of things to do in this state.

She'd be pissed at first, but I was looking forward to it. Her rage excited me.

If she wanted everything; I'd give her everything.

SEVENTEEN

"We didn't realize we were making memories,

we just knew we were having fun."

~ A. A. Milne

DONATELLA

"You've got to be kidding me." I stared out at the barely clothed bodies, covered in fake tattoos, body glitter and jewelry, all of them holding clear cups which were definitely not filled with water. There were blow-up chairs, fake Bohemian print blankets, and tents on top of the grass. I looked at what lay before me with a mixture of astonishment and exasperation. "You brought me to TLSM?"

"Is that what this is called?" he asked me, tossing the duffle bag he'd taken off the helicopter over his shoulder. He was the one who'd brought me so why did he look like he no idea where we were? Noticing me ready to beat him to death, he lifted his phone. "I just searched things happening within a hundred miles of the city and saw this music festival."

He's an idiot.

I'm an idiot for thinking he was anything but an idiot.

"I'm going home—"

He grabbed my hand and pulled me back.

"Donatella, have you ever lived life like normal twenty-six-year-old?"

"No, because I'm not a normal—"

"Me either," he said seriously, looking me in the eye. "Tomorrow we can go back to being not normal people. My secrets will start to come out and when that happens, I don't know when either of us will get to have *normal* day of youthful stupidity. You don't trust me. You don't know me. Fine. But everyone here is the same. No-one knows anyone. They don't care; they just want to have fun. So, let's join them and have fun."

"WOOOOOOHHHHH!" Three random guys ran right in front us, holding flags behind their backs as if they were capes. No sooner had they gone before the music got louder as a new band took the main stage.

"You could have at least gotten me shoes," I muttered, lifting my heel to stop from sinking further into the grass.

He flipped the bag down slightly and unzipped it, pulling out a pair of sandals. Bending down, he put them at my feet. "Anything else, your majesty?"

Saying nothing, I stepped out of my heels and into

the sandals. He extended his hand to take the heels, but I took them myself and walked forward. He was so damn annoying and doing far too much.

A private helicopter ride to The Last Summer Music Festival? Who was he trying to be right now? And of all places, TLSM? The festival took place on the last day of summer each year, but because most teens and young adults were already back at school, it had just become a festival for post-graduates who didn't have to go to work the next morning or had nothing else to do with their lives. In the middle of the damn clearing of Foster Woods.

"TLSM rules! Whoa, yea!"

"Dude, you're like forty; shut the hell up," I muttered at the man to the left of us as we made our way through the crowd.

Gabriel, who must have heard me, snickered but didn't say anything. It was only then that I realized he was still holding my hand. When I tried to pull it back, he just held on tighter. Too tired to fight him, I let it go. He kept us good distance away from the massive crowd, until finally we got to where a green blanket was spread over the grass beside the tree. A thin, frail woman was standing guard over it.

"Thanks." Gabriel handed her a wad of bills.

"No problem, hot stuff." She winked at him then happily skipped... Yes, skipped, away from us.

"Hot stuff? What is this, 2003?" I asked myself as I watched her go.

"Be nice, she's a paying customer of yours," he said to me, finally letting go of my hand and bending down to bring out containers of food.

"A customer of mine?"

He glanced up at me like I was stupid and I must have been because it took too long for that to connect. Shaking his head, he finished setting up and said, "Sit."

"I'm—"

"I know you're not a dog, I'm just saying you're free to sit so we can eat," he said as if he could read my mind, lifting the box for me.

Saying nothing, I sat down on the blanket, dropping my clutch to the side. Inside each of the boxes were more of my favorite foods. Tomato galette with fetta and fresh thyme, deep-fried shrimp fritters with cornichon dressing, and honey lemon chicken with artichoke bites. "You made all of this?"

"Chef Carluccio is warming up to me," he replied, shifting to lay on his side, his legs off the blanket. "I promise it's edible," he replied, taking a bite of the food. However, it must have been much harder than it should have been because he had to keep chewing.

"It is edible, right?" I asked, trying to not to laugh.

He reached over and took the box from me. "Eat the others."

"Nope," I snatched it back, taking one and popping it into my mouth, only to have the same problem as he did. It was so hard.

He broke out, laughing at me. "You really can't help yourself, can you? If I say left, you will say right, even if it means going over a cliff!"

I handed him the box back, still chewing, and he smiled, shaking his head at me. He handed me a bottle of water which I didn't want to take, but decided to man up and take it when I noticed the way he was trying not to laugh at me, fully aware I was just fighting him and choosing to suffer.

"I can't help it," I told him after drinking. "People

have been giving me orders I've had to follow my whole life. I don't like it."

"People as in your parents?"

"Most kids could rebel... But if I did, I'd end up in a ditch somewhere and they'd have to come and save me, and then lecture me to death on why I should have listened to them and their all-knowing selves," I muttered, stuffing a chicken bite into my mouth which thankfully tasted the way it was supposed to...amazing.

"I'm guessing that actually happened?"

I paused mid-bite, not liking how casual he was again. "Let's talk about your parents."

"New topic," he said quickly, looking back over the crowd.

"What, I thought we were going down memory lane?"

"Today you are the most beautiful and happy I've seen you since I got here," he replied, changing the subject completely.

"Nice try but—"

"You don't laugh like that at home," he said, still not looking up at me. "At home you... You're the princess of the mafia; bloody-thirsty, ambitious, cold, and ruthless. That's beautiful in a tragic way. But today, you are just beautiful. You saw another person and decided to change their lives for the better. You gave them hope and you enjoyed it. You laughed with her, teased her, and even made faces." He laughed to himself before turning to stare at me. "You were beautiful in an organic way."

"What happened to accepting me at—"

"I do accept you. I accept the darker parts of you and the brighter ones. You weren't acting out of character today. That is who you are under those conditions. That was you, too."

Reaching over, I grabbed one of the napkins and reminded him, "That was me working. It's good to make sure people think we are generous."

"True, but there were other kids sitting alone. Other kids there who could have used that generosity. You chose her because there was something about her you liked. That's why you sat down with her, too. If not, you could have just bought the drawing and left."

Sighing, I nodded. "Thank you, Dr. Gabriel. Are you going to become my new primary shrink?"

"Do you want me to be?" he asked blankly.

I frowned. "Why do you do that?"

"Do what?"

"Act as if you're willing to do or become anything I need you to be?"

"Because I am. That's what people do in relationships."

I rolled my eyes. "We aren't in a relationship."

"Only because you're so damn stubborn."

"Thank you very much." I bowed to him, and he knocked on my head.

"Did you just..."

"What?" He grinned, taking a chicken bite and stuffing it into his mouth. Leaning over, I smacked his head and he smacked my thigh. "Do you really want to start a war right here, *Donny*?"

"Do you have alcohol in that magic bag of yours? I feel like I'm going to need it to survive however long we are here."

He reached in and pulled out two bottles. "Red or white?"

"I thought you knew everything—"

"Both then," he cut me off to say. Gabriel uncorked them both and then handed me one bottle. "We'll switch back and forth."

"Are you trying to get me drunk?

"Do you change when you get drunk?"

I nodded, lying. "I get much more violent."

When he reached over to take the bottle away from me I moved back, drinking straight from the bottle for the first time.

"I'm going to regret this, aren't I?"

"Here's to being young and stupid," I said and drank, and so did he.

"If we are going to be young and stupid, then let's go all the way," he said, rising up and pulling me up with him. He spun us around.

"Dance with me."

"No."

"Dance with me, please. I love this song." he pouted, holding me closer and swaying with me.

"What's the name of the song?"

He paused.

"You're such a liar." I couldn't help it; I laughed.

GABRIEL

I learned four important things about her today.

One: She could be very sweet when she wanted to be.

Two: She loved the band, Saturn Sun.

Three: She was a weird dancer.

Four: She didn't become violent when she was drunk; she simply got sleepy.

I wished I had more time to find out all of her quirks and habits, but I didn't. Tomorrow was the day everything had to come together and I had to have her decision. We couldn't be normal longer than this.

"Where have you two been—"

"Wyatt, I went to TLSM. It was so lame and so fun at the same time." Dona giggled…yes giggled. Leaving Wyatt to just stare, I carried her into their house on my back. Shock covered Wyatt's face.

"Are you drunk?"

"Me?" Dona asked, shaking her whole body and making carrying her much harder for me. "A little tipsy, but a bottle and half of wine will do that to a person."

Right, I'd learned five things. Donatella could drink wine like water, and even I, who loved a good strong red in the evening, could hold no candle to her.

"Gabriel?" she asked in a sweet voice right into my ear, making me shiver. "Thank you for the ride, but I can walk."

"That's what you said before—ouch." I sighed, putting her down on her bare feet. Where the sandals I had given her had disappeared to, I had no idea.

"Peace and good night." She actually gave us both the peace sign before heading up the stairs, leaving Wyatt and I standing alone. Ethan came out of the elevator and nearly did a double-take when she waved to him and said goodnight with a smile on her face.

"What's the matter with her?" he asked us both.

"That's what I want to know."

"She had fun. That's it. We had a fun time out together," I answered, walking up the steps as well.

"She isn't going to marry you," Wyatt called out from behind me. The uncertainty in his voice gave me hope.

"We'll see. But if I were you, I wouldn't bet on it."

EIGHTEEN

"So…

you want to be tough?

You want to be rebellious?

You want to be a badass?

Then show your heart to everyone…

EVERYONE."

~ Michael Xavier

GABRIEL

"Let's try to avoid bullets today," I said to my refection before I stepped out of my room. Part of me expected to see Dona waiting outside, ready to strike swiftly. Luckily, my expectations were not met and my trip to the elevator and down to the dining room was a quiet one. I could hear muttering and saw two familiar men standing in front of the door, eyeing me like dogs… *Well they are dogs.*

I snickered at the thought and decided to name them. "Morning, Rocky, Coco."

They looked at me as if I was insane and were about to say something when I nodded to the door. "I would open it myself but, ahh…" I reached up to my arm. "I think one of you might have pulled my arms back too far…not to mention the bullet."

"The bullet our boss gave you."

"The one that didn't kill me, yes I know. The door…" I waited and the big Irish one opened it but held his hand out to stop me from entering the room.

"Sir. It's him," Rocky said.

"Him has a name," I asserted but he ignored me. He

nodded to the other guard before opening the door wider for me to enter. The Callahans all sat, Dona included, in a different arrangement than before. Ethan was at the head, with Wyatt on his right and Ivy on his left. Donatella sat next to her and Helen her other side. The butler nodded for me to sit two seats down from Wyatt; they were putting distance between us. Dona drank some sort of hangover juice, rubbing the side of her head.

"Gabriel," I said to Rocky. He looked confused. "My name is Gabriel, not *him*. I'm saying this for your sake, Rocky. I'm sure your boss prefers you to be more descriptive when announcing his guests. I mean, you wouldn't want him to seem *rude* and *ill-bred,* now would you?"

He glanced to Ethan and I watched from the corner of my eye as he continued to eat his breakfast as if he couldn't hear us. Meaning he wouldn't allow Rocky to wiggle out of accepting this defeat… It would look bad on him.

"Excuse me, Mr. Gabriel," Rocky said to me.

"Leave us, Grayson," Ethan finally said to him and nodded to me. "Gabriel, welcome. We didn't expect you'd been joining us for breakfast."

"Your expectations are correct," I said when the doors closed behind me. "I'm not here for breakfast."

Casting the helmet in my hand over my shoulder, I walked around the table aiming directly for her seat. She ate her toast calmly, as if she didn't notice I was in the room, so I leaned over until my lips were touching her ear and she froze, "I came for you. Let's go."

"Gabriel, my brother invited you eat at his table." Wyatt scowled at me, tearing his bread with more violence than necessary. "You wouldn't want to seem *rude* and *ill-bred* rejecting that offer, now would you?"

Standing up straighter, I rested on Dona's chair. "Seem? Wyatt, didn't you notice? I *am* rude and my breeding is quite questionable."

"I did notice."

"Then why bother talking?"

He bit his tongue and I snickered.

"You aren't off to a good start this morning," Dona finally spoke before sipping her drink.

"How so, my love?" I asked, making Ethan pause for the first time. I ignored him and focused on her.

She inhaled. "Not only are you late, and I abhor tardiness, but your greater offence is expecting that I'll stop everything I plan on doing today to go off with you again. I already have a migraine."

"I cannot be late to a function I didn't plan on attending as I told the maid this morning, which is why you were not expecting me. And I was not expecting you to stop what you have planned today. I checked with your assistant; we'll be done in time and I'll drive you over. As for the migraine… Well, was the wine at least worth it?"

"Wait, go back; you did what?" She looked over her shoulder at me. "How do you even know who my assistant is?"

I smiled, reaching down to steal a piece of her bacon. "Did you know your grandmother is one hell of a tough negotiator? I had to promise our first daughter would be named after her. I told her you might want to name her after your mother so she said she would settle with Melody-Evelyn but it must be hyphenated because she would not be regulated to a shitty middle name."

"Why am I not surprised by that?" Ivy muttered behind Dona's back.

I wasn't sure what was funnier, remembering that conversation or the look on her face; it was a mixture of surprise, shock, and horror. Dona raised her hand to speak but then paused, shaking her head.

"If this your idea of trying to woo me..."

"Woo?" I laughed at the word. "No, that was yesterday. This, right now, is me trying to make you an accomplice in a bank robbery."

Her mouth dropped open and I laughed. Not just me, but Ivy and Helen did as well.

"Are you insane?" she asked me.

"Only as much as you are. So...you coming or not?" I asked.

She just stared in shock before shaking her head. "Seventy-seven percent of all bank and casino robberies end in capture or death. Nineteen percent only make the annual salary of a cafe barista."

"First, I'm glad to see you've thought about this—"

"I read!"

"Who casually reads up on the statics of bank robberies if they don't want to rob a bank?" I questioned, my eyebrows rising in honest confusion.

"Who doesn't read up on it when they do want to rob one?" she yelled at me. She was really getting worked up which just made her more beautiful and hilarious.

"Secondly," I went on, ignoring her outburst, "in all your reading you must have noticed that four percent of robbers make it big. Think of it like Ocean's 11, but with nine less people."

"Why eleven and not twelve or thirteen?" Ivy asked, seriously thinking about it. I'd forgotten where we were for a moment.

I leaned over to look at her. "Ivy, is that really a question? Twelve and thirteen were horrible."

"Plus, they were arrested in twelve and thirteen," Helen said.

"One of them got arrested in eleven, too," Ivy defended.

"But not for robbery," Helen and I said at the same time.

I glanced down her, nodding. "Bloody well done."

"What the hell is happening!" Dona screamed, drawing our attention to her. Her brothers looked at all of us as if we were modern art the MET museum. "They're crazy…all of them!"

"Well, that's hurtful," I said, moving to lean on the edge of Helen's chair and looking to her. "Apparently our fearless Dona is scared and I'm going to be late, so would you like help me rob a bank?"

She tilted her head to the side and pursed her lips; "Which bank—?"

"I am not scared; I'm just not an idiot!" Dona said to us.

"Neither am I. It's not like I'm going to go in there shooting up the place. I do have plan. So, if I'm not an idiot, you must be a scaredy-cat."

"I'm not five. That isn't going to work on me." She made a face.

"I'll be leaving in ten minutes; if you have the time, I wouldn't mind the help…" I said to Helen, winking at her before getting up and heading to the door, which opened as I approached.

"Coco, Rocky." I nodded to the guards as they moved to tell Ethan whatever it was they needed too.

"The bank you're robbing…" Ethan called out to me, finally speaking up. "Is it Wilson's Bank?"

I glanced over my shoulder. "Why do you ask?"

"If so, I have another account for you to rob, unless you plan on taking the whole bank down?" he asked, placing his elbows on the tables and folding his hand over one another.

I turned and politely said, "You have two options. Option one: you may ask for a favor and be in my debt. Option two: you may send a representative on your behalf to do what you need while I am there, preferably a female one. Preferably."

"See you eight minutes." I looked over to the ladies.

DONATELLA

I looked at the paper in Ethan's hand.

"What account do you need the money from?"

"Tobias's," he answered, looking up at me. "We just found where he was hiding the money the other cartels were paying him; great timing, wouldn't you say?"

"Or a set up," Wyatt added, not looking at me.

"Well, should I leave this to you or not?" Ethan

asked. Now he was asking me when he should or shouldn't act like a giant asshole.

"I'll handle it," I muttered, reaching over to take the paper before heading to door.

"Looks like someone really wanted to go," Helen muttered then pretended to be interested in the detailing on her silverware when I turned to glare at her.

Ignoring them all, I headed towards the front doors, which were already open. Gabriel leaned against a chrome and black motorcycle, the make of which I didn't know. The handlebars were high and there was just barely enough room for two.

"You may want to consider changing," he said, looking down to the black Christian Louboutin peep-toe spike heels I was wearing which matched perfectly with my high-waisted black trousers, white crop-top, and chain necklaces. "Not that you don't looks stunning, as always."

Rolling my eyes, I turned to see one of the maids waiting, and I outstretched my hand to her. She looked confused.

"Hair-tie," I finally said.

Nodding, she took her red hair out of the bun,

picking off the strands on the band before giving it to me. Reaching up, I pulled my dark hair into a tight ponytail as I walked down the front stairs of the mansion, up to Gabriel and his bike.

"Let's go. You're on a time crunch, aren't you?"

His eyebrow rose. "You aren't going to argue? Demand to ride your own bike?"

"No matter how many times I tell you, you seem to think I am idiot," I said, brushing him out of my way and throwing my leg over the bike before looking back at him. "I don't know where we are going and if anything goes wrong, I'll simply abandon you and there won't be any trace that I was there. Let's get this over with."

"You look so beautiful," he said randomly before sighing, "and yet I hardly notice because of all the venom coming out of your mouth."

"Me and my beauty don't exist for you or anyone else to notice," I reminded him.

He grinned and I didn't know why. He didn't explain, instead handing me a helmet that I didn't take it, much to his annoyance. He didn't comment, instead throwing the helmet to one of the butlers. He took out two pairs of aviators, putting one on me and then himself before lifting his leg over and taking a seat in front of me.

"Don't say hold on tight... It's cliché," I said into his ear, wrapping my arms around his torso. Even through his leather jacket I could feel his hard stomach. His whole body was nothing but solid muscle. I didn't know why I noticed; it's not like he didn't look strong. But I did notice. Just like I noticed he smelled like peppermint.

"You don't have to hold on tight," he said, revving the engine. "You just have to make sure I can feel your breasts pressed up against my back."

Before I could speak, he kicked off and we were on our way, gravel kicking up as he went around the fountain, then out the gates and on to the street. Like a bullet, we cut through wind. I could feel my heart pumping in my chest, though not from fear. I liked how he rode—fearlessly, dangerously, speeding faster and faster. He swerved through traffic, not stopping for anything or anyone. When others slowed down as the light turned yellow, he sped up. If I wasn't holding on as tightly as I was, I would have flown off long ago. I was thankful my heels fit my feet like a glove, because one wrong move and they'd come off before I did.

The wind and his speed made it impossible to speak, and I didn't need to until he suddenly reached up and placed his hand over mine. He slowly moved our joined hands to the spot right over his heart. I wasn't sure what he was trying to pull until I felt it. His heartbeat. It was racing just as hard as mine...and...and each beat came right after mine. My heart would beat, then his, and then mine, as if—as if they were having a conversation. I was so awed by it, I didn't realize he wasn't holding my hand there anymore... I was willingly leaving my hand over his heart.

Once I did realize, I dropped my hand back down to his torso, which made the bastard laugh. I couldn't see his face, but his body shook and in return shook me.

He's so annoying, I thought as I saw the W logo of Wilson bank on the glass tower up ahead. He didn't slow down, and within a few seconds we passed it. Driving a couple blocks over to the new Obelisk Hotel, one of the tallest buildings in the city, he waved something to the guards as he drove into the underground parking garage. Not a single vehicle was there. Slowly, he pulled up in front of elevator, then stopped, parking, He cracked his neck and checked his watch.

"We don't have much time," he said seriously, much more serious than he'd been when he talked about this.

"This isn't the bank," I stated as I stepped down, brushing off my clothes.

"It isn't," he agreed, getting down too and taking my hand. I pulled away. He glanced over his shoulders. "You're in unchartered territory, don't fight me too much..."

"This is Chicago," I stepped into his face. "It's not unchartered. It's my territory."

"Yes, love, can we go now?" he asked, waving his hand towards the elevators.

I didn't say anything, stepping into the elevator. He followed me inside. "Also, just because I'm not fighting you on that nickname doesn't mean I enjoy it."

"Tell me what you'd like me to call you and I'll say that instead," he said as he texted on his phone. "Love."

"Dona," The moment I said it and saw his grin, I regretted saying anything.

"Dona is something only family calls you, correct?"

I walked right into that one, I thought. *Wow,* I mused, stepping into the beautiful Egyptian lobby. The walls were covered with hieroglyphs all the way to the top.

The ceiling was a point, where light came down right over the fountain which spurted water upward and back down like an umbrella.

"The final numbers, Sir," a woman with tan skin, long brown hair, and big hazel puppy-dog eyes said as she handed Gabriel an envelope. When he took it and checked the contents, her eyes shifted to me. But when I looked back, she quickly looked away again.

"They're wrong," Gabriel said to her and she froze before leaning in.

"Everything looks fine to me—"

"Don't worry, I'm sure it's just a mix up at the bank. We were planning on going later, but..."

"I can go. What's the matter?"

"It's fine." He smiled at her and reached into his pocket, pulling out a list. "Can you help get all of these for me instead?"

"Of course," she said, frowning as she read.

I couldn't help but be curious. However, before I could see, Gabriel took my arm and linked it with his, walking me out the front doors.

"I have many questions," I said as I noticed the staff

and security nod to him as we exited onto the street.

"Then ask," he said, putting his phone back in his pocket before looking over to me. He grabbed my hand as we started walking.

"Do you own this hotel?"

"No, but I know the person who does," he replied.

"So, this person just trusts you to handle the management of it?"

He shook his head again. "They don't trust me, but I don't make it easy for them, either."

His mouth was moving; I knew he was answering my questions but it didn't feel like I was getting anywhere.

"Okay," I paused right outside a bakery, the line of which was annoyingly long. "What's your connection to the hotel? Why do you—"

He stuck a piece of cake he'd stolen from the vender outside between my lips, before licking his fingers. "On second thought, why don't you just observe, and when it's all over I'll explain?"

Licking the frosting off my lips, I glared at him, but he didn't even have the decency to look back. Instead he placed a hundred dollars into the tip jar of the vender before taking my hand again. When I tried to pull away, he held on even tighter.

"It's a beautiful city," he said, looking at the skyscrapers. "In an industrialist type of way."

When I looked up at the buildings, I couldn't help but think of my father. "Of course, it's beautiful. It was built by us... From digging for potatoes to sitting on clouds. Under smoke, with dust in all our mouths, raging winds trying to lift us from the ground, and the terrible burden of destiny on our shoulders; we built this mighty, chaotic, passionate, vicious, and unforgiving wonder of the world. So, when we say *I am from Chicago*, the rest of the world knows you are a fighter."

Blinking rapidly, I looked over to him to find him staring at me, but the look in his gray eyes was odd. He looked sad...and worried. "That's what my father used to declare proudly until my mother let him know many Italian immigrants helped... Why am I telling you this?"

The question was more to myself than him, but he answered with a soft smile. "I'm not sure, but I'm enjoying it. Tell me more once we're done here."

"I'll pass. Wait, here?" I looked in front of me, and

sure enough across the street was Wilson Bank.

He's seriously robbing a bank? I thought as we walked inside, however that question left my mind as I saw him reach for a deposit slip and actually begin to fill it out.

"What are you doing?"

He glanced up and scanned the room before looking back at me. "Banking."

Urgh! This man! I'd actually never felt the need to face-palm, but he made no sense to me. He didn't act normally, nor did he seem to have a care in the world. Finishing up, he walked to one of the lines for the teller, checking his watch as he went.

"Love," he said, pulling me to him and wrapping his arms around my body, his lips at my ears, "my life is about to be in your hands. I just need you to intercede on my behalf. But don't fight them..."

"What? Let me go and who—"

Before I could question further, he pushed me down to the ground as two men came into building, firing bullets into the celling.

"EVERYONE DOWN NOW!" The first man in all black with a monkey mask on his face yelled.

"MOVE IT!" I heard to the right where the second and third gunmen was already behind the teller glass. With a semi-automatic pointed in their direction, he slowly kicked the tellers out until they were in the main lobby with us.

I glanced over to Gabriel, who quickly rolled something in the gap between the base of the door to the teller both. However, whatever it was beeped as soon as it entered the booth and grabbed their attention. All three of the monkey heads, still pointing their guns, turned towards him. Gabriel stared at them wide-eyed.

"What did you just do?" the first monkey asked, walking out of the booth towards us…him.

"I…I…noth…nothing," Gabriel stuttered…and I didn't know him well, I didn't know him at all really, but I knew he wasn't the type of man who stuttered. He was acting. All of this was an act.

BANG!

I was shocked when the robber fired, but the bullet didn't hit Gabriel, instead hitting the ground beside him.

"Lie to me again and the next one is going through you!" The monkey yelled, grabbing his shirt.

This is some acting…kinda wish he'd told me to bring a snack.

Gabriel grabbed on to his wrist and said, "It's an alarm. You can kill me, or you can take what you want before the police get here, and they'll be here much quicker than you think."

"FUCK! You little shit!" The man yelled, taking the end of his gun and hitting it into Gabriel's face. You'd think once was enough for the cameras but he kept going. Gabriel blocked it with his arm and glanced at me wide-eyed, as if he was telling me to do something. I'd seen him fight. He could easily take the idiot on his own.

"Intercede," He mouthed to me.

I shook my head and mouthed back. *"Not my fight."*

And I wasn't going to get involved. It was only when I saw blood from his arm—the arm Ethan had shot—that I moved. I wasn't sure why, but I did.

"Stop!" I sat up, pushing the gunman away. "He's bleeding, you fucking dumbass!"

"Who the fuck are you talking to?" He turned to me.

Rising to my feet, I dusted off my shoulders. "I'm talking to you, Curious George! How many other people in here have monkey heads on?"

"You must be stupid, bitch—"

"I'm stupid?" I laughed. "You come in to rob a bank, you don't take anyone's cellphones or tie anyone up? And you lose your cool over a freaking alarm? What is this, amateur hour? Someone oughta smack the ape out of you all—"

"SHUT UP OR YOU CAN TASTE A BULLET!" he hollered, pointing a barrel at my face.

In a flash, Gabriel was on his feet and in front of me, standing between myself and the barrel of the gun. "Best be pointing that thing at me, *mon ami*. Your odds of living are higher that way."

"Let's try it—"

"One. ONE! ENOUGH! ONE!" One of the other monkeys yelled, coming over to us and pointing his gun at me. "Both of you on the ground and shut up, or I swear, we will shoot you."

I glared at him. It was because Gabriel grabbed on to me and pulled me down that I even got back on the ground. They kept their guns on us as they moved back behind the teller counter.

"Where the hell did you get these guys? They're morons," I whispered to him.

BANG!

It happened so quickly that it took me a second to realize one of the other prisoners had tried to make a run for the door. Now he was lying face down on the ground, just a few feet from freedom, a bullet in his spine.

"WE AREN'T FUCKIN' AROUND HERE! SIT DOWN! SHUT UP!" It was then that we could all hear the sirens outside. "SHIT!"

I looked to Gabriel and he just stared at the teen's body before looking over to me, his eyes cold, deadly, as he said, "These aren't my guys."

"What?" My mind started to work overtime as I replayed the last ten minutes in my head. If they weren't his and they weren't mine, then they were real bank robbers. But what were the odds of them robbing the same bank as his on the same day...*wait.* His words from earlier coming to mind.

He'd said, *"Don't fight them..."*

He had known they were coming. But he wasn't working with them.

I looked at him again but his head was down, his hand on his arm. Anyone would think he was hunched over from pain. But since I was so close, I could see the wicked grin on his face.

He's robbing a bank while it's being robbed. They were his Trojan horses.

He must have known I was looking because he lifted his head slightly to look at me. The grin on his face widened. "I'm one-eighth Greek and the hotel is not mine. It's yours. A wedding gift. And when this is over, we'll rest there for the night."

"You're telling me this why?"

"Because you're smiling and it isn't fake, and so I'm glad."

I paused. Reaching up to touch my cheeks… I was smiling. I didn't know when that had happened. It didn't matter because I couldn't look away… Part of me was once again in shock, knowing this wouldn't be the only the last time I was Gabriel surprised me. But knowing that made my heart race.

What was going to happen next with him?

NINETEEN

"It's not exactly love at first sight.

It is more like soul recognition."

~Lynette Simeone

DONATELLA

The great poet Virgil once said, "Whatever it is, I fear the Greeks even when they bring gifts." As I stood on the balcony of the tallest building in Chicago, my building apparently, I wondered if I should be at least one-eighth concerned about this gift and the man gifting it to me.

"Hello, big brother, how are you this evening?" I asked, lifting the phone to my ear, not looking away from the city lights.

"I've been trying to reach you all day," Ethan stated.

"You may not have noticed, but I was held hostage in a bank robbery," I said cheerfully.

"We noticed," Wyatt's voice came on the line. "What happened? Are you alright?"

"I'm fine. The S.W.A.T team took out two of the three men, and the only hostage shot is apparently recovering—"

"What happened with Gabriel, Dona?" Ethan questioned much more directly.

"He reopened his wounds, but a doctor came by to see him as said he'll be fine just as long as he doesn't have too many days like—"

"Donatella, don't be coy."

"Don't be demanding," I snapped, then took a deep breath, not wanting them to kill my mood. "Ethan, Wyatt. I'm fine. In fact, for the first time in a long time, I feel great. I'm with Gabriel; I don't know when I'll be home, don't wait up and don't bother me for now. Love you both. Bye."

Hanging up, I slipped the phone back into my pocket, shifting my gaze to the W of Wilson Bank, the light of the sign now dimmed. It had taken over four hours before we were free to leave. While the S.W.A.T team snuck into the building and helped people get out, Gabriel did something to the computers. He was wounded but acting chivalrous, demanding the women be saved first, just to give himself more time. By the time we made it back to the hotel, the coverage of the robbery had been played at least half a dozen times on every major network.

BUZZ.

Turning around and heading back into the massive suite, I saw Gabriel come down the stairs dressed in jeans that hung off his waist and a dark shirt he hadn't bothered to button. He was still drying his wet, brown-blonde hair.

"Are you expecting someone?" I asked him as he moved to the door.

"Someone, no. Things, yes," he said, opening the door to the same shy, puppy-dog eyed woman I'd met earlier. She wasn't alone this time.

The first two people who came in after her brought dinner trays. They didn't just set up in the dining room but the entire living area, moving the couches back and placing them around the coffee table. They set the small table and even lit candles, while another two workers wheeled in two separate carts; the first held clothes, the second contained shoes and handbags.

"Stop," I held my hands out to them, walking to the second cart and lifting the velvet red box. They were Christian Louboutin, but the box indicated that they were a one of a kind custom shoe; like two I'd been able to get previously, yet here there were *seven* boxes. Lifting the lid, I stared at a pair of butterfly bow-tie pumps. I was tempted to try them on but didn't want to look too excited, especially knowing that Gabriel enjoyed pissing me off. Closing the lid, I put the box back down and stepped back, nodding for the workers to keep going.

"You like?" Gabriel asked from behind me.

"They look a little small for you," I said.

I heard him snicker, "You're probably right, you're free to have them instead."

Crossing my arms, I watched the worker bees hurry about the suite. "I'm rich enough to buy all of this and more."

He leaned over, his lips once again to my ear, making me feel warm with each word he spoke, "But isn't it nice when someone else buys it for you?"

"No," I said, turning to face him. "It makes me wonder what that someone is up to. I'm here, Gabriel. I'm waiting. Why don't we lay our cards on the table before exchanging gifts?"

"Exchanging?" He smiled. "What did you bring for me?"

"Being on my good side. Having me on your side is gift, didn't you know?"

His gray eyes did it again, mentally stripping me naked as they looked over my body. "I'm well aware."

"Then why did you ask?" I didn't wait for his answer, walking to the set table. One of the workers pulled out my chair for me while another pulled out Gabriel's who waited for me to sit before sitting himself. Putting the napkin my lap, I lifted my glass and waited. One of the workers carefully poured the red wine then looked to Gabriel as he buttoned up the rest of his shirt before filling his glass.

We both waited, quietly drinking as we watched each other.

"Will that be everything?" one of the workers asked.

"Yes," Gabriel replied but didn't look away from me, his chest rising and falling slowly. "You all may go."

It felt like it took forever for them all to leave when in reality it was only seconds. The air was so heavy, like the moment right before a rainstorm. Reaching over, he lifted the tray cover and in fluent French said, "*le Homard bleu aux baies de myrte et gingembre*."

"Blue lobster and myrtle berries?"

"Blue Lobster with myrtle and ginger berries," he nodded at the beautiful dish before us and refilled my wine glass for me. "You don't understand French?"

"Why would I understand French? I'm Italian and Irish." I reminded him, picking up my fork. But it was me who needed a reminder; I was here to question him, not the other way around. Putting my fork back down, I gave him my full attention. "And you knew that. You know a lot about me already yet I don't know anything about you. You want it that way. If you don't answer my questions, I will walk out and when I walk out, no one can make me come back. Not my grandmother, not even my mother, if she were alive."

"Ask then, Dona," he said before taking a bite of his food and lifting his wine glass.

"What is your name?"

"Gabriel."

"Last name?"

"I do not have one," he stated. I could feel myself getting annoyed when he said, "That is the truth."

I didn't want to get caught up on the smaller question now. Fine. "What mafia are you linked to?"

"None."

I knew it! He was just playing around. "Gabriel, I'm going to need more details from you."

"Ask more detailed questions."

Oh, this little— "Fine." I sat up. "Did you choose the

Wilson Bank for a reason or did you choose it because you knew a robbery was already being planned there? If it was for a particular reason, what is it? Is it connected to my family? How did you manage to pull it off? Is that detailed enough for you?"

He swallowed the food in his mouth, putting his glass down. "I did choose the Wilson Bank for a reason, and it wasn't because I knew a robbery was being planned there." He decided at that point to drink, relaxing.

"Go on."

"It's odd…the bossier you are, the more turned on I get," he whispered, placing his hand on his lips. "I'm torn between putting you in your place and seeing just how much more I can push you."

"You push, I shoot. The dead don't get turned on so it's your choice," I replied, lifting my glass to him.

The asshole lifted his glass as well, tapping it against mine. "The dead also can't speak, meaning you'd never get answers you want."

Lifting the glass to my lips, I drank all of it, taking a deep breath afterward before setting it back on the table. I lifted the napkin from my thighs before standing. "Thank you for the wine Gabriel, it's been interesting."

Just as I moved, he spoke again.

"The reason I chose the Wilson Bank is because after your Aunt Coraline gave away control of the bank to her uncle, he and his partners made it corrupt. Much of the money coming in was from corrupted officials overseas. They now take the assets of various ingrates and spread them throughout the United States and off-shore accounts. Some of those people have been targeting me for a very long time. I didn't have the power to stop them before, now I do."

The way he said it, without doubt, eagerly, like he'd been locked up and finally set free to cause chaos... It sent a shiver down my spine. I wanted to know what he was going to do with this power and how he got it.

"On top of that, Wilson Bank has been scamming average people," he went on without missing a beat. "The moment your federal government and people found out, Wilson started hiding their secret funds even deeper. I didn't have time to be chasing down accounts so I secretly tipped off two lifelong employees - who happened to be in anger management - to the fact that they were penniless. I let their anger grow and then waited for today, where I used that small window of chance to copy all hidden accounts and then delete access to them. The money will be frozen there, untouchable, even though they know it's there. And if they try to get access to it, they'll expose themselves. So, other than the fact that your aunt once upon a time owned the bank, it has nothing to do with the Callahan family and everything to do with me. Detailed enough?"

It was at this point that I relaxed. I was already sitting back down by now and smiling as I too began to eat. "So, you, like everyone else, are out for revenge?"

"No." He shook his head, looking me dead in the eye as he said, "I'm out for what is *mine* by right, Donatella."

The look in his eyes as he spoke was like a raging fire. He looked dangerous… Even to me, who grew up with men that embodied danger.

"What does that mean?"

Buzz.

Of course, his phone would pick now to go off! I thought, annoyed as he picked it up and hit answer, only to say, "You may come in."

I looked to the door as it opened and seven men entered, dressed in black suits, one tall brown-skinned man stood in front of the two rows of guards.

"You really do enjoy making my job difficult, Your Highness," the tall man said to Gabriel.

What? I laughed to myself in disbelief, looking over to the man. "Please tell me that is an insult."

He looked at me, confused, and then back at Gabriel, forcing me to look at him, too. When I did, I saw that same wicked grin he'd had at the bank, and I couldn't bring myself to speak. So, he spoke instead.

"I don't have last name… I just have title," he whispered, then loudly stated. "Sebastian…my title."

"Prince Gabriel Honoré Déllacqua III, Hereditary Prince of Monaco, the Marquis of Baux."

"Thank you, Sebastian. You all may leave, I'll be here for the night," he said, and as they took their exit, I took a deep breath, only speaking once the door closed was behind them.

"While that does explain why you're such an entitled prick," I spoke as if it all meant nothing, lifting my fork and pulling the lobster meat from its small shell. "It still doesn't explain why you are in my city and not in Monaco."

"Is it your city, or your brother's?"

"It's the Callahan City. I am a Callahan."

"But a Callahan still under another Callahan," he stated as fact. Reaching it his pocket, he put a black velvet box between us. "You said you wanted power, respect, and recognition. You do not want to bow down to anyone...not even your brother. As my wife, you can have all of that. Your brothers will have to bow to you. Since I don't have a last name, once I take the throne, you'll forever be known as Her Serene Highness Donatella Aviela Callahan, The Princess of Monaco."

He opened the box and inside sat a large, red, radiant cut diamond on a thin platinum, diamond-studded band. It was beautiful. I wanted it. I wanted all of it. However, reason stopped me from jumping in head first.

Getting to my feet slowly, smiling, I walked the small distance over to his side of the table, leaning on the edge right near his hands.

"A prince comes out of nowhere, offering me everything I want on a silver platter, that sounds too good to be true," I whispered, pulling out my gun and pointing it directly at his chest. "And if it sounds too good to be true, my father told me to shoot first and ask more questions second. Seeing as how you've already been shot, I'll skip to my question. Why me? I'm sure there is a duchess or countess or whatever somewhere in Europe that can be your princess. Me, I'm just a girl from Chicago."

"Where in the hell have you been hiding that?" he asked, gesturing to the gun, baffled and amused but not afraid. He looked over me quickly as he tried to answer his own question.

I pulled back on the hammer.

"Just a girl from Chicago," he laughed, grabbing my wrist and lifting my hand up until the barrel of the gun was at his forehead. "So then…the rest of the world knows you are a fighter," he replied, using my own words from earlier against me. "Over the last two decades Monaco has become a growing power in Europe. It is one of the very few monarchies left in the world which hold any real power. As you know, with power come enemies. Before my mother died, she looked high and low for girl who would make my position stronger, but would still be intelligent, beautiful, and charming enough to be a princess. And your mother appeared, promising you'd be everything I needed, and she was right. What use is a duchess or countess who is only well read with a pretty face? I need a woman who is not afraid to get her hands bloody."

"And mine are already stained." I grinned, putting the hammer back in place and shaking his hand off. Switching the gun to my other hand, I said, "Some fairytale this is."

"Fairytales are for the weak-minded, Donatella. We don't love each other. We don't need to love each other. What we need is more power. One marriage and we both get it. Why rule a city when you could rule a nation?"

I stretched out my left hand and lifted the fourth finger. He took the ring from the box and slid it on to my finger. It fit perfectly, the flame of the candle reflecting in the red diamond. I couldn't see myself, but I knew my smile must have been just as mischievous and depraved as his.

There was only one thing to say, and I said it proudly, "Long may we reign."

"With all prestige and unwavering might," he said, looking me in the eye as he kissed the back of my hand.

It might have been the wine. It might have been the conversation. It might have even been the sheer excitement of what was to come. It might have been all of those things all at once that made us both look at each other with lust.

Within a second his lips were on mine, his hard chest pressed up against me. One hand on my ass as the other grabbed my breast through my top. His tongue was in my mouth, brushing around mine. He was overwhelming. Every one of my senses was taken by him. We moaned into each other mouths, and I could feel him getting harder against me. He kissed me to take my breath away, to give me no space to deny him. His kiss moved from my lips, down my jaw and to my neck, sending chills down my spine.

I wanted him…but…

"Stop." I didn't just say it, I grabbed a fistful of his dirty blond hair and pulled his hair back, forcing him to him to look me in the eyes. The look of pain in his gray eyes, most likely from the bulge I could feel pressed against my stomach, told me just how he felt about being stopped. "A ring only gets you this far. I'll need a crown if you want to go any further."

Letting him go, I pushed back and stood up straighter, fixing my top as I walked to the stairs.

"How soon do you want it?" he asked and inhaled through his nose as he tried to calm down. "The bank is finished; the ring is on your finger. I need nothing else from Chicago. My father will step down from the throne on my thirtieth birthday. I need to be in Monaco by then."

"And when is your thirtieth birthday?"

"Three days."

This son of bitch.

"Give me twenty-four hours," I replied, walking back up the stairs without saying anything else.

GABRIEL

Abandon everything you've ever known and follow me.

That was what I'd just asked her to do. She was born and raised in Chicago. When she spoke about it earlier, I knew she loved this city and I worried she wouldn't be able to leave. However, once again, she proved she was the woman I needed. Many people spoke about gaining power, but very few were willing to sacrifice to get it. Both of our families stood at the top because those who came before us were willing to put anything and everything on the line to get there.

My father used to ask me, "How can you rule men if you act like one?"

The answer was simple: you can't.

Like the Pharaohs of the past, you must be half-man, half-god.

"Sebastian," I spoke into the phone in my hand, pouring the rest of the wine into my glass, "we'll be returning home in twenty-four hours."

"Understood, Your Highness."

Hanging up, I took my glass, walking out on to the balcony, unable to stop the grin on my face as I looked up at the flickering light of the Wilson Bank logo.

"Soon," I whispered and drank. Soon they'd all be on their knees crying tears of blood, begging me to spare them.

And I'll place my heels on their heads so they can drink their own tears.

TWENTY

"If you really want to do something, you'll find a way. If you don't, you'll find an excuse."

~ Jim Rohn

DONATELLA

When I came out of the bedroom the next morning, dressed in an ash-gray, off-the-shoulder, cocktail dress and butterfly Louboutin heels, there were many more people within the suite, all of whom were buzzing around Gabriel like bees. I was surprised at his appearance, his choice of clothes. Since he'd arrived in Chicago, I had only seen him in casual, laid-back clothes designed and worn for comfort. Never looking bad, but still not as stylish as he was now; dressed in a slim fit, perfectly tailored, beige suit with a light blue shirt and gray tie and brown spectators. His hair had been freshly trimmed and styled.

Hearing me walk in, he turned to face me fully, and when he did, everyone else automatically stepped back, giving us space.

"Good morning," he greeted with a smile.

"Depends on who you are," I replied, looking him over before reaching for his tie and pulling it down so I could take it off easier. Looking over to the rack of clothes, I walked over and picked out another one. He lifted his collar up for me as I put it over his shoulder.

"You aren't going to tie it for me, too?" he asked, lifting his hands up to finish tying it.

"According to my brothers, I don't know how to tie a tie well," I admitted, crossing my arms. "And seeing as you're all dressed up for some reason, I'm sure you didn't want me to try and perfect it now."

"Your Highness," the same woman with tan skin, long brown hair, and the big hazel puppy-dog eyes came forward, handing him a box.

"Who is this woman and why is she always in my line of sight?" I asked him sweetly, which made him give me a look.

"This is Amelia du Bellay, who, for all intents and purposes, is your first assistant. She'll help you get acclimated once we arrive in Monaco tomorrow," he answered, taking the box from her hand.

"Good morning, Madame," she directed at me.

"Madame? That makes me think of a brothel-keeper," I made a face and laughed. "Call me Donatella; that is, until you call me Your Highness. And when we are together like this," I pointed between myself and Gabriel, "please make sure to be three steps away."

She stared at me like deer frozen in the middle of the road. I lifted my fingers up and said "*Un. Deux. Trois.*"

Blinking, she took three steps back, and I faced Gabriel again. He was holding a red carnation brooch, the stem of the flower made of white diamonds, and a red teardrop diamond on top of second row of white diamonds. Brushing my hair to the side, he leaned in and pinned it on my dress and whispered, "Try being tad less combative."

Leaning forward, I whispered loudly, for them all to hear, "I'm giving her a chance to prove herself. If I get to Monaco tomorrow and find out there are rumors of me being *mean* or *bitchy*, I'll blame her. And let my second assistant take her place."

"Second assistant?" he asked, straightening up to putting on a tie bar with the same carnation design engraved on it and ignoring everything I'd just said. Then again, it wasn't a message for him.

"You'll meet her when we leave. I don't trust your people. I barely trust you. Of course, I won't go alone," I told him, already walking to the door. And when I moved, a few of his guards moved with me. To them I said, "Gentlemen, where I come from, guards will gladly die for the person they are protecting. They live and breathe for that person. Their wives are jealous at the degree of their devotion. I tell you this because today you will be tested. Your prince," I pointed to Gabriel, "is going to face my brothers and explain why I'm leaving them and the city we all grew up in for..." I paused as the words hit me again, "for the rest of my life. I've made up my mind and there is no going back unless they kill him, so...make sure he lives through the next twenty-four hours."

"I'm sure I handle my own," he said, walking up to me.

I laughed. "Do you have a sister?"

"One, half-sister."

"Not the same and I'm guessing you don't like her very much," I shot back quickly. "So you have idea what you are about to face, my family doesn't handle goodbyes well."

He rolled his eyes at me. "I hardly believe your brothers are so attached that they're going to lose their minds because you are getting married. Speaking of marriage... They'll be at the wedding, so it isn't a goodbye."

I looked his guards. "You all do have wills prepared, correct?"

"Sebastian," Gabriel said as if he was bored. "Let's go before she claims they breathe fire, too."

I shrugged, saying, "Foretold our fate but, by the gods' decree, all heard, and none believed the prophecy."

Gabriel looked over to me. "Homer's Iliad? You're Cassandra of Troy now?"

"You're one-eighth Greek. I was speaking in a language I thought you would understand." I winked, stepping onto the elevator once it arrived and spinning back on my heels to face him.

He grinned, shaking his head and stepping in beside me. "Forgive me, Madame, I'll heed your warning. Happy?"

I pointed the space over my head. "Not until there is something expensive and sparkly sitting right here."

He sighed deeply. "What is the life expectancy in Monaco now?"

"Ninety-one point two-one years, Sir," Sebastian replied. "It's still the highest in the world."

"Brilliant," Gabriel muttered. "Only sixty-one point

two-one years of life with a mad woman to go…"

"Not if I don't kill you earlier," I muttered back. I felt everyone around me, with the exception of Gabriel, tense. He didn't say anything more.

"Donatella," Amelia whispered right behind me in my ear.

"Drop it," Gabriel ordered coldly. She didn't say anything, just moved back as the doors opened.

I now regretted not getting further information on him last night. After reaching out to Jackal and having her confirm he was who he claimed to be, I told her to gather as much information on him as she could and to bring it to me later. She'd been unable find anything the first time around but now, after our little hostage situation, she was able to confirm who he was. I had feeling he'd done something, liked stopped doing whatever he'd been doing to block information about himself from getting out. Then I had more personal things to arrange. Without the information I needed, I was lost at the conversation and mood change. That needed to change quickly.

"Have a good day," the valets said we walked outside.

There, three black range rovers were waiting. It was only when I was inside sitting next to Gabriel did I ask.

"What was that about?"

"Right now, according to you, I needed to survive your brothers before we get into anything else," he responded, adjusting his watch. "Any idea how to do that?"

"I'm not picking sides—"

"Wrong," He cut me off. We were back to that bullshit again. "You picked my side Donatella, or at least, I thought you did. I truly hope I'm not wrong and that you aren't secretly hoping your brother's wishes top yours."

"What is that supposed to mean?" I asked, glaring at him.

"You've been here at the edge of everything you've always wanted be," he said, looking out the window as we drove through the city. "And recently, you held back. You convinced yourself it was to save your family or something of that sort…either way, you stepped away from power, not towards it. Which means you didn't really want it, or were too scared to take it. Right now, you might be in that same position, pretending you want power and pretending you are strong, but hoping your brothers will give you an out. Hoping that they'll fight hard enough to stop you, allowing you to keep pretending you're sacrificing but in reality, you're too scared to go—"

"Keep talking and I will personally skin you alive, you motherfucking asshole. Here's a tip if you want to make it the next sixty-one point two-one years. Don't speak about things you don't know; you could lose your goddamn tongue!" I sneered at him, clenching my fist at the very familiar rage building up in me.

"What don't I know?" he asked coldly, looking over to me, all traces of humor gone from his eyes. "What it must be like to contemplate killing your siblings? *Love,* there is no monarchy on Earth that did not commit fratricide. Killing our own is what we are good at. And for the record, the reason I came to you now, and not weeks earlier, was because of rumors that you were going to kill them. I had to wait for you to choose. While I'm grateful you didn't kill them, because then leaving Chicago would have no longer been an option for you, I am left to wonder if you truly want what you say you want."

Kill him. I should have fucking killed him. "I'm in the fuckin' car, aren't I?"

"Then you'll fuckin' help with your brothers, won't you," he questioned back.

I couldn't reply; I was too angry. All I could think of was beating the shit of him, of taking off my heels and gouging out his eyes!

Prince, my fucking foot.

GABRIEL

I could feel the anger rolling off her.

I knew very well if I said one more thing she'd resort to violence and may very well kill me before we could reach her brothers.

However, I need to hold her feet to the fire.

I wasn't sure where her mind was. This morning she'd asked to be alone for the most part and didn't really speak. It was like she was playing chess with herself mentally. She didn't at all act like she was shaken with the idea of leaving home. However, she wasn't that cold or dead inside. In fact, she was the opposite. She didn't care about everyone, not even most people or things. She had a list. A very small list of people and things she cared about.

Those things she loved and defended passionately. Everything else was meaningless to her.

I needed to be at the top of the list…where her brothers were.

I was using her ambition for now but in time, after she was isolated from them, I could be there. It wasn't a good thing. I knew that.

However, I didn't come this far for nothing. I was already isolated. She'd understand soon. But in this war, I needed one strong ally. It needed to be just me and her against everyone else.

They may love her.

They may miss her.

They may even think they needed her.

But the truth was that I needed her more.

BOOM!

Jumping and turning back, I watched the black ranger behind us combust into a raging inferno before swerving into oncoming traffic, the cars around it swerving, trying to avoid it.

"He wouldn't dare…" Donatella muttered under breath, almost in awe as a large black suburban, the windows tinted so dark it would be impossible to see who was inside if not for the man pointing a motherfucking rocket-propelled grenade launcher at the bloody fucking car!

"Sir, get down!" Sebastian yelled, putting together a semi-automatic machine gun as our driver swerved off the highway into a single-lane road. They spun out of control right past us, crashing into tree. The blast from explosion was so strong that the car spun around several times. I tried to reach for Dona, but she was already moving to the front of the car.

"Ma'am! GET DOWN!" Sebastian yelled at her between firing out the window.

She ignored him and focused on the man behind the wheel "Take a left—"

"There's no road—"

"Do I look like an idiot? I know that! Make one and take a left!" she snapped at him, holding on to the headrest of the driver's seat. "...left! Another one now!"

The driver jerked to the left violently and she would have fallen had I not grabbed on to her legs, holding her steady. She glanced back at me, surprised. "Glad you're doing something—"

"DONA!" I hollered, pulling her as hard as I could towards me and wrapping my arms around her, pinning her under me. No sooner had I thrown myself over her than the whole car jerked forward violently, throwing us down. The glass shattered around us, flying in every direction. However, nothing compared to the heat steaming in from the front.

I glanced down at her and she stared up at me.

"Are you alright?" I could feel myself yelling but I couldn't hear myself. The ringing in my ears just seemed to get louder and louder.

Reaching up, she touched the side of my face, and I didn't know why until she showed me her fingers…my blood on them.

"I should be asking—" was all I could read of her lips before I felt hands on me then someone pulling me out.

Damn, it's sunny. It was such random thought, but given the pain I was in, that was all I could think as I stared up at the sky through squinted eyes. Rolling on to my side and pushing myself up from the twigs and grass, I wobbled as I tried to stand up. Around me, it was like a scene out of a bad action movie. There was at least a dozen men…some of them were mine. Men who'd stood with me just moment ago. It was one of my cars that had purposely slammed into us.

Us. Glancing back towards my car, I saw her; dark brown hair covered in glass, her dressed ripped, and a few cuts, but otherwise alright. The leader, who had a large discolored birth mark under his left eye held her arm tightly with one hand and pointed a gun at me with the other. Dona, of course, wasn't afraid, the look on her face a mixture of annoyance and astonishment as she shook her head, blowing a few strands from her face. Seeing her so calm seemed to calm me down. As if this was nothing but a dream.

BANG!

I glanced over at the man, the ringing in my ears dissipating enough for me to hear him as he yelled, "Get on your knees!"

I stared at him for a long time as if I didn't hear him. Then simply said, "No."

"On your knees!" he hollered and put the gun to her temple.

She raised her eyebrow as she looked at me and for some reason I felt like I could hear her asking me, "Well?"

And I so shrugged. "*Thought this was your city*."

Her head crocked to the side and her jaw set.

Did she hear me? No, not possible but it was amusing to think.

"I'm not going to tell you again—"

She gave two short whistles, and just like that the man beside her went down. Before anyone could move, a storm of bullets rained down on top of them. A few of them still in their cars pulled out, those that tried to escape with them only ended up shot in the back.

"You were thinking something along the lines of 'Don't you run Chicago?' earlier, weren't you?" she asked, reaching down and taking off her one of a kind, brand new, now utterly useless, broken heels and stepping over the man who'd held her before coming to me. "Is my answer sufficient?"

I glanced back over at the scene of the worst action movie in history; bodies in the mud, blood on the grass, cars on fire...and realized it wasn't an action movie, but a mafia one.

"Very much so, yes," I snickered, bitterly.

"Ma'am!" I heard whom I could only assume were the men who'd fired on her command. "Are you alright?"

Ignoring them, ignoring the pain, I rushed back to the twin cars now glued at the burning engine. I pulled at the door and Sebastian's body fell right towards me.

"You better not be dead after losing this fight," I said to him, reaching up to feel his pulse. Thankfully, it was still there. Dragging his body further way from the cars, I lay him down and turned to go back for the driver but before I could, the whole car exploded, engulfing him and everything else inside. All I could do was watch it burn.

"Retaliation for the bank?" she asked from beside me.

"I wish." I did wish it were that simple. "This is retaliation for living."

"Ma'am, your car is here."

"Thank you. Before you do anything else, take care of Mr. Sebastian here," she said to them. I wanted to thank her but I didn't have the energy for any words. "Gabriel, let's go."

She didn't say anything more and didn't wait for me

to speak instead, taking my hand and leading me to the white Jeep. Once we were inside, she ripped the side of her dress and cleaned the drying blood from my ear. As her driver took us away, I confessed.

"I lied," I said, unable to look from the window. "This is just as much about revenge as it is my birth right."

"That's hardly a lie," she replied and pulling my eyes from the fire, I looked at her and she smiled genuinely for the first time since the first day I'd met her. "You never told me it wasn't about revenge, so how could it be a lie?"

Shifting to face her better, I took in her whole expression. "I understand that being from a family like yours, this might be accepted as a normal experience. However, do you not think you are being much more...congenial than normal? You almost seem at peace with this current turn of events?"

"In a way I am," she admitted, sitting back in her seat.

"Excuse me?"

"I'm sure you're upset. And most likely annoyed you lost people, though from the looks of it, not that many were loyal to begin with." She frowned and pulled her broken heel up again. "I'm very annoyed about my shoes and hair being ruined after the amount of time I took to get ready this morning. But other than that, I'm pleased with these events."

"May I ask why?"

"No one wastes a grenade launcher on someone who isn't worth it," she said as if it were the most rational thing in the world. "They came for you in broad daylight, in middle of the highway, with a fucking grenade launcher, and even then, they weren't sure so they flipped your guards... Your death was worth all that trouble. No one has even used a grenade launcher on Ethan."

Reaching over I put my hand on her head, "I can't tell if you hit your head too hard or if you're just inherently mental?"

"You offered me power," she replied, smacking my hand away and glaring at me. "But did you really have it? Yes, you do—"

"Some power this is," I snapped angrily. Did she not get it? "Donatella, if it wasn't for you, I would have died today. The only person who had power today was you. And I...I, other than hand, was weak—"

"Borrowed power," she yelled back and glared at me. "It's frustrating, isn't it? Knowing you're alive thanks to the rule of some else! It makes you wonder… *If not for them what would happen,* right? Welcome the last twenty-six years of my damn life. Today, I didn't save you. My brother did. These are his men, it's his city. Like you so proudly reminded me last night. Ethan got all of this through birth and from there only made his position stronger. You are the same, if not greater. The people who are trying to kill you are terrified of you, that's why they did this. Even with you an ocean away, with barely anyone around you, they cannot sleep at night, feeling you breathe down their necks. I don't see weakness. I would have left you out there and thrown this ring back at you if I saw weakness. I see what your enemies see, a sleeping dragon. I'm the only woman who can make sure everyone knows you're awake."

She didn't know who I was fighting.

She didn't know what was I was facing, yet she said exactly what I needed to hear…and still managed to make herself the most important part of the conversation. It was a gift, one-part vanity, one-part sapience.

"Aren't you worried you'll only be borrowing power from me then?" I asked.

"No," she replied reaching into her hair to take out a few leaves, tiny pieces of glass coming out, "the moment you put this ring on my finger, you sold half of everything you have to me."

"Just like you did when you accepted?"

She sighed, frowning at me. "Must I say it?"

"You must." I nodded eagerly.

"You're alive, in the car with me… Aren't I already sharing?"

"You just can't say the words, can you?"

"Aren't you in a mood now?" she retorted, obviously trying to change the subject, but I was having too much fun to turn back now.

"Nope." I shook my head. "My fiancée made me feel much better."

"Men are so damn fragile, always needing some part of themselves stroked," she muttered under her breath, snickering, I looked from her to the "men" driving, however they looked like they didn't even have any hair on their chests yet! The one in the passenger seat was even pressing the buttons on his video game.

"I must have hit my head much harder than I thought because I'm seeing teenagers..." I thought back to the where we'd come from. At that moment, I'd blocked out everything around me but now I couldn't remember seeing anyone who wasn't young. "Did they..."

The one driving caught my eye in the rear view and reached into his eardrum to pull out a small wireless earbud, music coming from it. "Did you say something, Sir?"

I shook my head. And he nodded, putting the earbud back in.

"When we were little, my mother would take my brother Ethan with her on these camping trips. As you can see, nothing in my family is normal. Camp for us was the place the guards went as a sort of pseudo vacation and training session," she said, but I didn't understand the connection until she went on. "When Ethan took over, he took her concept and applied it to under-privileged and orphaned teens throughout the country. Our shelter and community center helps give people part-time jobs in their community and with us. From there he finds the most...

broken ones."

"How broken?" I asked looking between the two in front.

"On the edge losing their minds broken. They may look like teens, but they've seen the worst of the world and the people in it. Ethan offers them a chance to be guards or part of our darker business. They get a safe place, shelter, food, and on top of that they are surrounded by people just like them. That makes it easier for them to form bonds with people without worrying that they're being pitied or that people think they're insane for having a much darker view of the world. In return, he simply asks for their best, and of course loyalty."

"He's growing an army," I whispered to myself, more impressed than I cared to admit.

"Not just for him," she said, looking out the window. "But for the next *Ceann na Conairte*...his future son. I hope he only has girls," she muttered the last part under her breath.

I laughed. Why did I find that cute? I didn't know. Donatella was like a box of fine chocolates. I never knew what I was getting with her. One moment she was ordering the death of multiple men, the next she was pouting like a toddler out the window.

"Sir, we're here," the boy in the front said as the gates of the mansion opened and we drove inside.

I glanced over to her and outstretched my hand.

"We aren't that close yet," she said to me, opening the door herself before the car had even stopped and stepping out gracefully.

"This is going to be a long sixty-one point two-one years." I smiled to myself as the door opened for me. O'Phelan stood at the top of the stairs staring down at both of us, and what a sight we must have been; bruised, blood, dirt, and smoke covered. A maid rushed down offering Dona a hot towel.

She didn't say word, just walked up the stairs and inside without me. Ignoring the rest of the people around us, I followed.

"ETHAN! WYATT!" Donatella yelled from the center of the entrance way. A few seconds later, the elevator at the top of the double-grand staircase opened and both men stepped out, dressed in button-down shirts and dress pants. "Good, you're down already."

"Dona, I'm sure you're aware the house is soundproofed, so you have no reason to yell," Ethan said, looking over. "What happened out—"

"I am aware. I knew you'd be close by. I thought you'd all want to be the first to congratulate me on my engagement!" she cut him off before he could even open his mouth. "There is nothing you can say. There is no changing my mind. We leave tonight."

They were both quiet. I just scratched the back of my head, not sure what the hell to do or say after this mess. However, Wyatt laughed, walking down the stairs. "Sis, you look kinda nuts, rushing in here covered dirt and yelling that...it's too early for jokes—"

Even Ethan snickered, shaking his head, which was more than odd because out of the three of them, he was always the level one. The hardest to read and the coldest. Wyatt was like his sister in that he couldn't keep his anger checked.

She turned and marched back to me. I wasn't sure what she was planning until it was too late, and her lips were on mine. She kissed me like she didn't care if we screwed right there, her tongue in my mouth and body pressed on mine. I was so shocked, I couldn't react until it was too late and she pulled away, flipping them both off.

"Nice ring," Wyatt said when we broke apart. His eyes narrowed as he replied, "You must be out of your goddamn mind if you think I'm going to let you get married to a motherfuckin' prince who can't even protect himself."

"You must be the one whose gone mad if you think I need to ask your permission" Donatella said, not even bothering to look back at him. Staying in my line of my sight, she spoke directly to me. "I didn't and I'm not going to back down, nor am I going to make an excuse. Now you finish your end while I get my things are packed and take a shower."

Somewhat shaken, I looked back up to them both and all the amusement in their eyes was gone. They weren't even looking at her… Both of them were glaring at me as if I'd committed the greatest sin in the history of mankind.

Just like that she turned, gracefully passing Wyatt who didn't even bother to look at her.

"Little sister," Ethan spoke up again and stopped, looking over to Wyatt as he came down the stairs to stand right beside her. "Don't you think you're being a little rash, especially considering the current turn of events? You're usually much more level-headed, Donatella. I'm disappointed."

She stood up straighter. "Your disappointment is your choice. I don't live to match your standard of who think I ought to be. And I do not remember hearing you ask for my opinion before you married Ivy. What was it you said again?" She snapped her fingers as though a lightbulb came on. "I'm the one getting married; how does that involve you?"

"I knew everything about her. You are flying blind," he replied.

"Blind or not, it still does not involve you, *big brother*."

"Why are you two arguing?" Wyatt asked, his voice calmer than I would have thought as he looked to me. "Because of him? He's not worth that. I don't care if he's the prince of the universe. He's not us. We've been polite despite the shit he stirs. I'm done with politeness. Get the hell out of our house or I will personally saw you in half and mail you back to your country. They may even send me a thank-you note."

He was different. More like Ethan now. The humor, the brashness he'd often displayed were gone. He honestly and whole-heartedly wanted to kill me.

The best thing about this family was knowing that by surviving them, nothing else would be as hard. "Why don't we talk—"

"Or I hurt you," Wyatt replied, reaching into his pocket and when he lifted his hands back up again he had on brass knuckles. "I like my option better."

"Fine, let's talk," Ethan said now, coming towards us and placing his hand on Wyatt's shoulder and squeezing.

"Ethan," Wyatt sneered.

"He wants to talk. Let him talk," Ethan said, looking at me directly. "My sister may be fine with being kept in the dark, but I am not. After the bank incident, your identity became much easier to find, Prince Gabriel. I'm also assuming that's why you, and most importantly, my sister was attacked this morning. Let me ask these questions once, so don't make repeat myself; who is after you and what do you need from my sister?"

"She's the dragon-whisperer," I smirked and

glanced over to her. "Can your shower wait? I prefer telling this story once."

She nodded walking back over to me.

"After you, *Your Highness,*" he said, stepping aside for me to walk. When he said Your Highness, it felt like an insult.

"Thank you," I said, outstretching my hand to Dona. She said we weren't that close, but when it came down to me or her brothers, she chose... herself. She walked forward without any of us.

TWENTY-ONE

"The road may be rough, the journey may be tough and the experience may be bitter, but they are stepping stones to our future thrones."

~ Bamigboye Olurotimi

DONATELLA

My feet hurt like hell.

My hair felt disgusting.

I just wanted to soak in hot bath for a while.

But thanks to the pack of alpha males around me, of course I couldn't do what I wanted to. And to make matters worse, when I stepped into the living room, not only was Helen there seated by the piano, but Nari, Sedric, and Darcy were all seated around the room. Darcy was lying on the couch, Sedric was on the floor in front of it, while Nari was in the corner on the phone.

The icing on this morning's shit cake was of course the news broadcast they were watching.

"Thank you, Randel. Residents here are still reeling from yesterday's attempted bank robbery at Wilson International Bank, which left one teenager paralyzed from the waist down. The police are saying the gunmen were disgruntled employees of Wilson Bank. Randel, our sources can now confirm two of those gunmen are confirmed dead and the third is in custody. We also received breaking news that one of the hostages was none other than twenty-nine-year-old, Prince Gabriel Honoré Déllacqua III, the Hereditary Prince of Monaco, next line for the Monacan throne. Eye witnesses inside say his quick thinking was the only reason why there wasn't any more casualties. And he stood in between the gunmen and Donatella Callahan, only daughter of former governor Melody Callahan and business mogul Liam Callahan. This incident, on top of this morning's accident on 93 Kingsway North, and last month's church bombing has citizens wondering if Chicago is reverting back to its violent past. CDN News have been pressing the commissioner—"

"A little turbulence in the air and everyone goes running to the commissioner," I said, turning off the television and getting all of their attention.

"That's what commissioners are for," Helen said, walking over to me and hugging me tightly. "Are you okay?"

"You mean before or after you choke me to death?" I said, trying to push her off. She was like a damn octopus.

"You're hurt!" she said, lifting my hair.

"I'm fine. If anything, *Prince Gabriel* is the wounded one," I said, and just like that she turned to him.

"We prefer him that way," Wyatt said, moving to sit on the arm of the couch, next to Darcy who sat up, and Sedric who glared at him.

"What happens if you kill a prince? Does that put you at war with the country?" Sedric asked looking up at Darcy, who shrugged, looking to Ethan.

"Can we wait till after the playoffs before we start a war?"

"Ignore them," Helen said to Gabriel, handing him glass of bourbon. Her annoying good nature disrupted the ominous atmosphere everyone else seemed so keen to put on. However, Gabriel seemed more doubtful of her than the rest of us, taking the glass but not drinking it yet.

"O'Phelan, can your people call the doctor?" Ivy said, walking in and standing beside Ethan near the door. "It seems like Wyatt's off the clock again."

"Are you going to talk or not?" Wyatt asked, ignoring the rest of us, and I'd never seen him so tense. Ethan moved to sit in a chair by the fireplace, Ivy following and then sitting beside him.

Gabriel's gray eyes looked at every one of them, before turning to me. "I'm sort of jealous… Your family loves you quite dearly."

Lifting the glass, he threw back the brown liquid, before bringing the glass back down. He stared at it. "Unfortunately, my family isn't the same. Like I told you, the nature of the monarchy is the willingness to kill your family if need be."

"Are you getting to the point?" Wyatt asked, cleaning his ear with his pinky. I was getting ready to beat the shit out of him.

"You want answers; you're going have to shut up and listen to my fucking story," Gabriel stated back, moving to the bar and pouring another glass. "Where was I?"

"Killing family," Ivy said eagerly, sitting up on the chair and eating nuts from a bowl as though this was some sort of show.

"Right," Gabriel nodded, turning back to us. "My father, Davet-Jacques Florestan Déllacqua I, was one of the most aggressive, zealous, underhanded, and resourceful sovereigns Monaco had ever seen. Under him, the country grew rapidly. He tricked, stole, and took land right under France's nose. When it came to ruling, he had no faults. It was his personal life which caused all the scandal. Like many other sovereigns, he enjoyed women—as many of them as he could have. He was not fond of the institution of marriage.

"However, under the Monacan charter, the heir to the throne can never be a bastard. Already in his late forties, pressure mounted for him to marry; to either marry one of the women who had already given him a child or marry someone new and produce an heir. At that time, two of his mistresses were pregnant. One, the youngest daughters of the then prime minster, and the other, the daughter of the palace cook. He chose the daughter of a cook out of his hatred for the prime minster, and thus my mother Adésme Benoîte became the Princess Consort and Her Serene Highness of Monaco. Six months later, both I and my half-brother, Prince Xavier, were born. I was born a day after him, but was the official heir to the throne."

"Wait, why is he a prince if he's bastard?" Sedric questioned, sitting up on the couch and scratching the side of neck.

"Because," Gabriel answered, sitting on the piano stool, "his mother and grandfather had my mother poisoned daily. The poison making her slowly lose her mind, their goal to make my father not simply divorce her, but have the pope declare the marriage was never valid to begin with."

"Thus, making you a bastard, too," I whispered, and he looked up to me, nodding.

"My father suspected her father was somehow behind it, however, Sylvia is very good at pretending to be innocent. And so, the fool believed there was no possible way someone as *kindhearted* as her could do such a thing. The doctors tried to find a cure for my mother. They changed everything; her clothes, jewels, bedding, everything was stripped and redone but she still got worse. They didn't realize the poison wasn't spread by a thing but a person...my very own father. They had poisoned the Jewel of Le Coeur Battant, which all sovereigns wear around their necks, and each time he went to see her or come around her he poisoned her. The only reason he didn't get sick was because they also gave him the antidote. On my sixth birthday, my mother threw herself off the west palace balcony. A year later my father married Sylvia, making her the new Princess Consort and

Her Serene Highness of Monaco... Thereby making her children, my step-siblings, legitimate children and in line for the throne. So even though Xavier is older than me by a day, I remain the heir, as my mother was the first wife. For him to take the throne, I must either abdicate or die."

"You said you take the throne on your thirtieth birthday? Why thirtieth? What about your father?" I asked him, not understanding.

"The poison..." He sighed, drinking. "Being poisoned and cured repeatedly eventually made him sick. When I left Monaco eleven years ago, he was unable to get out his bed and stand on his own. I've heard since then that he's barely able to lift his hands. Though it could be much worse, Sylvia has kept the palace silent. Nothing gets in or out with her knowledge. She's still loved and her father was recently reelected as prime minster once again. She plays the role of the dutiful, loving princess, kneeling by her sick husband's side. There are songs of their great love," he chuckled, unable to stop himself from laughing. "She's made the whole country think her and my father were soul-mates, that he chose the wrong woman the first time. So, people also believe Xavier was meant to be the heir... After all, he is the elder one. All of Monaco is under their control currently."

"The only problem is you," Wyatt finally spoke. "So, you are telling me you want my sister to marry you and move to a country where not even the people within it think you deserve to be their king?"

"Monaco doesn't use the kingship title—"

"Not my point," Wyatt snapped. At this rate, Ethan wasn't going to have to say anything. Apparently, Wyatt was channeling his behavior.

"My parents made a deal with you, correct?" I cut in, trying to remind my dear little brother how we'd gotten to this point. "When?"

"I don't know," he replied and paused.

"What?"

"I left Monaco under direction of my father. He told me to go to school in England. At first, I thought he was doing it to get rid me. The heir of Monaco usually studies in Monaco, so I thought he was trying to position Xavier to take over. I refused. The next morning, I found myself on a plane landing in Heathrow. The only person beside me was Sebastian. He gave me a letter from my father, telling me it would be safer for me to not return. That he was doing what he needed to do to protect me. He told me to stay hidden and when the time came, he'd send one final letter to me. That letter come thirteen months ago, and it only had sentence… *The door to sovereignty can only be opened with a single key, Donatella A. Callahan is your key.* Under it was a number for your grandmother who then told me about the arrangement. We both agreed to wait until was closer to my thirtieth birthday before I approached."

"Why Dona?" Darcy asked confused.

"Think of a family stronger than ours," Ethan asked him.

Darcy didn't answer because he couldn't.

"Now think of family other than ours with a female the right age to marriage him." Ethan asked, walking over to the bar, and Ivy slid into his chair. "Around the same time, you left Monaco, our family increased the amount of cocaine entering the country by over thirty percent, thanks to a set of laxer screening processes."

"So, they sold her for thirty?" Wyatt asked, and I was officially at the end of my rope.

"No one sold me!" I snapped at him. "No one has

that power. He gave me an option and I made my choice." Looking to Ethan, I asked, "Has he provided you with enough clarity now? As much as I am thrilled about this little history lesson, it doesn't change my mind. If anything, it only makes me more excited to meet Queen—"

"She's a princess—" Helen interrupted.

"Not the point," I said through clenched teeth, "They chose us...me because they knew that when it comes to being ruthless, no one compares to us...to me. So, I'm going to my room to make sure my things are packed and to take a long, hot bath. You all are free stay here and keep listening."

GABRIEL

When she left, we were all silent and I wished more than anything to escape with her.

"I don't care." Wyatt rose to his feet. "I don't care if you are the Prince of all of Europe and the goddamn moon, too. I don't care about whatever deal was made with my parents. I don't care about you or your sad prince life. I don't like you and I trust you even less. Find someone else.

Or, here's a thought, grow some balls and fix your damn country on your goddamn own."

He looked over to Ethan as he moved to the door. "I'm going to talk to her before she thinks she's Queen Katherine."

"Monaco doesn't have a kingship—" Ivy said to him, and he replied by slamming the door.

Leaving me with the rest of her family.

"All of you leave," Ethan declared, and they all got up just like that. Ivy stayed until he gave her a look. They exchanged nods before she got up, taking her cashews with her. True kingship, apparently.

When the door closed, I was left face to face with him, the eldest and hopefully most rational of them all.

He needed to know. "Whatever happens, I'm either leaving this house dead or with your sister."

"Kings...princes...monarchs, you all are very good at ordering the deaths of others," he said as the doors opened again and Rocky and Coco dragged in two of my former guards. Two other men put down plastic wrap because before Rocky and Coco dropped the traitors to the ground. Both looked around them as they shook their heads, trying to beg for their lives but the tape over their months muffled all their efforts. "For some reason, when it comes to killing men with your own hands, you all stumble." Ethan went on, "I do not know why. I do not care why. But it is good to know you are different than that...which is why I brought you gifts."

He reached behind his back and pulled out a gun, handing it to me.

Without blinking, I took it and shot them both through the skull. "Thank you. You shouldn't have."

"You seem eager to get this over with."

"I've came too far to let anything or anyone get in my way," I said, returning the gun. "Even if the devil himself tries to stop me, I'd burn alive fighting against him."

"That's why you are in this situation." he frowned, putting the gun away. "Don't fight the devil...be him and let others burn trying to fight you."

"Thanks for that advice. I'll stitch it on my royal pillow."

TWENTY-TWO

"Saying goodbye is a little like dying."

~ Marjane Satrapi

WYATT

When I got to her room, both doors were wide open and more than a dozen maids were already packing her things in large brown boxes. I was stunned to see how much was already done. The longer I looked, the angrier I became.

"ALL OF YOU, GET OUT!" I hollered making them jump, staring at me wide-eyed for a brief second before my words must have hit them and they left quickly. Waiting until the door was closed before looking over to her; she laid in the middle of her bed, legs crossed, staring up at the ceiling.

"I hope you aren't waiting for true love's kiss. You'll get bedsores," I muttered, walking over to her.

She smiled but didn't look over at me. "I'm a princess. I'm sure there is some special magic for that. When do you think I get the power to talk to birds?"

"You're not a princess," I replied, laying down next to her and staring up at the spinning ceiling fan that she had for no other reason than to watch it spin.

"What am I then?" she asked softly.

I didn't have to think. "My sister."

"I'll still be your sister even in—"

"You're a hypocrite." I didn't want to hear it. "For five years you told me to come home. To come back to Chicago. That Chicago was our home. That nowhere on earth will ever feel like home except Chicago. I'm finally back, and now you're planning on moving not even to another state but to another damn country!" I bit my tongue, breathing in and trying to keep calm.

"I'm a hypocrite," she replied.

"Don't agree with me. Just don't be a hypocrite," I whispered back. "Don't—"

"Don't do this to me, Wyatt," she replied. When I finally looked from the fan over to her, her face was calm and emotionless, but her eyes... Tears slipped down, rolling down the side of her face and neck.

"Dona—"

With one hand, she took mine and with the other she brushed the side of her face. "I love you, Wyatt. I love this city. I'm happy you're home. I'm happy you came back. But I can't stay. Gabriel said part of me might be hoping you'll stop me...and he's right."

"Then let me stop you," I begged, squeezing her

hand tightly.

Finally, she turned to look at me, her green eyes coated with tears she wouldn't let fall. "The part of me hoping you'll stop me is smaller than the part of me that will hate you for making me stay."

"In time, you'll get over—"

"I'm a dying wolf-dog here, Wyatt," she frowned. "I'm dying. I didn't even realize it. Until he said it."

"He's just trying to get in your head."

"Maybe, but he's not wrong," she said, smiling. It had to be the saddest smile I'd ever seen. "Time will only make this worse. We aren't kids anymore, Wyatt. Ethan's married. He was going to be father. Soon, he will be. And one day you will be, too. You'll get married and have a family, and what about me? If you make me stay, if you beg me to stay, you're just forcing me to watch as I become less and less important to all of you."

"Dona, that's impossible." I turned over, feeling my eyes burn as I stared at her. Reaching over, I put my hand on her head. "You're my sister. My twin. No one can—"

"You don't know that because you've never loved anyone that deeply," she reached up, taking my hand off her face. "And I want you to love like that. I want you to love like Dad did."

"What about you? You don't love him—"

"If I can't learn to love him... I won't love anyone else," she said seriously. "You know how I am. It takes a special type of person to be willing be with me. And an even more special person for me to want to be with them, with all of my heart. Gabriel... He's the closet I've come."

"Because he comes with a crown and country," I muttered, bitterly.

"Exactly." She nodded. "He comes with power and influence. I've sucked up all the power there is for me to take in Chicago. I've grown as much as I can here. So, it's either I get relegated to the background behind you and Ethan, or I became center focus in another painting. Wyatt, this is how we survive. Deep down, we are nothing but rational animals. And I know that if I stay, I'll butt heads with Ethan because I need to rule in my own sphere. This marriage is how we will all survive as a family."

I hated how rational she was being.

I couldn't work with her when she was rational. I couldn't fight.

"You aren't the type of person who'd want to be stuck in some damn palace, hosting charity balls and…whatever other monotonous thing princesses do. He's going to parade you around like some damn trophy and you'll go insane from boredom. Or insane from all the stuffy rules they try to make you follow."

She looked away from me and back at her fan. "Your lack of faith in me hurts, little brother."

"Good. Stay," I said selfishly.

She snickered and then took a deep breath. "Since Ethan got married, I kept feeling this tightness in my chest and didn't realize what it was. Ivy kept taking my place within the family. And I kept feeling so…erased. I woke up one morning thinking, '*So this is what dying feels like… How painful.*'"

I swallowed the lump in my throat. She wasn't giving me any space here. Any room to change her mind. She just kept digging my grave.

"I kept wondering if this is how mom felt," she whispered.

"What?"

"Mom wasn't from Chicago. She didn't know Dad.

She uprooted herself and everything she was comfortable with and married for more power...just like this. Just like me. I never thought about it. But now that it's me...I keep wondering if she felt this way. Sure, of what she needed to do, but a small part of her still uncertain, sad, and afraid. She must have, right? So that means, when they chose Gabriel, she must have been certain... That this moment of sadness, fear and uncertainty would be worth it in end. All I need to be is strong enough to take the same step. I trust Mom, Wyatt. I trust her, so I'm going to take this step...even if you hate me for it. But please don't hate me."

I'd lost.

Rolling back over I blinked the tears away from my eyes. But they came kept coming. Goddamn it!

"Thank you," she whispered, rolling over and hugging me.

Looking away, I found the strength to say, "You better not let them change you or talk down to you. You're just as— you're better than them. The moment you say the word, we can tear the whole damn country apart. *You're a motherfucking Callahan.* There was a crown on your head before them. The one they'll give you will be visible to the naked eye and they can take that back, but you'll never lose the one you were born with."

She snickered and hugged me tighter. "First of all, in what twisted world would I *ever* let anyone, royalty or not, change me? Secondly little brother, I'm going to be happy, I promise. So, promise me you will, too…and you'll look after Ethan."

"I'm the younger one. He should look after me," I muttered, and she punched my side. "Ah! Dona!"

"He does look after you!"

"Whose side are you on? Weren't you just a week ago thinking of killing him!" I pushed her away, trying to get up, but she grabbed a pillow and smacked me on the side of my head.

"I have no idea what you are talking about? I've always been a kind hearted, good natured, team player. How could you ever excuse me of—"

Taking one of the other pillows I smacked back.

She stared at be wide eyed, shocked…appalled even and I grinned saying; "A kind hearted, good natured, person wouldn't hit me back."

Her green eyes narrowed back on me as she said; "I

also said team player and right now you aren't on my team!"

She hit me so hard the pillow broke open, and of course Dona's pillows would be made of goose feathers, and of course they would fly everywhere. She sat up on to her knees to look at me for quick second before pointing and laughing like a damn six-year-old. Taking another pillow, I smacked her on the side of her face so hard, the pillow burst open and her hair whipped around. Smiling, I pointed back at her, "Should I laugh maniacally or just grin sheepishly?"

"Off with your head!" she screamed, grabbing a pillow and rushing after me.

ETHAN

This wasn't supposed to be my position.

My father was supposed to have the honor of some great terrifying speech for whoever came to marry Dona. I didn't even have time to get my uncles to do it. So unfortunately, it fell on my shoulders. We stood in living room, right by the unlit fireplace, under the family portrait.

"What are you having?" I asked him as I moved to the bar in the corner.

"It's a little early—"

"You're marrying my only sister, without warning. Without asking, after being disrespectful and willfully irritating. Yet here I am, offering you a drink. Are you refusing that drink?" I asked him as I poured myself a brandy.

"Brandy is good," he replied, holding out his hand. I handed him a glass before moving to sit in the chair as he took the other one.

Sitting in silence, I drank staring up at the portrait, realizing it was going to change. Not because of him… But because of me. It was only my father, my mother, and their children in that image. Soon, it would need to change to me, Ivy, and our children. And on and on it would go. I never thought about it before. It never occurred to me that I'd needed to change until now, that the structure of my family would change. Dona sat here often… I wondered if that was what she was seeing.

I wasn't sure how long we sat quietly. I didn't mind the silence, but apparently, he couldn't take it anymore.

"Despite everything else, I will take care of her," he said sternly, breaking my concentration. I looked over to him, somewhat surprised by his statement.

"Of course, you will," I replied and he seemed surprised by mine. "You don't have a choice. Your life, your country, anything else you care about depends on how well you treat her. I would have thought you weighed all the risks before making it known that you wanted to marry the daughter and sister of the most power mafia in the history of the world."

"Hubris seems to be a family trait," he snickered, lifting his glass to me before drinking.

"One your family must also share." I glanced up at the painting. "Of all my family members, I'm least eloquent. I don't have a speech or wisdom to share with you... And even if I did, I'd rather not speak with you at all. The sight of you upsets me. You marrying my sister upsets me and that has nothing to do with who you are... But who my sister is to me."

I paused, drinking and he didn't say word, thankfully.

"Do you have sister?" I asked him.

"Half-sister but apparently she doesn't count." He grinned. I didn't find anything funny in the least.

"Then you don't understand what we are feeling," I spoke for Wyatt, too because I knew he'd be broken even more so by this.

He shook his head. "In all honestly, no. I understand she won't be in the city. But it's not as if she's disappearing for all time. It's not like she won't be able to call or video chat—"

"She has always been here," I cut him off before anymore stupidity came from him and drove me to shatter my glass over his head. "In the middle of Wyatt and I…is Donatella. She has always been our referee, our judge, our support, in everything big or small. To me she has been my biggest threat but also my greatest ally. Because she has always been strong I've had to be strong. She pushes us even when we do not want to be pushed…or at least she did. Now she's going to be on the other side of the world dealing with whatever mess I'm sure you're needing help to fix. She isn't going to be there for us. But you. For the first time, we'll be on the sidelines, and the sidelines are not a fun place to be when you've always been center stage."

That's why she needs to go. He was doing to me what Ivy had done to her. I didn't understand it then but now did.

Damn it.

"I don't want to talk for much longer. Just know, whatever happens in my life, in Wyatt's life, we will always stop whatever we are doing to be at her side if she calls. Hurt her in any shape, in any form or way... And even I do not know how *far* I will go and how *depraved* I will be when I get my hands on you. I tried. I tried to think about what I would do to the man who hurt my baby sister and all I see is red. Not anger red. Not blood red. But fire red. As if I know, somewhere in the back of my mind, whatever I would do, would be so horrific, atrocious, and unspeakable it would damn me to hell for eternity. All I can see, when I think of Donatella being hurt by you in any way, are those red flames." Finishing my drink, I stood up and he stayed sitting. "That's all I wanted tell you."

Turning from him and heading towards the door when he had the balls to say, "We haven't begun negotiations."

"Excuse me?" I turned back to him.

He rose from his chair confidently, not at all what I was expecting from him and yet I was not surprised by it. He was foolishly confident even when he didn't have the upper-hand. It must have been a mental condition princes were born with.

"You were the one who said that I'm marrying the daughter and sister of the most powerful mafia in history of the world, did you not?" he smirked, finishing off his drink. I didn't reply even as he stepped in front me. "Your sister is marrying the crown prince of a rising economic giant; a nation of thirty-seven million, bordering four other nations and the Mediterranean Sea. You've done an excellent job of being the dutiful, protective brother, now I'd like to hear from the Don of that almighty mafia."

"They're one and the same. So, I'd suggest you choose your next words carefully," I said, looking him in the eye. "I don't negotiate, I simply take."

"What confidence," he replied, the amusement in his face gone, "considering that's how I took your sister."

I felt my hand twitch. I could see it almost in slow motion, how easily it would be to pull out my knife and slit his neck right open. Reason won over instinct, and I replied with words, not blood, saying, "Big words for a prince who only an hour ago was pleading for his life."

"You're mistaken," he glared at me. "I don't plead for my life. My life is guaranteed. I'll explain, seeing as you've never been in this position before."

"What that position is that?"

"Weakness."

I snickered at that. "You're right, I don't know that position, nor will I ever."

"Donatella." He lifted his right hand out and then his left as if it were a scale. "Your family's image."

A year. That's how long Donatella was going to put up with this bastard before putting a bullet threw his skull while he slept.

"As the head of the Callahan family, our marriage makes you even look stronger. For the first time in your history, people won't whisper about how powerful you are, or what your connections might be. They will know your family extends into royalty. By connection to me you all now have permanence in history. They will talk of you all as they talk of the Medici family."

"Is there a point or do you simply wish to see how long I can maintain my composure?" I asked.

"With such a legacy, don't you think I should get something in return?"

"My sister isn't enough?" Now he was insulting us.

"If I go down, your sister goes down too," he frowned. "And with her, so do the years of persevered, untouchable influence and power your family has created. With great families, image is everything, isn't? How does the image of my death or defeat for the throne look to you?"

"I thought your life was guaranteed?"

"You all are that guarantee." He grinned.

Weakness... Donatella on one had. Our family's image on the other. I now understood what he meant. However, he didn't understand who I was.

"You do realize she isn't married to you yet. I've become very well-equipped in cleaning up messes. Your death will be a hassle, but can be cleaned up as well." I laughed because it was funny and he just grinned.

"You do realize now that she's seen me and what I can offer, should she lose that, she'll never get another chance to have what she wants. At least not without coming for your throne again. Her ambition is dangerous like that. So, you're free to kill me now, knowing that it will most likely hurt your precious sister in the future."

A year? I gave him a year? Dona is going to kill this motherfucker within six months if not less.

"What I want is simple, and nothing you wouldn't want to do anyway," he spoke again, his shoulder relaxed, as were his eyes. "I need men. I need them to be from Monaco. What happened today can never happen again, anywhere, for any reason. And I do not mean men loyal to you or men who can trade their loyalty to the highest bidder. Their first and only priority should always be your sister and I."

For a brief moment I wondered what type of man I would be if I'd been born into his life, and I wasn't sure if I found it reassuring or disturbing that I'd be somewhat like him. He was thinking and becoming the devil he needed to be… No, he already was that dark-hearted, he just needed the army to do follow through. I couldn't fault him for that. Not when I'd had a ready-made one when I'd come into power.

I briefly thanked God that my father hadn't been as much of a fool as his had but then again, I should also have thanked my mother for not being as weak as his.

The strength of their marriage was what saved me from the chaotic irrational soap-opera that was his life.

"You'll have your men," I replied, turning as I realized I did have a speech for him. "Gabriel, men like you and I aren't supposed to be just men. We're leaders. We're rulers in two different spheres but still rulers, nonetheless. The women we marry will feel pain and will get hurt, yes. But the pain I'm speaking of, the harms I am warning against, aren't small. It is not forgetting an anniversary or even fighting with one another. The harms I am warning you against...are the types kings and princes seem so prone to... My sister can and will handle anything you throw at her, but if you, Gabriel, make her your wife and then decide you want a mistress, too, I'll kill you.

"If you allow her be embarrassed or disgraced, I will kill you. She ends up gravely injured because of fire directed at you, I will kill you. Your life is not guaranteed. My sister is not your insurance. Do not test me and this vast benevolence that I am bestowing on you. Because if I even hear whispers of her being treated like your mother was... You'll see those flames I was talking about earlier. Now excuse me, Your Highness, I have an international drug empire to run."

I said nothing more and didn't wait for him to say anything either, not that he should have had anything to say. Ignoring and walking past the men taking out her boxes, I headed towards my study, hoping for peace to outrun the reality around me. But my mind wouldn't stop.

I understood everything.

Why she was going to leave.

Why she wanted to leave.

Why my parents chose him.

Even why he needed her.

And yet, despite it all... I couldn't imagine coming home and not seeing her. I couldn't imagine Chicago without Dona...without my baby sister.

I didn't want to think about either but it was going to happen.

"You alright?" Ivy asked when I entered.

Leaning against the door, I shook my head. "Give me one good reason to stop him from taking her."

"If you couldn't think of one, I doubt I can."

Right. That was the problem. Because I knew and understood everything, I knew I didn't have a reason to force Dona to stay.

"So, I have to accept this?" Accepting something I didn't want was an odd feeling...

"It's okay to say it hurts to lose her," she said, hugging me.

And I looked down at her as she held on to me. Realizing only then that the odd feeling was...pain. Not physical, but emotional.

I hugged her back. I nodded slowly, admitting it to only her, "It hurts."

Saying goodbye to my sister hurts.

TWENTY-THREE

"I, with a deeper instinct,
choose a man who compels my strength,
who makes enormous demands on me,
who does not doubt my courage or my toughness,
who does not believe me naïve or innocent,
who has the courage to treat me like a woman."
~ Anaïs Nin

DONATELLA

Lifting the slim crystal vial on my dresser and dabbing the perfume behind my ear and my wrist, I rubbed them together before putting the vial back. I looked back at my own reflection, fixing the curl of my hair. If beauty was a woman's armor, I had more than enough to slay a dragon. That's what I was doing. Slipping into my beige heels before rising from the bench in front of my vanity, touching the bare skin over my breast, I smirked. I wasn't sure why my heart was beating as fast as it was, however I could feel the humming in my chest, making my blood warm…all of me warm. Excitement. It was the feeling I got when I when I was excited and yet this shouldn't have excited me as much as it was.

Stepping back and walking towards the door, the gray satin robe-style dress I was wearing with slits up both thighs and a plunging neckline flowed with each step I took. I glanced over my shoulder at the room of boxes still waiting to be taken away before closing the door behind me. The walk from my room to Gabriel's wasn't far, and I didn't even bother knocking, instead, stepping inside. A voice came from the bathroom.

"Rest for now, Sebastian, we can leave early tomorrow morning," I heard him say; I noticed a beat-up leather notebook on the dresser closest to the balcony, I walked forward and lifted it up carefully. "It's fine. She's still saying goodbye to her family, I'd rather not rush her. I still have time." He went on, followed by the sound of the faucet, and I didn't bother to listen more than that. I looked to his journal, captivated by his drawings.

The first set were just random people on the streets.

A few birds and other animals.

But in between that there many drawing of a woman who looked very much like him. They had the same eyes and I just knew she must have been his mother. His drawings were in color, so detailed. Almost every other page of the first half of the book was of her until...

Until it got to me.

Nothing else, just me.

Me, angry. Me, laughing. Me, looking out the window, swimming and me...naked. He seemed to have spent plenty of time imagining my breast size, waist, and hips as they were slightly different in each drawing.

"Who knew you were such an artist?" I said when I heard the bathroom door open.

"Almost everyone is an artist in Europe… The only difference is if they are known or not." His steady voice replied behind me, he didn't seem startled or even thrown by me being there.

Since his arrival, that's all he had done to me; he'd startled me, thrown me off my balance. He'd upset, confused, conflicted, doubtful, and excited me. Like a tornado, he came in and ripped everything out of place, became the focus of my and everyone else's attention. The power shift was so swift, I barely had time to grasp it, to grasp that I was being sucked in and there was no saving me because part of me wanted to be uprooted.

"Donatella," he whispered, standing directly behind me now, his voice sending a shiver down my spine. He reached around me and tried to take the notebook from my hands, but I pushed his hand away. "Did you need something?"

"We can't leave tonight," I said, flipping to another page. "I want to see my parent's grave with my brothers in the morning. I came to tell you that. But it seems you aren't ready to leave yet, either."

"I wanted to give Sebastian at least one night of rest before we flew out," he answered.

"You really care about him."

"He's loyal. I honor loyalty. Doesn't everyone?" he asked.

I didn't reply, merely flipping through his book. He sighed softly and took a step back from me. It was only then that I turned around and saw the bandages on his bare back and the one over his arm. He was only wearing his trousers. He didn't complain or even act as if he were hurt. He simply kept it in.

"Gabriel," I called out to him and he turned partly, his eyes immediately looking down my body slowly.

"Do not do this to me now," he snapped stepping forward, pinning me between himself and the desk, his gray eyes filled with lust. "I've spent the day fighting for my life. First with the men this morning, then with your family. Verbally sparring with your brothers is exhausting, as you already know. I do not have the energy to pretend I'm not turned on by you and this display of...whatever it is you are seeking to do. I'm on the edge of sanity, Donatella; do not push me unless you're willing to fall alongside me."

Reaching down to undo the tie of my dress and allowing it fall down around my feet, I said, "I have a beauty mark on my left breast and a crescent-shaped scar on my right thigh, so next time you draw me properly—Ah!"

I gasped, my mouth dropping open as he, without shame, cupped my breast, his hands so cold it made me shiver. Leaning over, he licked my nipple. His tongue running circles over and around it before he sucked on to me. His right hand dipped between my thighs, stroking my pussy. Stunned, I couldn't do anything but let him grope and suck on me, grasping on to his shoulders and moaning loudly as he slipped his middle finger into me…and then another one.

"Ahh!" I couldn't form words anymore. I just rocked up and down on his hand. Standing straighter and licking his lips, he pumped faster, staring down at me like he wanted to tear me apart in the best sort of ways.

"What happened to needing a crown?" he smirked as my eye twitched, and I held on to his arm. He looked too fucking smug.

Reaching into his pants, I grabbed his cock, trying to ignore how big it was and how hard it throbbed in my hand. As I slowly ran my finger over the tip of him, my fingers coated with a layer of his arousal. "There already is a crown on my head. Can't you see it? There's no turning back now, Gabriel. The moment I stepped in here, the second you touched me, you sealed your fate indefinitely."

Just like me, his mouth parted as he tried to breathe through the pleasure. Leaning in again, his lips were on mine, his tongue in my mouth and mine in his. Both of our tongues brushing against and over the other's. Wanting more, leaning into him, my breasts bouncing on his bare chest, I rode his fingers as I stroked the length of his cock. "Now be a good husband and make me moan."

Without a second to waste he had us both on the floor.

"Do you want to moan like wife or a whore?" He pulled his fingers out of me only to bring them to my lips. Leaning forward, I licked.

"Both," I answered.

His nose flared and the grin spread on his lips as he grabbed my thighs, forcing me on to my back and pulling me forward. He lifted my leg on to his, spreading me wide before sucking on me.

"YES!" I cried out, grabbing on to his hair and rocking against his mouth. My whole body shivered as his tongue entered me. My nipples were so hard, my breasts bouncing so much that I had to grab on to them. My eyes rolled back as I pinched my hard nipples, the pain and the pleasure. It felt so good I could feel the pressure in my stomach rising.

"Cum for me," I heard him demand and I wanted to, but the way he commanded me made me want to fight back.

Not yet.

It felt as if I was at his mercy. I didn't want that. I want him to feel this… I wanted him to be immobilized by my mouth. Kicking my other leg on to his shoulder, with all the force I could muster, I pushed back.

"Urgh…" He groaned in pain but only brief as I got on top of him. Staring down at him, I smiled and kissed his lips before turning around so my ass and pussy were in his face. I stuck out my tongue, licking from the tip of him all the down to his balls. Feeling him moan against me only made me shiver more.

My whole body felt like it was being electrified. I felt wild, bolder. I craved him, wanted all of him in my mouth.

"Mhm!" I heard him moan again on my pussy.

It was music to my ears as I sucked harder, my head going up and down his as his fingers sped up in me.

"OH!" I cried feeling my toes curl as I came…only a few seconds before he did. I drank all of him like he did me.

Rolling on to my back and closing my eyes, I wiped the corner of my mouth, "Not bad, Your Highness."

He didn't say anything and I thought he may have been spent, when all of sudden I felt his strong hands on me, lifting me off the floor. Opening my eyes, I looked up to see his jaw tensed…a moment later, I felt the soft sheets of his bed under me.

"Not bad? You say that like we're finished," he said. He stripped out of boxer briefs, his cock still hard, still twitching for me.

My eyebrows raised and with a smile on my face I said, "Forgive me, I forgot I wasn't dealing with just any mere man."

"After tonight, princess, you'll never forget again,"

he said, climbing on to the bed.

GABRIEL

I knew she was dangerous but I didn't think she'd be this hazardous to my life. There was so much I still wanted to do, no, *needed* to do in my life. And yet at this very moment, as I thrust my hard cock deeper into her wet pussy and heard the noises her body made, I knew I could die happily like this.

"Harder!" she cried out as sweat rolled down my face and dripped onto her back.

"Please...please..." she begged and it was beautiful. She was...perfect. Her body, her voice, the look in her eye, everything.

"Cum with me," I said, hunching over her and grabbing on to her breasts. They bounced from the force. "Come on."

"Ohh!" she cried out and bit the side of her shoulder to keep from crying out more as I came inside her. We stayed like that a few seconds before I pulled out and collapsed beside her. Both of our chests rising and falling.

"Jesus Christ," I laughed, reaching up to rub my eyes. I'd fucked her so hard, I was seeing spots. I'd lost count how many times we'd done it. And what made it was worse, I still wanted her. It was like she was a drug; the more I had her, the more I wanted. If this was just the first night, how was I going to make it?

She moved to rest on top of me and feeling her breast on my chest, I wanted to cry out in frustration, at being too tired to have her again.

"Give me ten minutes," I said, between breaths.

"What are you made of?" she asked, and I opened my eyes to see her smiling down at me, her dark hair a beautiful wild mess on her head, a few strands even sticking to her face. "We've fucked four different ways already."

I frowned. "Only four? I must be out of shape."

She laughed softly, and I smiled at that, reaching up and brushing her hair off her face.

"Why are you out of shape? Not enough women in Europe?" she asked.

"Out of respect for my future princess, I've been out practice for the last ten months," I said.

"I haven't," she said without shame.

I frowned at that. "Are you trying to make me jealous?"

"No, just telling you the truth," she said, drumming her fingers on my chest. "I can't promise much more than that."

"What?"

"I told you: I'm temperamental, prone to violence, and hostile to authority," she smiled down at me. "I've never been able to see myself as a wife to anyone. I've never liked anyone to that extent. I always figured I'd marry for power, if I married at all… When that time came I'd tell my future-husband…you, not to expect too much from me. I'm loyal to those who are loyal to me. I will respect you if you respect me. And I'll always be honest if you are honest with me."

"And if I love you?" I asked, bringing my thumb over her lips. "If I love you, will you love me?"

She stared at me for what felt like forever, but I did not mind because it gave me an excuse to shamelessly look into her beautiful green eyes.

"Yes."

I was shocked she had admitted that. "Yes?"

"Yes," she repeated, never looking away for me. "If you truly love me, respect me, and are loyal to me, in time, I will love you back."

She really was honest. So honest, I wasn't sure what to say.

"You weren't expecting that answer?" she asked, rolling off me and lying beside me. "But loving people is easy even though it may not seem like it. But if two people are trapped on an island with only each other to rely on, they will fall in love. Attraction is important. But love… That comes from two people forming a bond. Knowing that one other person is always in your corner. Will always stand by you. Fight with you. Love is what happens when you are fully and brazenly able to trust and depend on another person."

I stared at her. No, I stared at her lips, beyond amazed by the words coming out of them.

"What? You're shocked, I think. Why?" She snickered. "Most people think because I'm so…"

"Bitchy?" I offered, as she couldn't seem to find the right word.

"Crazy coldhearted," she corrected, kicking me. I laughed. "They think I don't believe in love or loving people."

"I'm not one of those people," I told her, this time moving and lying on top of her. "You're a lot of things, Donatella, but incapable of love is not one of them. How else could you write such passionate novels? I was merely shocked that you'd admit all of that to me."

"You read my novels?" she asked, her eyes wide. I didn't know why that shocked her so much.

"How can anyone not know you are Odette Odile?" I asked, grinning. The name was perfect for her.

"You only know because of my grandmother, don't you?" She frowned. "She really is a loose cannon now, isn't she?"

"Don't be too hard on her. I quite like your grandmother," I replied.

"Someone is already getting comfortable telling me what to do."

"Here we go." I groaned. Most days she was the dangerous and seductive black swan, but as she laid under me, naked, calm, speaking honestly of herself and the future with the smallest and rarest of smiles on her face, I saw all the beauty and gentleness of the white swan. She was both. “You’re like a pillar of ice on fire,” I said to keep her calm.

“What?”

I nodded. “Everything I heard about you before coming and everything I’ve seen of you since I’ve been here, tells me you are unexplainable. You are two opposite things at once. You are... You are a crazy, coldhearted person, but you aren’t that way all of the time. Sometimes you’re sweet and cute. You just can’t show that part of yourself because of your family so you write it. The heroines of your books are all different versions of the you you’re unable to freely show. I enjoyed reading your work...”

“You’re being very sappy—”

“All of them but the last book. That one was crap,” I cut her off to finish and just like that I saw the fire light up her eyes.

She pushed me off her, and got up. “I’m going to shower, don’t follow me.”

“But shower sex is the best kind.” I pouted,

watching her ass as she got up to leave, with a stupid grin on my face.

"Once I come back we'll go over what happens next," she replied.

"Next?"

"What happens when we get to Monaco? What have you planned for your family? When will the wedding be? Did you really think I came here just to fuck you?" she asked from the bathroom door.

"Yes."

SLAM.

Smiling to myself, I lay back and closed my eyes, trying to relax, but instead her words replayed on a loop in my mind.

"Love is what happens when you are fully and brazenly able to trust and depend on another person."

When I asked her if she'd be able to love me if I loved her, I wasn't expecting any sort of serious answer... It was more so a gentle joke. I knew now I couldn't joke about things like that that with her. I said those words not even sure if I'd ever love her. Loyalty yes, faithful yes, kind and caring to what she needed, yes. But love was not my strong suit. Sex I could do, happily, along with flirting, however love in the way she spoke of it... The way I should have thought of it, that intimacy between a husband and wife wasn't one of my strong suits. She was much more passionate than I'd actually realized.

I wanted her to *"fully and brazenly"* trust and depend on me. She wouldn't until I did ...but how could I when I kept lying to her face?

"Gabriel?" I heard her voice and the bed shifted but I didn't open my eyes. She was screwing with my mind as much as she was screwing with my body. I feared if I spoke more, I'd ruin everything before we even started.

"So much for being superhuman," she muttered and I wished I could see the facial expression that went along with the annoyance in her voice.

Instead I felt the sheets cover me, then the heat of her body beside me. I waited a few minutes, feeling her relax before shifting onto my side, my arm draped over her.

Only then did I open my eyes, allowing myself to see the side of her face... She looked even more beautiful sleeping like this.

Shit. I'm going to fall hard for her.

I might have already been falling.

Glancing up at the camera in the corner of the room, I glared, holding her tighter, before closing my eyes again. I swore to never tell her the truth of my past but to always tell her the truth of present and future.

It was my only option.

TWENTY-FOUR

"Some are born great,

some achieve greatness,

and some have greatness thrust upon them."

~ William Shakespeare

DONATELLA- 8 YEARS OLD

"Do you feel better now, Super Dad?"

"Do not start with me, Mel; I'm doing all I can not to—"

"NOT TO WHAT?"

My eyes snapped open and I rolled over in my bed…my bed?

"Keep your voice down, she's sleeping!" Daddy yelled.

Rubbing my eyes, I sat up and looked over to Wyatt's bed, but he wasn't there.

"You do this all the time, Liam! You are always undermining me!"

"I apologize for not letting you lock our daughter—"

"She was one room over, Liam!"

"She was crying!"

"SO WHAT?"

"I will not tell you again. Lower your fucking voice, Melody!"

"DO NOT BARK ORDERS AT ME!"

Walking to their door, I looked through the tiny opening just as my mom's hand made a fist. She stood on the other side, her whole body shaking.

"You are always hard on her. She'll grow up thinking you hate her. Worse, she might even hate you! For fuck's sake, Mel, she doesn't need to be —"

"Strong? Independent? A Callahan?" she asked, looking up at him.

"You know what I mean—"

"Yes. I do. She's a *girl*. She's your little princess. When she cries, it breaks your big soft heart. Fine! I won't bother with her. You can keep her locked away, feed her ice-cream and cake all day. When she turns grows up, she'll be the type of woman who gets used then thrown away; she'll be like Natasha."

"Watch your mouth!"

"Or what, it might say too much of the truth?"

"Goddamn it, Mel!" Daddy raised his hands and balled his fists, but Mommy just crossed her arms like she did when she was waiting for us to get ready and we were late. "She's eight; she's already doing self-defense, you have her swimming before the sun is up, running before the sun goes down. Let her breathe! Let her enjoy something!"

"There you go again! Making it seem as if I don't want her to enjoy anything in life! As if I'm torturing her for the fun of it. As if I don't love my own daughter! Fuck you!"

"When you push her like this—"

"I *was* her!" Mommy yelled, pushing Daddy away when he came close to her. "I hated my father for pushing me, too. I was miserable as a kid. I don't even remember ever being a kid—"

"Exactly! Why would you—"

"Because if not for my father, I would be dead!" she screamed. "Dona was born a Callahan and a Giovanni. That's two strikes against her. She was born a female; three strikes! She doesn't get any more, Liam. That's it. Being born our child and a female, she gets the short end of the stick. I know this. The only gift I can give her is fearlessness. So, no matter what, she knows she has the ability to protect herself."

Daddy put his hands on his face and took a deep breath, "I understand, baby, I do. But you can't make her super-girl in one day."

"I can't teach her anything without someone complaining!"

"What does locking her in an art gallery teach her?"

"Ugh!" Mommy moved like she wanted to strangle him but just took a deep breath, too. "I wanted to teach her to think beyond what she sees in front of her! I asked her how many people were in the painting and she said seven. I wanted her to realize there were eight! The person who made it. The person who saw the big picture. The creator of it! I wanted her to understand the most important person is the one who creates situations! I want her to know she can create the world she wants for herself and not just accept whatever it is she's been given! And before you go on about, *why I didn't explain that to her,* I would have but she began to whine, yell, pout, and stomp her feet like a spoiled brat. Then you came along and rewarded her with bloody ice-cream! If Ethan or Wyatt had acted like that, would you have done the same?!"

"I—"

"No, you fucking wouldn't!"

"Can you just let me speak, goddamn it?!"

"No, because you say stupid shit that annoys me when you open your bloody Irish mouth! If all she becomes is pretty and useless, it's on you, Liam!" She grabbed the door handle and her eyes snapped to mine. I wanted to run away but I couldn't move. I was stuck there. "There she is; go buy her a pony, Super Dad."

SLAM.

"Donatella, come here."

I didn't want to, but I opened the door and stepped into their room. He sat on the bench in front of his bed so I had to walk around to get to him. It was weird because he didn't look at me once, he just kept looking at the carpet.

"Daddy?"

"Sit," he told me and I moved to sit next to him. He blocked me and pointed to the spot on the ground in front of him. Sitting at his feet on the floor, I crossed my legs and looked up at him. He stared and stared, and so I stared back, opening my eyes wide to make sure I didn't lose.

"Hey!" I yelled when he faked throwing something at me and made me blink. "That's cheating!"

"That's life," he laughed. "Besides, that's what you get for just staring at me all bug-eyed."

"You weren't saying anything."

"I was thinking. Now, hush." He pointed and I crossed my arms but kept my mouth closed. "Your mom said you were acting spoiled."

I opened my mouth to say something but he gave me The Look so I didn't.

"Donatella, do you know why I love your mother?"

I looked to make sure I could speak before saying, "You always change the answer!"

"No." He smiled. I loved when Daddy smiled like that, his eyes looked like they were laughing, too. "I just find new reasons each time."

I took a deep breath, "What's the reason this time?"

"Because she is so selfishly in love with herself, she never once doubts her choices."

"Huh?" I tilted my head to the side to look at him, and he laughed at me.

"You won't understand this until you are older," he said, and I could tell he was serious when he sat up, leaning in front of me, "but all the things your mother puts you through are so you'll have strong heart."

"A strong heart?"

He nodded. "The world might hate you for your choices, people will expect you to feel things, but don't cater to them. Cater to yourself and what you believe is right. Make your heart strong enough so that it can withstand everyone hating you even when you love them... I see it, Dona... Your heart is getting stronger day by day."

"But Nana says not to be too strong or I won't get married?" I frowned, and he frowned too, flicking my forehead. "Ouch! DAD!"

"Who said I'd let you get married?" he yelled at me.

"You can't stop me!" I stuck my tongue out at him and tried to make a run for it, but he grabbed me, tossing me over his shoulder.

"Your mother's right; looks like you've gotten spoiled!"

"Daddy!" I laughed as he spun me around as fast as he could.

"Say no boys until you're forty!" he yelled at me.

"DAD!"

"Fifty!"

"MOMMY, HELP!"

"Ugh!" I heard him yell, dropping me back on my

feet. The world spun and I fell on my butt.

Looking up, I felt her brush my hair from face. The corner of her mouth turned up into a smile. "You couldn't take him on your own?"

"That's your job," I muttered.

She laughed and nodded, "You're right, it is my job. When you want to get married, I'll hold him down and you make run for it, okay."

"Can we drop this whole marriage talk?" Daddy grumbled, rubbing his side.

"Who's getting married?" Wyatt asked, coming inside with a bowl of ice-cream in his hand.

"No one!" Dad yelled at him. "And how many times have I told you to stop walking around while eating!"

"I want some! Share!" I got up, rushing to him.

"Get your own, Dona!" he frowned, lifting his ice-cream and pulling away. But Ethan, because he was taller, took the bowl out of his hands and gave it to me. "Hey!"

"You should have brought her some too," Ethan said to Wyatt.

"Yeah! Thank you, Ethan. You're the best brother ever," I grinned, taking a big bite as Wyatt glared at me.

"I hope you get fat," he said to me.

"I hope you starve," I said back.

"Guys." Ethan pinched us both.

"Ouch!" We yelled, but he just nodded to something behind us.

When we turned, Mommy and Daddy were watching us.

"Are you all fighting with each other?" my mother asked us.

"No," Wyatt and I said quickly, and I handed back the ice-cream.

"They look like they are to me." Daddy put his hand on Mommy's shoulder. "What should we do with the three of them?"

"Three?" Ethan gasped. "It was just them."

"Nope, three." Wyatt crossed his arms. "If you didn't give her the ice-cream, we wouldn't be fighting."

"You're supposed to deny fighting!" I kicked him.

"Ouch…Urgh! Kick me one more time, Dona!" Wyatt yelled at me.

"I say we drop them somewhere at the border and see if they can make it back," Daddy said to Mommy.

She smiled, tapping her chin. "That sounds fun."

"No, it doesn't!" I looked at Ethan to see he was grinning.

"I can find my way back from the city—"

"The city border? Think about it, son." Daddy was now smiling like Mom.

"The state?" Wyatt asked, slowly.

They still didn't answer.

I took a small step, turning around and I opening the door before grabbing both their hands. "RUN!"

And we did. Laughing, we ran as quickly as possible.

DONATELLA - NOW

"Mom, Dad, your plan worked," I said. The black headstone had an image of them embracing engraved into it. "Like all your plans, it worked. We're all on the same page again... Even though I'm leaving Chicago. It's too soon for me to thank you. This could all go terribly wrong and I could hate him very much—"

"Not going is also an option," Wyatt muttered behind me.

"Wyatt misses me so much already, he's sobbing behind me right now," I said, making him snort. "And Ethan..." I glanced over my other shoulder to look up at him, and he emotionlessly stared right back. "He's basically helping the maids move me out... He's really happy he has no more competition. Dad, he's kinda been a bully to me."

He huffed, crouching down beside me and shoving me lightly with his shoulder. "Just so you know, Father, your daughter planned a coup against me."

I frowned, shoving him back. "It was a fake coup!"

"Now, just a few days later, she about to run off and marry a prince," Wyatt said, kneeling down on the other side of me. "I know she was your little princess, but did you really have to make her a real fucking princess? Her head is already big enough."

"Let's be grateful she's only a princess," Ethan added, placing a tulip on the grave before standing up again. "If she became a Queen, she'd float into the atmosphere and explode."

Wyatt laughed. "I didn't think about that, but you're right. She'd walk outside her castle and her head would rocket her to the moon."

"You don't need to thank me," I said, ignoring them as I put my tulips on the grave. "Your sons are back together because I've stopped them from killing each other over the years." I paused, putting my hand on their picture. "As you can imagine, it's been a very exhausting job; Ethan pretending he doesn't care, Wyatt pretending he doesn't care. It was like watching two idiots run into each other. Which is why I'm retiring and leaving it up to you two to watch out for them while I'm trying on crowns. I won't be able to visit as much... At least not in person. But I'll talk like you're listening wherever I am, I promise... Oh and I better have a one hell of a letter from you, Mother, waiting on my wedding day. And..."

"Enough, you'll talk their ears off," Wyatt grumbled as he stood up. "If you have anything to tell them, call me. I'll come up here and hold the phone up."

"I'm so going to hold you to that." I couldn't help but laugh as I stood up and turned around to see them both staring at me, the corner of Ethan's lips turned up and Wyatt trying to force himself to not look upset. I outstretched my hands and they both looked at me, confused. "My goodbye gifts?"

They both rolled their eyes before turning around and leaving me. Watching them leave, I glanced back down at my parents' tombstone, placing my hands on it before following them. This wasn't the end; it was just the beginning of a whole new story.

The proof of that was the man standing dressed in a dark gray suit in front of the awaiting car, beside him Sebastian and...doe-eyed Amelia du Bellay.

"I thought you died?" I asked her when I reached the car.

"No, ma'am, I wasn't in the cars." She bowed slightly at me.

"Suspicious," I said, looking between her and Sebastian as he opened the door for us. He was alright for the most part. A few cuts and bruises and a cast on two of his fingers.

"Should I get rid of them, *Your Highness*?" Gabriel asked me, a smirk on his lips.

"We'll see," I replied, sliding inside before him.

It took a few moments before we finally started to move and no one said a word. It was as if we were going to a cemetery, not leaving one. I didn't mind it though. It allowed me time to take in the scenery as we drove to the airfields. In the distance, I could see his hotel…the one he'd supposedly built for me.

"Why did you build a hotel here? If it's for me, it seems like a waste of money since I'll rarely be back."

"But you will be back," he said, and while I didn't turn to look at him, I could see looking at me in the reflection of the glass. "You will be back and when you are, there will be place for you to call just yours, without your family… Though I'm not sure it was good investment. This city is quite violent. People who come here must be mad."

"Or criminal, or royalty, or all of the above," I replied, and as we stopped in front of the aircraft. The first thing I noticed about it was that it was a commercial plane and the second was the aircraft livery which boasted the letter D; which I could only guess was for his family name.

I looked over at him, but before I could even ask he said "Yes, it's commercial. Sebastian and I thought it would be best if we didn't make a big show and announce my return. It will look like any other international flight when we land in Monaco."

I didn't speak and Sebastian open the door for us.

Gabriel stepped out, unbuttoning the top of his suit jacket and then reaching back for me. I didn't take his hand, stepping out on my own. There were a dozen men dressed in casual clothing, waiting in front of the plane. In front of them was none other than Jackal. A black scarf was wrapped around her neck, hiding the only scar she didn't like people to see; the scars all over her face were as clear as day. She walked up to me, taking my purse and nodding to Gabriel, who blinked slowly, taking her in before looking to me.

"Does your family hold interviews at the gates of hell for these people?"

"Jackal meet Gabriel. Gabriel, Jackal; my second and favorite assistant," I said to him before looking over to Amelia, who seemed about ready to piss herself.

All our attention shifted when four other cars pulled to stop just a behind our car. Ethan, Ivy, Wyatt, Helen, Nari, Sedric, and Darcy all stepped out. None of them came closer, so I walked the short distance between us alone. When I got closer, I opened my mouth to speak but no words came out.

Helen took that opportunity to latch on to me.

"Once you're settled and ready to start wedding prep, you better call," she said, hugging me tightly and kissing my cheeks.

When she let go, Nari, who usually prided herself on not being emotional, sniffled and wrapped her white arms around my neck.

"Show them what a real powerful woman looks like," she whispered and quickly let go, stepping back.

"I've changed my mind," Sedric frowned at me. "You shouldn't go."

"Agreed. Who's going to stop Nari and Helen from—Ahh! Ouch!" Darcy bared his teeth at his sister.

"Children. Children. Behave," I said to them both. They both grumbled but hugged me anyway.

"Be safe, cuz," Darcy said.

"If you need back up…" Sedric started.

"I won't call either of you," I teased, letting go.

"So hurtful." Sedric put his hand over his heart but smiled at me.

Leaving Ethan, Wyatt…and Ivy. Both Ethan and Wyatt looked as if they were doing everything possible to numb themselves. Anyone observing might think they were just standing there and staring at me, but they were looking through me, not at me. I could tell.

So, I gave them a moment and focused on Ivy, who smiled. "Last time we were on this airfield, you were welcoming us back, and now here we are, sending you off."

"That is how airfields work... People come and people go," I reminded her, hating the feeling of pain in the back of my throat. "Take care of my brothers, Ivy, or I'll be back faster than you can reach for a bowl ice-cream."

"You get to be a princess, and I get to be a barrier to stop these two from killing each other?"

"Exactly." I grinned.

Wyatt huffed, saying to Ethan, "You'd think we were a pair of brutes the way they speak about us."

"If anything, she's one of the reasons we fought so much," Ethan replied, glancing down at me.

Rolling my eyes, I moved first, hugging Ethan, kissing his cheek, and whispering into his ear, "I love you so much, big brother. To the moon and back. I'm sorry for always pushing and hurting you. I can never say how grateful I am for everything you've always done for me...for all of us."

I pulled back quickly and he swallowed slowly and just nodded. "Love you, too."

"Good, so at my wedding, you're going to be Gabriel's best man. Start thinking of your speech now because I'm not helping you with that one."

"Why in the hell would I do that?" He frowned, thoroughly unhappy with the idea.

Ignoring him, I let go and moved over to hug Wyatt tightly...then tighter...then even tighter...

"Ahh! Are you hugging me or are you strangling me?" he yelled, smacking my arms.

"You will always have me. You will always be a part of me. And I will always love you, unconditionally and forever. No distance or person can get between us," I whispered, kissing the side of his face and pulling back, laughing as I added, "I would make you my maid of honor but Helen might kill me, so that means you're stuck walking me down the aisle."

"Of course, I am. Were you planning on walking down by yourself?" he snapped, peeling me off of him. His eyes glistened.

I knocked my forehead against his. "Don't get all

mopey when I leave."

"Will you get on the damn plane already; it's hot out here!" he said as he squeezed my hand tightly and then…let go.

Taking a step back from them, I smiled. "Next time you all see me, you'll be bowing."

They groaned and even Ethan rolled his eyes as I laughed, fighting the burning in my eyes.

"We'll hold the wedding a soon as possible," Gabriel's voice came from behind me, and when I turned around to look at him, I realized I didn't want to turn back to look back at them.

"*Au Revoir*," I waved over my shoulder and then walked forward.

No longer Donatella of Chicago.

But Donatella of Monaco.

EPILOGUE

"This is the first verse of genesis. Holy art thou, chaos, chaos, eternity, all contradictions in terms!"

~ Aleister Crowley

GABRIEL

"Another reason I built that hotel," I said, lifting the panel so she could look out the window. "Was so that you could see this."

"What are you...?" Her voice trailed off as she looked out. We had taken off a little bit ago and she'd been quiet...too quiet. I didn't want her to miss it. "I can still see it."

"I told the pilots to fly as low as they could until you couldn't see it anymore," I told her, looking out as well to see the Obelisk in the distance, the only thing still so clear because of the light reflected in the glass. "In ancient Egypt, the Obelisk represented the mound from which a cry awoke creation and set life in motion and it also symbolized another cry, which would mark the end of life."

She snickered to herself, leaning on the windowpane and watching until we were too far to see anything else and the plane began to rise. She inhaled deeply, closing her eyes. When she opened them again I saw a familiar look of determination.

"Amelia, tell her everything you know," I said, rising

from my chair. "I'll be back."

I walked to the front of our cabin and into the guard's cabin. They all began to rise to their feet, but I shook my head. I noticed two who didn't move. Sebastian stood in the aisle beside them.

"They gave us kids?" I frowned. The two teenagers were familiar.

"When do you think they're going to ask us our ages instead of calling us kids?" The one on the right said as he clicked away on his video game again.

"I think we're always going to be called kids," the other yawned, tugging on his eye-mask and shrugging his shoulders as he relaxed into the chair.

"That's going to get annoying," the second replied and Sebastian looked at me as if I had some damn answer as to why they were on my plane. Last, I remembered seeing of either of them was when they were driving me and Donatella to the mansion.

Finally, the second one rose from his chair and put his video game on the seat. His brown hair was buzzed on the sides and kept high at the top. He had two small black birthmarks, one by his right eye and other over his left lip.

"I'm Gunner, short for Guthrie, full name Jerome Guthrie. If it shoots, I can shoot it, and I don't miss. I'm seventeen," he looked Sebastian. "I'm not kid. Don't like being called a kid." He looked back at me. "Behind me is Loïc Landry, they found him in a ditch in De La Fontaine, so I don't know if that's his real name but you can call him either Loïc or Landry. If you need something or someone, he'll find them and get it. Nice to meet you, Sir… We look forward to working for you."

He said the last part with no emotion, as if he were reading off a cue card.

It was quite funny. I put my hands-on Sebastian's shoulder as I moved them forward. "Teach them the rules and don't call them kids…at least to not their faces."

I didn't hear whatever else was said between them as I walked to the cockpit of the plane. The steward there bowed once, taking his leave. I knocked once right over the keyhole and the door slid open.

Stepping inside, the door slid closed behind me as I sat in the seat closest to the door.

"Don't you think the two of you are being quite bold?" I asked, leaning back in the chair.

"You obviously don't know us very well, Gabriel," he replied coldly, looking over his shoulder to ask, "How is our princess?"

I glared into his green eyes, the spitting image of hers. "How in the name of God can you both sit here so comfortably, knowing your daughter spent the morning putting flowers on your grave?"

He got up, taking off his hat and running his hands through his dark brown and gray hair. He walked the two steps it took to get to me then bent down and smacked the side of my leg.

"I sit the same way you're sitting; the same way you will continue to sit knowing full well you've been lying to her face. That your father didn't give you any letter. He didn't tell you to go to England for school. You were exiled by your step-mother. When we found you, you were waiting to die, not planning revenge. You haven't been speaking to Evelyn but to us. Lie after lie after lie and now you want to take the moral high ground with us? Us, who saved you from hopelessness. We spent the last ten months teaching you everything you needed to know about our children and walk out alive. We picked up that crown, dusted it off, and put it back on your handsome little head. We did this not for you. I couldn't care less about you. We did this for her. It's her country, her throne; we're just letting her share it with you. Have you forgotten?"

How could anyone forget selling their souls?

GABRIEL - TEN MONTHS AGO

"What do you think? Could I be the next Monet?" I asked Sebastian, looking up from the painting back at him only to see his old brown face frowning at me. "What? It's good!"

"It's a bowl of fruit," he stated.

"It's a *painting* of a bowl of fruit," I corrected, wiping the red paint off the tip of my brush.

"Yes, another painting of a bowl of fruit to add to the world's never-ending collection of painted bowls of fruits."

I didn't say anything, gently cleaning off the paint, which made my hands look like they were covered in blood.

"But yes, sir, your painting is nice."

"No point flattering me now," I snickered and looked to him again as he walked over to the kitchen sink. "Tell me, Sebastian, what is an exiled prince supposed to do with his time?"

He paused for only a brief moment before slipping the dishwashing gloves on to his hands. "One of two things. Option one, forget he was ever a prince at all and live as all normal men live."

"Option two?" I asked, rising from my stool and moving to the sink beside him.

"Be a prince, take back your birthright."

"Two impossible options, thank you," I said bitterly, washing my hands before reaching to take the second pair of gloves but he stopped me. His brown hand on my wrist. His brown eyes serious as he said, "Only one of those things is impossible and it's not taking back your country. Don't wash the dishes; it's beneath you."

"It's beneath you too, and yet here you are."

"I know it's beneath me." he replied, snatching the gloves from my hands. "So, let's just think of it as an investment."

"In what?" I turned around to watch him complete

the task that he thought was beneath me.

“One day when you return, when you are crowned sovereign, you will remember my many long years of suffering beside you and you shall drape me in honors so high even my great-grandchildren will brag.”

I laughed at that. At least one of us still dreamed. Putting my hand on his shoulder, I told him the hard truth. "For you to have great-grandchildren... You’re going to need children, and I don't know how you are going to do that when you've decided to spend the rest of your life hovering over me."

“You *must* be a prince; you have to have the last words on everything.”

“I do not!” I said, walking over to the refrigerator and reaching inside for a bottle of water. All of sudden, a chill went down my spine.

Lifting my arm up slowly, I watched as the hair on it began to rise.

“What now—” Sebastian looked over to me. The look on my face must have terrified him so much that he forgot to take off his gloves before rushing to me. “Gabriel! Gabriel!!”

I tried to speak but I couldn't. My throat burned hotter than hell. It was like someone was pouring lava down my throat. My legs buckled...my body fell forward...was like my mind was disconnected from my body and I lost complete control of myself... "Gabriel hold on! Dear me, hold on!" I could see his lips moving but couldn't hear him. He rolled me to my side and I don't know when he managed to get ahold of his gun or why he even needed it until glasses and plates above me shattered, raining broken shards all around. I could only see their boots as they attacked.

Peaches and vinegar, I could smell it. It was coming from me...

MOVE, Gabriel! FUCKING MOVE! My mind yelled for a brief second but just when I tried the burning intensified. One minute I couldn't feel anything and the next, I could only feel the burning; as though my flesh was being scorched off my bones.

Please, God, please... I begged as I saw a pair of black combat boots stop in front of me. The boot rose and kicked me to my side.

No. I'm a goddamn prince! I won't beg! I will never

BEG! With all the strength I could muster, I found the will to say, "Fuck you."

Breathing through the pain, I could barely see anything but the slender object in his hand. Bending down, he brought his hand back and I didn't look away. He was not going to see fear in my eyes. Like a hammer, he brought his hand down into my chest. Whatever he stabbed me with, spread like ice throughout my whole body. As if I were coming up for air, I inhaled greedily and rolled on to my side.

"Fuck me? That's not what you say to the people who just saved your life, now is it?" An older woman, not a man, with an American accent spoke. She took the black mask off her face, revealing her shoulder-length black hair and brown eyes.

"Do you plan on lying there all day?" I glanced past her towards the brown-haired, green-eyed man walking up to us. He reached into the open fridge and took out an apple. His accent was more... Irish?

"Really?" the woman said to him.

"What?"

"You're going to eat an apple from the fridge of a

prince whose evil stepmother's favorite method of murder is poison."

"What? She wasn't poisoning the food; it was his paint."

I glanced over to my canvas...then back at them.

"Who...who are you people?'

"Who we are isn't the question you should be asking," the man crouched down in front me, taking a bite of the apple. "This is the part where you ask me what you should be asking."

The woman beside him didn't speak, merely putting her elbow on his shoulder blade...in her hand a silver gun. She smiled, but it wasn't comforting.

"You saved me to just kill me?'

"We've done crazier things," the man replied, shrugging before taking another bite. I believed him.

"What is the question I should be asking?" I asked, as he had requested.

He stood upright, offering his hand to the woman who took it, rising beside him. She spoke for him, "Can we help you kill your stepmother and punish your enemies...can we make them bow at your feet...so you can cut their heads off?'

"Can you?' I asked.

This time, she was the one who grinned. "We're the mafia, we can do everything."

"The mafia?" I snickered. "Do you both know what year it is?"

"Apparently, it's the year of bitch-ass princes locked in towers," the man stated, walking over to Sebastian, who lay bleeding the ground but still breathing. The man pulled out his gun again and pointed.

"Stop!" I pushed myself off the ground, my legs still so weak I nearly fell. I forced myself up right and I grabbed onto his arm. "He's my guard."

"He's a shitty guard," he replied.

"He's with me." I could only repeat because my throat still ached when I spoke.

"When you're with us, you don't need anyone else," the woman said and the man glanced down to my hand on his arm, telling me with his eyes to release him. I only held on tighter.

"I didn't say I was with you."

"That doesn't save him; it just means you die with

him," he countered.

"And here I thought the mafia honored loyalty—"

"Only until it comes against self-preservation," she said, walking over to us. "He's old; what you need to do is beyond him. He can't protect you anymore—"

"I'll protect him, then! He's family! MY FAMILY. SO PUT DOWN THE FUCKING GUN!"

"Yell at my wife again and I'll shove this gun down your throat first," he snapped, the barrel of gun pointed at me.

"Go ahead, then. You're the ones who have wasted your time. Or does the mafia go around saving bitch-ass princes in towers for free, now?" I snapped back.

There was silence.

They glanced at each other for moment and when the man took his hand off the trigger, I finally let him go.

"Fine, he lives. But if you want to win this fight, you're going to have to leave him, your morality, and any sort of compassion left in you, behind," he said, staring me the eye. "You'll never take the throne with how weak you are now. Abandon him and everything else and we'll make sure you're stronger than even you thought was possible."

"Why does it sound like I'm selling my soul?"

"What good is a soul when you're not even free to live in a shitty apartment in West London," she stated, waving her arms around the hellhole I'd been calling a home. "Do you want this or do you want Monaco? If so, there is a price. That is how your stepmother took it out of your family's hands to begin with. You can only beat evil with a greater evil. So, I will ask you once and only once: do you want to rule or do you want to die in this shitty apartment?"

I didn't have to think about it which said a lot more about me than I was willing to admit aloud yet. "My humanity never helped me, anyway."

"Then let us introduce ourselves," the man said and outstretched his hand. I outstretched mine but instead of taking it, he balled his own hand into a fist, pulled it back, and punched me in the face so hard I felt blood pool in my mouth, and stumbled back. "I'm Liam, the beautiful woman standing behind me is my wife Melody. You can call us Mr. and Mrs. Callahan until you earn the right to call us by our first names. It's an impossible goal, but you should still put in the effort. Now pack. We have less than a year to break and remake you."

Callahan. I knew that name. But I wasn't sure where from… All I knew was I'd asked for help from God and two devils had walked in, instead.

GABRIEL - NOW

"Liam," Melody's smooth voice spoke up from behind me but it wasn't harsh like it normal was; it was softer now, gentle. "He's already been interrogated by our sons. We don't want him to secretly hate her, now do we?"

He frowned, showing the lines on his face. "Would it kill you to let me have fun, too?"

"I'm already dead, baby, didn't you hear?" she replied, causing him to snicker before focusing back on me.

Rising from my chair as he rose from the ground, I didn't back down from him. "I never want to see or hear from either of you ever again. Your version of events never happened. You hold no power over me and if you think you can use me to do anything, I will tell her that neither of you is rotting away at the Callahan cemetery."

"You'll die before you can even open your mouth,"

he responded and once again I saw where Ethan got it from.

"Maybe," I grinned, too... I wasn't the same man they had met back then. They'd made me into one of them. Now I knew the Callahan family rules. My favorite was Rule #2 *take no prisoners and have no regrets about it.* I disagreed with it. Prisoner make great leverage. "Maybe you'll kill me before I can out you... But I'll make damn sure to take your daughter to the grave with me."

The smile on his face dropped as he glared at me, "Watch yourself—"

"Better yet, you watch yourself," I sneered back. "There is a saying... Even the devil loves his kids? Your daughter...your only daughter... Has now invested her whole life and ambitions in me. She's ripped herself from everything knows and cares about... Kill me, you shatter that."

"Are you hiding behind my daughter?" His jaw cracked to the side. "She's isn't that weak—"

"Not yet...But what happens if I make sure she loves me so deeply, so insanely, that if I die, she'll want to die too? Luckily, she knows that type of love from watching you two. And we both have something to bond over…parents who left scars. So, you go ahead, the best time to pull that trigger is now…Liam…or should call you *Dad*?"

He huffed then snickered until he just laughed like the madman that he was, leaning back on the chair his wife sat in. The way he smiled, the way he stared, it put all of his children to shame… The real devil of devils, the true Mad Hatter of Chicago.

"Finally, you sound like a son-in-law I can tolerate. I would applaud you but again, we did all the hard work." He said in a serious tone before dangerously adding, "Don't worry, you won't see us again."

"But you'll be watching, correct—"

"Liam," Melody spoke up again, rising up from the pilot's chair and ignoring me completely as she handed him her phone. His eyebrows bunched in confusion for a brief second before looking down at the screen… The moment he did, his whole body went stiff. He grabbed on to the phone tightly, his nose flaring.

Melody, coldly glanced over at me, her brown eyes like daggers, "Play time is over. Go back to her and don't make a habit of leaving her alone."

"What's going on?" I knew that look on their faces. I'd seen it once before, and they only had it when they thought one of their children was in danger.

"Gabriel, you'll never be good enough for my daughter. I know that, he knows that, and most importantly, Dona knows that," she said in a voice even icier than before, her stare even harsher. "Nevertheless, I chose you. I chose you because you are the only person who can make Dona do what she needs to do; focus on herself and what she wants and needs, even when she does not realize it. Do you understand?"

The words coming out of her mouth? No. I did not understand. But the reason for her to speak so seriously, that I understood... *Something, somewhere had gone terribly wrong.*

I had nothing to say, even though I had so much to say... Luckily or unluckily, there was knock on the door and they both turned, grabbing their hats and sitting back in the pilot seats.

"Goodbye, Gabriel. Let's not meet again," she added... And Liam never said a word, he just sat like sculpted stone.

"Sir," Sebastian said, looking over my shoulder in confusion then back at me. "Your Donatella is—"

"We're going back!" The very woman herself hollered, rushing up the aisle, towards the cockpit and I quickly shut the door behind me.

"Dona—"

"Turn the plane around!" she screamed; she was near manic, her eyes wide, her hands shaking. In her hand manicured hands, she gripped a cellphone with the same fury her father, who stood just beyond the doors, had shown only mere seconds ago. "Are you fucking deaf? MOVE!"

When she reached around me, I grabbed on her and pulled her in the small bathroom stall. She tried to yank away from me, but I held on tighter. "Let go! Let me go!"

"Calm the fuck down!" I hollered.

"MY FAMILY WAS JUST ATTACKED, DON'T TELL ME TO FUCKING CALM DOWN!"

"What?"

She yanked her arm way, trying to open the door but I blocked her once again, "Dona, talk to me. STOP!

Just...fuck! DONA!" Holding her still and forcing her to look in my eyes, her nostrils flared. "WHAT happened?"

"Do you need me to paint you a picture?" she snapped at me. "My family was just attacked..."

"I heard that but by who, when—?"

"I don't know who! And now! Right when we took off! We need to go back, so why are you still standing in my way?"

It was only now, like usual when concerning Melody Callahan, did I understand her words.

"To do what?" I questioned, releasing my grip on her.

She stared at me as if I were insane, "Do I look like I'm in the mood for one of your jokes—"

"Does it seem like I'm joking?" I wasn't. "You want to go back home...to do what?"

"My family—"

"Was attacked, I heard that. But what can you do?"

"Excuse me?"

"You got on this plane because you don't have the power to do anything without your brothers. Now you want to do what? Run back to them—"

"I know your family life is so fucked up that you might not give a shit—"

"Did they ask for you?" I cut her off and she froze for a second.

Getting her bearings back, she said, "They could be hurt."

"No-one called you back home. Whatever is going on in Chicago, it is mafia related; you're royalty now, that is not your fight."

"My fight is my family's fight—"

"I'm your family!" Again, she looked stunned and I pushed further. "When something bad happens to them - and it will, as violence is an occupational hazard of being in the damn mafia - will you go back each time? You still have your last name but when you stepped on this plane, you left the Callahan Family behind. Your family will survive without you. You have your brothers, uncles, cousins, half of Ireland. Whatever happened, your family will come out on top... I'm sure of it... But will you, Donatella, individually, be able to do the same if you go back? Nothing. You're not their cheerleader, you're my queen."

She stood there staring at me with a mixture of horror and shock before blinking and taking a deep breath, glaring at me again, "We aren't married yet. So I'm not your queen yet. *So* you can either move or be moved. The choice is yours, Gabriel."

She was finally calm.

The coldness in her voice would have put Melody to shame. Opening the door, I let her step out first and when she did, she glanced over to the cockpit. Part of me, the part that enjoyed a little chaos, wanted her to walk towards it. But a much greater part of me was grateful when she turned, facing the aisle again. She'd almost returned back to our section when the long-lost daughter of Edward Scissorhands, Jackal, stepped in front of her. She placed her hand over the scarf around throat, swallowing hard before opening her mouth. The words would have been inaudible if not for the absolute silence in the cabin, every last person now facing her...

"Who?" Dona demanded.

SECOND EPILOGUE

"Mostly it is loss which teaches us about the worth of things."

~Arthur Schopenhauer

WYATT

"Anddddd… She's gone…" Ivy spoke first, speaking as if she were baseball announcer, most likely to break the tension. However, I just kept watching the plane fade into the distance behind the clouds until I could barely see it in the distance.

"Don't mope…" Ivy said, coming up beside me and linking arms. "After all, you still have me!"

Smirking, I shook my head, "Careful Ivy, if you hang around me long enough, you'll realize I'm the better brother."

Ethan snickered in actual amusement as if the sheer possibility of it was laughable. Before I could comment, he outstretched his hand to her.

She laughed to herself, letting go of my hand. In that spilt second, I saw a glint from the corner of my eye. The type of glint that meant only one thing…

"ETHAN—"

BANG!

Unable to move…unable to speak…the warmth of the blood splattering right across my face…

No!

The doctor me in me knew…just knew…that it was over…no one could have survived. And hearing the only word he screamed erupting through the air, sent chills down my spine to the point that I felt sick.

"IVY!" Dropping to his knees, he held on to her limp body, her blonde hair soaked in crimson blood; he pulled her into his arms like a broken doll looking up to me as he screamed "IVY!" He smacked her face a few times. "IVY! WAKE UP!" Angrily, he looked at me, "WYATT! WYATT! WHAT THE FUCK ARE YOU DOING? HELP HER!"

I'd never seen him like this... My older brother didn't panic, he didn't lose his cool, and he never asked me to do the impossible.

"I can't help the dead," I whispered, my body still unable to move forward or back. I just kept staring into her lifeless blue eyes that were still open, blood pouring down her face. It felt as though the world had slowed down...No, frozen and I was stuck. And yet it hadn't and I wasn't. Our men were already all around us, their guns drawn, panning out to find... To find the person who'd just started what was going to be a very bloody war.

In the back of my mind I heard my mother's voice, *"Every last person we kill is for family. If we don't kill them, they kill us. It is the way of the world. It is self-defense..."*

Like always, my mother was right.

COMING SOON

Donatella's role as the princess of the mafia is now over. Her rise to power as Crown Princess of Monaco has just begun.

COMING SOON

THE HOUSE OF DÉLLACQUA

The spin-off

of

the spin-off...

SNEAK PEEK AT CHILDREN OF REDEMPTION

PROLOGUE

"I am as my creator made me..."

~Minnie Smith

WYATT

I knew exactly when it happened...When the monster inside of me woke up. I was different from my siblings. I'd always known that. I didn't know how, but I knew I was different from them. Whether they would admit it or not Ethan and Dona, were the real twins in our family. Yes, Dona and I were close, in fact there were times I had a feeling she'd need me or she'd have a feeling I'd need her; twin telepathy, as it's called. But at the end of the day, no matter how close I was to her, in my mind, Dona was my sister, but she was Ethan's twin...not mine. The reason why I'd never tell her that was the reason why I knew I was different.

Ethan and Dona were children of Machiavelli, masters of

manipulation, champions of cunning thoughts and actions. While I knew how to manipulate and on occasion was cunning...I hated it. They loved deceiving people, loved watching as people fell into their traps. Like the Greek gods, they found amusement in watching people come to tragic ends. They were the eye of the storm...while I was merely a chaos monster. Like my father did for my brother, he gave me *The Prince* to read as boy. Out of respect for him I read it...once I finish however I chucked it out the window, along with *The Art of War, the 48 Laws of Power, Crime and Punishment.* The pile of books that been tossed to the sky from my window before plummeting back to earth never to enter my room again was enough to fill a small library.

Why?

Too many fucking words.

And I don't mean that in the Neanderthal '*I do not like reading*' sense...but in the '*why the hell are there so many goddamn books on power*?' sense. Why? Power has always been simple to me...people want to do whatever the fuck they want to do, but can't because they fear retaliation. So they seek a position that allows them to do just that...a position that allows them to fuck others and never get fucked over in returned. It was for that reason Ethan and Dona plotted and schemed…I on the other hand did not like it. I don't see the world like that.

Yes, I like everyone else, whether they admit it or not, like power.

And yes, I, wanted to do whatever the fuck I wanted, and I always did; because unlike other people I did not fear retaliation, I welcomed it.

When I was younger, my parents, my siblings, even I thought there was this softness in me…that the reason I didn't connect to power or manipulation like Ethan and Dona did, was because I was kind, or merciful…in my family that was akin to being born with a tail. So I worked hard, I pushed myself, all to prove I was just as ruthless as my brother and sister…until one day I realized I wasn't kind, I wasn't merciful.

I was fucking bored with it.

Why fight people who can't fight back?

Why manipulate people who could never do the same to me?

Those thoughts came to me when I was sixteen because that was the first time I'd ever fought a real opponent…a chaos monster just like me.

My father.

WYATT - 16 YEARS OLD

His fist collided with my nose so hard, the blood came down like a broken faucet, and when I stumbled as I reached up to stop the flow, his foot collided with my chest. Down on the ground, he kicked me all the while screaming down at me.

"How much longer are you going to be such a little bitch?!"

I'd never heard such rage in his voice, and in that moment, his words hit me stronger than his boot in my rib. I felt it and it sent chills down my back...it was fear. I heard someone call out to him and he stopped, but not before bending down, grabbing me by the hair, and lifting my head up so he could see my bloody face.

"Your weakness will get your siblings killed one day. If your mother was alive, she'd be ashamed of you." He stared down at me, his green eyes glaring in frustration and anger.

I smiled, tasting the blood in my mouth, and said, "Are you trying to provoke me?"

Before he could answer, I spit the blood at his face.

I broke out of his grasp, rushed him, tackling him to the ground, and pinned him under me. I punched over and over again. His arms were pinned, and he couldn't block, so he took it. And the more he took, the harder I hit until all of sudden I felt arms around me pulling me off him and throwing me to the ropes.

"Wyatt!"

Blinking, all of a sudden, I saw Ethan standing in front of me staring wide eyed. My legs shook a little, but I managed to stand straighter. Ignoring him, I looked around him to my father, who now stood with his back turned to us, fixing the tape on his arms.

"Mom would be ashamed of me? What about you? Since she died, you walk around like a kicked dog—"

"Wyatt enough!" Ethan hollered at me as I laughed. I wiped the blood from my mouth with a collar shirt.

"Ethan," my father said as he stood up straighter. He rolled out his arms as he turned to face us, "If you ever interrupt your brother and I again, I'll break your arms and legs before tossing you out of the ring myself. Am I clear?"

The stunned look on Ethan's face, how his green eyes widened, while father's only got calmer, deadlier, just brought me so much joy. I couldn't help the grin on my face.

"He's interrupting still, old man, why don't you break one leg and arm now so he gets the picture?" I asked, not realizing that I was hopping in place, more than ready, until I saw my father lift up his fist.

"You worry about yourself."

"I have nothing to worry about," I replied.

He tried to hide it, he tried to be cold, but I saw it, the small grin on his face, and I didn't care if Ethan was in the ring or not. I charged him…ready to kill him…and he charged me, ready to do the same damn thing.

I wasn't a kid anymore.

I wasn't even his son anymore.

I was just another motherfucker in his ring.

We fought till the sun began to set, blood, sweat and saliva on each other's fists. The more I hit, the he stronger he seemed to get, and the harder he punched back. Grabbing my head, locking it into his arm, he squeezed, choking the air out of me…

"So this is where your monster lives huh?" He snickered right into my ear as I tried to elbow into him. But he just held on to me tighter.

"I'm going to kill you!" I sneered at him through the

pain.

"You can try...but you'll need to get in line, son. When I'm done killing those in front of you, we can try again!" he replied. My vision started to blur. My legs went numb and all of a sudden, I was on my back, gasping for air. Crouching down beside me, blocking the light from my eyes, I saw two of him as he spoke. "You think because you are my son that I will not kill you…you are wrong."

"Rule 1…" I managed to sit up, trying to grab my breath.

"You kill for family. You die for family…because you can't trust anyone else," he recited back to me. "What about it?"

"We don't kill family…you're bluffing…"

He huffed as if he were going to laugh. "None of the rules say you can't kill family. Rule 15 makes it clear—"

"If you betray the—"

"Being weak is a betrayal," he snapped at me. "Being stupid is a betrayal. If it comes down to you over your siblings…my business…I won't choose you." He stood up straighter and walked to the edge of the ring. Pietro lifted the ropes for him to step out.

"Would you have chosen Mom?" I asked, placing my

hand over my stomach, slowly sitting up from the mat. I watched as he paused a few feet from the door. "I call bullshit. Either bullshit on you killing me for family's sake…or bullshit on you loving Mom so damn much."

"One day, Wyatt…you will learn…chaos for chaos's sake is just brokenness."

What? "Which dead philosopher did you steal that from?"

He didn't bother saying any more than that. I wish I could have seen his face. He just kept walking forward until he got on the elevator, leaving only Ethan and I around the ring.

"You're a fucking idiot," Ethan said as he got into the ring. I tried to get up from the ground. All of me hurt, worst of all my legs. Stumbling forward, Ethan caught me, lifting my arm over his shoulder.

"I'm fine," I said, even though I didn't have any strength left to move away from him.

"You're a fucking idiot is what you are," he muttered again moving to set me in the corner of the ring.

"I heard you the first time!—Ugh!" Gritting my teeth, I held on to my side trying to fight back the pain.

"Biggest fucking idiot I've ever met," Ethan said one

more time as he handed me a water bottle.

"I think you might be malfunctioning...run back to Dad so he can reprogram you to kiss his ass like a good little solider," I snapped and snatched the water from his hand.

Just like my father, he didn't react, just shook his head. "What good comes out of going against him? Of provoking him with Mom?"

For a smartass, he was often a total dumbass.

"Why don't you provoke him? Why don't you push back?" I asked.

He frowned. "I would if he was wrong! Don't you see—"

"No I don't see! I'm told. This or that. Now I want to see...I want to see if he'll keep to his word...if he'll really kill me." I grinned up at Ethan before taking the rest of the water and splashing it on my face.

"Wyatt," he said in his warning voice...the one he used on the fucking guards.

Rising back up to my feet...without him...I placed my hands on his shoulder. "Big brother...it's no fun working inside the rules. Dad might be right...or maybe...just maybe even he doesn't know what he'd do."

"So your plan is what? Cause chaos until he kills you?"

"Want to take bets?" I grinned so wide my cheeks hurt.

Ethan shook my hand off of his shoulder and moved away from me, but not before saying, "Dead men don't pay."

"Fuck you are annoying."

But I wasn't going to ruin this. If our father couldn't kill me…that meant no one could…this was going fun.

Let the games begin…

DISCOVER MORE BY JJ MCAVOY

Ruthless People Series
RUTHLESS PEOPLE
THE UNTOUCHABLES
AMERICAN SAVAGES
A BLOODY KINGDOM
DECLAN + CORALINE

Children of Vice Series
CHILDREN OF VICE
CHILDREN OF AMBITION
CHILDREN OF REDEMPTION

Single Title Romance
MALACHI AND I
BLACK RAINBOW
RAINBOWS EVER AFTER
THAT THING BETWEEN ELI AND GWEN
SUGAR BABY BEAUTIFUL
CHILD STAR

ABOUT THE AUTHOR

J.J. McAvoy was born in Montreal, Canada and graduated from Carleton University in 2016 with an honours degree in Humanities. She is the oldest of three and has loved writing for years. Her works are inspired by everything from Shakespearean tragedies to modern pop culture. Her first novel, Ruthless People, was a runaway bestseller. Currently she's traveling all across the world, writing, looking for inspiration, and meeting fans. To get in touch, please stay in contact via her social media pages, which she updates regularly.

https://www.facebook.com/iamjjmcavoy

https://twitter.com/JJMcAvoy